PRAISE FOR JUST A TASTE

'Fun, fresh and always sex[...]
Ha[...]

'This flirty, slow burn roma[...]
holiday charm. *Just a Taste* has [...]
It's easy to root for Alex and [...]
Far[...]

'Anise has a magnetic, tender and butterfly inducing way of writing.
Just a Taste gave me all the feels her last books did; giggling, kicking
your feet and stuffing your face into your pillow type of romance'
Soraya Nadia Bouazzaoui

'I burned through these pages for the hot kitchen
scenes and the cold nights, and to watch how love
can thaw an icy heart and an icy room'
Joya Goffney

'The perfect cosy Christmas read – getting snowed-in never tasted
so sweet!! I adore getting swept up in Anise Starre's swoony stories'
Lizzie Huxley-Jones

'*Just a Taste* serves the perfect blend of sizzling slow burn
romance and deliciously witty banter in this sweet, cosy
holiday romance. I devoured it and adored every page!'
Chloe Liese

'*Just a Taste* was delightful from page one. Though this
is my first book by Anise Starre, it won't be my last'
Tif Marcelo

'Trapped in a mansion, in a snowstorm, with a full pantry
and sexual chemistry bouncing off the walls . . . sign
me up! *Just a Taste* is the perfect read to snuggle down
with when it's cold outside. Noelle and Alex's sweet and
spicy romance warmed the cockles of my heart'
Jenny Bayliss

'Starre combines the sexiness of a wealthy man and the aphrodisiac of delicious food in a way that will have even the Grinch's cold heart melting. Hoxton and Noelle are enemies with a chemistry that could light up a whole Christmas tree farm, and I was hooked for every page. It's the perfect romp in the snow this holiday season'
Allie Samberts

'Anise Starre serves up the perfect blend of forced proximity, slow burn steam and delicious enemies-to-lovers banter. I devoured every page – just don't read hungry'
Camilla Isley

'*Just a Taste* is a wonderfully charming and cosy romance that'll coax you into the holiday spirit (no matter how grumpy you may be)'
Deanna Grey

'Anise Starre's warm, witty writing makes *Just a Taste* the perfect holiday romance, as sweet and cosy as a cup of tea on a snowy winter day. Noelle and Alex's love story could make the Grinch-iest sceptic's heart grow three sizes!'
Kaitlyn Hill

'*Just a Taste* is the perfect antidote to a cold winter's night: warm, comforting and joyful! Bonus points for making me crave delicious food. Noelle is a Christmas delight!'
Jamie Wesley

'*Just a Taste* is so much more than a taste. It's the entire delicious meal, one I thoroughly enjoyed. He and Noelle are wonderful in this grumpy/sunshine slow burn romance, and I can't wait for Anise's next book!'
Beverley Kendall

Anise Starre is a born and bred Londoner who now travels the world with her husband. She loves writing sweet, fluffy romances featuring Black women being loved on and adored, with a hint of steam and spice to get the heart going. Anise is the author of *One Week in Paradise*, *One Last Job* and *One More Shot*. Her fourth novel is *Just a Taste*.

You can follow Anise on Instagram @authoranisestarre and TikTok @anisestarre. Her website is anisestarre.com.

Also by Anise Starre

One Week in Paradise
One Last Job
One More Shot

First published in Great Britain by Simon & Schuster UK Ltd, 2025

1 3 5 7 9 10 8 6 4 2

Simon & Schuster UK Ltd, 1st Floor
222 Gray's Inn Road, London WC1X 8HB

Simon & Schuster Australia, Sydney
Simon & Schuster India, New Delhi

www.simonandschuster.co.uk
www.simonandschuster.com.au
www.simonandschuster.co.in

The authorised representative in the EEA is Simon & Schuster Netherlands BV,
Herculesplein 96, 3584 AA Utrecht, Netherlands. info@simonandschuster.nl

Simon & Schuster strongly believes in freedom of expression and stands against
censorship in all its forms. For more information, visit BooksBelong.com

A CIP catalogue record for this book is available from the British Library

Paperback ISBN: 978-1-3985-4418-5
eBook ISBN: 978-1-3985-4419-2
Audio ISBN: 978-1-3985-4439-0

Typeset in Bembo by M Rules
Printed and Bound in the UK using 100% Renewable Electricity at CPI Group (UK) Ltd

MIX
Paper | Supporting
responsible forestry
FSC
www.fsc.org
FSC® C013604

JUST a TASTE

Anise Starre

SIMON &
SCHUSTER

London · New York · Amsterdam/Antwerp · Sydney/Melbourne · Toronto · New Delhi

To everyone who loves, celebrates and looks
forward to Christmas with a smile . . .
and also for anyone who despises it.

May this book warm your heart – if not
your frosty outlook on the season ;)

TWO YEARS EARLIER

Noelle

The vegetables are burnt.

In quick succession, my heart leaps into my throat then sinks to the bottom of my stomach as I yank open the oven door. Thick, dark smoke wafts out of it and that unmistakable, charcoal–like burning smell invades my senses.

Shit.

They're not just burnt. They're utterly unsalvageable.

'Who was supposed to be keeping an eye on the veggies?' I call as I pull on my oven mitts and yank the tray out. There had been rows and rows of perfectly sliced carrots and parsnips on the tray just two hours ago. Now it's just one blackened rectangle. I swallow down a sob.

'Uh,' says Jamie, barely lifting his head to spare a glance in my direction. He's been 'working' on the same dish – the cranberry sauce of all things – since he arrived this morning. 'Pretty sure veggies were on you.'

'No,' I grit out. 'They most definitely were not on me.' I stride across the kitchen and toss the remains into the bin. 'The pheasant was on me. The lamb was on me. The potatoes were on me. The scallops were on me. The gravy was on me. The Brussels sprouts were on me—'

'And, last time I checked, Brussels sprouts are a vegetable,' Will cuts in with a smirk. He's over at his station kneading a giant bowl of stuffing into precise little balls. 'Like Jamie said, veggies were on you.'

It's an unfortunate testament to how used to this kind of behaviour I am, that I don't turn around and march out of the kitchen, middle fingers held high. Though it is getting more and more tempting.

You're a professional, I remind myself as I pull out a fresh bag of carrots from the fridge. *Don't sink to their level.*

Sometimes, being the bigger person really sucks. If Eve, my twin sister, were here, she wouldn't have thought twice about tossing the tray straight at their heads. A smile tugs at my lips as I lean into the daydream of smacking both my annoying co-workers with a tray of burnt vegetables.

It wasn't always like this.

When I first started at The Avalon, a four-star restaurant attached to one of the city's most luxurious hotels, I would have bet good money that nothing could douse the excitement I felt for the job. I'd spent years working in kitchens that should never have passed the health inspection; they were grimy, cramped spaces with unimaginative menus and the only thing more filthy than the floors was the attitudes of my fellow co-workers.

Food standards, who?

Health and safety, where?

That, and the fact that they barely paid minimum wage, has left me feeling like a cog in a relentless, greasy machine. I'm just another line chef in a sweat-soaked kitchen where the stench of old oil clings to my rapidly yellowing uniform and the closest thing to a break I ever get is a five-minute respite in a grimy staff room that smells like cigarettes and burnt coffee.

In short, my current career status is most definitely *not* what I spent thousands of pounds on culinary school for.

But working at The Avalon was supposed to be different. Here, the walls were pristine, the countertops gleamed like polished silver, the air smelled like fresh food instead of stale cigarettes, and the staff had a level of professionalism I'd never seen before.

It was like a dream come true.

Until it wasn't.

The decline snuck up on me so gradually, it's hard to pinpoint the exact moment things started to fall apart. All I know is that, in the last six months, we've gone from a team of eight to three, and Will and Jamie have lost any kind of enthusiasm and commitment for the job. They're like ghosts floating through the kitchen. Anything and everything they can push on me, they do.

And I let them.

I let them because I genuinely love cooking. I love the way the ingredients come together to create something magical. I love seeing a table of full, satisfied customers and knowing that I did that. Me. Something I made. Nothing beats that feeling.

And Will and Jamie know that about me. They know I'll never say no and let the kitchen fall into chaos, because cooking is my passion. I'm the one who comes in early every morning to prep for the day, even though we're supposed to be on a rota. I'm the one who stays late every evening to clean up and make sure we don't lose our perfect health rating. I'm the one who meets with Gareth, the restaurant manager, to fine-tune the seasonal menu every three months. They know it all. They know I'll always be there, picking up the slack and putting in the extra hours.

'*Not for long!*'

Eve's sing-song voice trills in my mind as I place the newly sliced carrots into an oven tray and reach for the parsnips. She's the constant recipient of all my work-related woes and her advice hasn't wavered even once over the last three years:

'*Quit and start your own restaurant.*'

I wish it were that easy.

If it were only about passion and dedication, I'd have started up my own place years ago. But there is a mountain of obstacles standing in the way, and each one is more daunting than the last.

First, there's the financial aspect. My savings are embarrassing at best, dire at worst, and it doesn't look like that will change any time soon.

Then there's the location. Finding the right spot is crucial. It has to be accessible, attractive and affordable. I've seen the wrong location doom a restaurant before it's even opened its doors.

And that's not even thinking about all the—

'*Excuses.*'

The Eve in my mind cuts me off, rolling her eyes exactly as I know she would if she were standing right in front of me. '*You can have all the excuses in the world, Noelle. Sometimes you just have to take the plunge.*'

I shake my head, ridding myself of the vision of my disappointed-looking sister, and refocus on the task at hand. Outside the double wide doors, I can hear the faint sound of a live band playing a jazzy rendition of 'Jingle Bells'. Even for a place like The Avalon, tonight is *fancy* fancy. I don't know exactly who we have dining with us tonight – all I know is that they paid enough to book out the restaurant for just their relatively small party of ten for a decadent Christmas meal.

I'm no stranger to the insanely rich and famous descending on The Avalon, but tonight feels different. When I poked my head out earlier, the wait staff were setting out gold-plated cutlery on the large table that cuts across the middle of the room, and even Gareth has been more twitchy and overbearing than usual, paying actual attention to the menu I suggested for tonight. Usually, our quarterly meetings consist of me shoving a painstakingly researched seasonal menu – complete with a list of local suppliers – under his nose, and him simply grunting before signing off on it and leaving me to do what I do best. Not that I'm complaining; I work best when I'm left to do my job, and I'd expected the same for tonight's meal, but he'd actually been moderately helpful – although a shadow of the restaurant manager he once was – and we pulled together a menu I'm actually proud of:

Appetisers and Starters

Truffle-infused caviar blinis served with a delicate
dollop of crème fraiche and microgreens

Wild mushroom and black truffle soup topped with a
drizzle of truffle oil and a sprinkle of chive blossoms

Mains

Pan-seared scallops accompanied by a cauliflower
purée and a champagne butter sauce

Roast pheasant with a cranberry glaze served with a
thyme-infused bread pudding, stuffing and Brussels sprouts

Herb-crusted rack of lamb accompanied with a side of
garlic mashed potatoes, and roasted root vegetables

Desserts

A golden Christmas pudding flambéed tableside
with brandy and served with a rich custard sauce

A selection of artisanal British cheese featuring
Stilton, Cornish brie, aged cheddar, and served
with quince jelly and artisan crackers

Definitely a little fancier than the massive meal I'll be preparing with my grandmother at our annual family Christmas get-together in two days, but it's the first time in what feels like years that I've been able to get this creative with a menu and I'm practically bouncing at the thought of getting it in front of our guests.

At least, I was. The excitement I felt this morning when I entered the kitchen has been snuffed out, replaced by a gnawing sense of irritation and anxiety as I lay the newly sliced carrots on the tray and reach for the parsnips.

'Focus, Noelle,' I murmur to myself, shaking my head. I try to force my mind to zero in on the task at hand, pushing away any lingering murderous thoughts towards my two co-workers. Instead, I picture the plates being sent out – vibrant, colourful, delicious, the kind of food that can't help but put you in the Christmas spirit.

'Hey, Noelle?' Jamie's voice breaks though my concentration. 'You need a hand with anything?'

I look up and see immediately that his show of camaraderie is laced with hostility. What a dickhead. 'Just make sure the cranberry sauce comes out well,' I snap back through gritted teeth.

Jamie gives me a mock salute and for the second time in less than an hour – surely this must be a world record – I conquer the urge to fling a metal tray at my co-worker's head.

★ ★ ★

'Everything ready?' Gareth glides into the kitchen, wringing his hands and nervously looking around. The wait staff for tonight file in after him, all dressed in perfectly pressed and neat uniforms. 'The guests have all arrived and they're ready for their appetisers.'

I open my mouth but Will cuts across me and says smoothly, 'We're good to go, boss.'

Gareth smiles at him. 'Thank you, Will.'

Thank you, Will.

Thank you to the man who has done nothing but roll stuffing into – admittedly perfect – little balls for the last five hours? I'm not even entirely sure how he's managed to stretch out the task for that long.

My eye twitches and I swear I'm about five seconds away from short-circuiting.

You're a professional, I remind myself for what has to be the umpteenth time today. *Just keep it moving. You'll be finished soon.*

The light at the end of this tunnel is knowing that by the end of tonight, I'll be making my way to my grandmother's house, ready to settle in for a week of nothing but (mostly) good-natured family arguments, delicious food and Christmas cheer.

Just a few more hours to go.

'Let's go then,' says Gareth. He nods to the wait staff and they immediately snap into action. I step aside and watch as they started loading up the first round of dishes – the truffle caviar blinis – to present them to our guests. There's always something about the first time someone eats a meal I've made that sends a jolt of adrenaline buzzing through my veins.

I know I've got things to be finishing off, but I can't help myself. I slip over towards the doors that lead to the dining area and peek out. The music from the live band and the laughter from the guests intermingle as the sound spills into the kitchen and my heart skips a beat as I catch a glimpse of our guests for the evening.

I don't recognise any of the laughing men and women sitting around the table, but there's an unmistakable energy to them. It's almost like there's an electric kind of magnetism radiating from the room. The men are wearing sleek, expensive-looking suits as they laugh boisterously and down glass after glass of champagne, and the women are decked out in elegant gowns and glistening jewellery that looks like it costs more than what I earn in a year.

It's clear that this isn't just any event; it's a gathering of the elite, and the pressure of perfection suddenly weighs heavier than ever.

A waitress scurries past me, and I catch snippets of conversation as she whisks away the appetisers.

'That was exquisite,' one of the guests, a woman in a midnight blue gown, remarks. There's an unmistakable hint of awe in her voice. 'If that was just the beginning, I can't wait to see what else they've got in store for us.'

Pride blooms in my chest.

Another voice – a man – chimes in. 'We've been assured that it's all locally sourced ingredients, you know? Isn't that incredible?'

'Simply amazing.' The woman nods before taking a sip

from her champagne. 'Do you know if we're expecting Hoxton tonight, by the way?'

The man frowns. 'I don't believe we received an RSVP, but you know how—'

'We need those scallops ready in about five minutes,' Jamie hollers suddenly.

'On it!' I call back, pulling myself back into the rhythm of the kitchen. I move quickly, plating the pan-seared scallops with almost surgical precision, and sprinkle the finishing touches – a drizzle of champagne butter sauce and a healthy green garnish – before sending them out with a flourish.

The rest of the evening passes in a blur of hurriedly plating dishes, barked orders, slight tweaks to the menu – '*Could I have the pheasant with the potatoes?*' – and stolen snatches of conversation from our guests. Every time the wait staff file in and out of the kitchen, I strain to hear as much as I can from the dining room.

Praise floods in every time the doors swing open, and the pride blooming in my chest has spread out to encompass every inch of my body. By the time dessert swings around, I'm fairly certain I have a constant glow from the endless stream of compliments being thrown my way.

'Noelle!' Gareth barks my name as he comes striding through the doors. As the doors swing open, I hear a flurry of gasps and cheers from the guests, followed by a loud:

'Alexander! What a surpr—'

The door swings shut and all I can hear are the noises from the kitchen again.

'They're asking for you,' Gareth says.

I freeze on the spot, suddenly aware of every speck of flour, every dollop of gravy, every splotch of mashed potato, splattered across my chef whites. 'Excuse me?'

Will and Jamie both sidle up beside me with identical looks of confusion. 'Why her?'

'They're asking for the chef behind tonight's menu.'

'It was a team effort,' Will starts, but Gareth rolls his eyes.

'I don't have time for this. Noelle, tidy yourself up as much as you can, and then we'll introduce you as we present the dessert. You've got five minutes.'

As he disappears back into the dining room, I get another snippet of conversation from our guests before the doors swing shut:

'. . . *shame you missed most of the meal but try some of the lamb. Here. It's to die for, and I'm not exaggerating.*'

'*I don't—*'

'*Oh come on, Hoxton. Where's your Christmas spirit?*'

Once Gareth is gone, both Will and Jamie turn to glare at me, but for the first time in longer than I can remember, I don't feel the need to argue with them. Instead, I fix a smug smile onto my face, lift both middle fingers high in the air and turn towards the bathroom.

⋆ ⋆ ⋆

I don't manage to get the gravy stains out of my whites entirely, but I must do a decent-enough job because Gareth doesn't immediately send me back to the kitchen to swap me with Will or Jamie. Instead, he just gives me a mildly disapproving once-over, nods reluctantly, and then gestures for me to follow him out into the dining area along with the wait staff carrying plates of Christmas pudding.

As soon as I step out into the room, the table erupts into over-the-top, slightly drunken – I'm assuming – applause and cheers from everyone. Well, almost everyone. There's a man sitting at the furthest end of the table, in the chair closest to the exit, with a sour look on his face. He's glaring determinedly at his plate, as if it's personally wronged him somehow, and doesn't so much as flinch as the rest of the table devolves into raucous applause.

'There she is!' a man at the head of the table says, grinning broadly. 'The mastermind behind tonight's menu.'

I feel my cheeks start to warm as I approach the table. 'I'm glad you enjoyed it.'

'Enjoyed is an understatement, my dear,' says a woman with a lofty kind of accent. 'This was truly divine. Even Alexander managed a smile eating his plate.'

Everyone laughs and several heads swivel towards the man

at the furthest end of the table. He looks up just as I glance in his direction, and my heart skips a beat.

This man, this Alexander, might just be the most handsome man I've ever seen in my life.

Warm, tanned skin; short, dark hair with a subtle hint of curls; an impossibly chiselled jawline and a sprinkle of a beard that somehow manages to straddle the line between scruffy and groomed in an effortless kind of way.

Damn.

I think I go a little weak at the knees.

His dark eyes settle on me for a long moment and then he glances away, back to glaring at his plate like it's the source of all wrongs in the universe.

'And what was your name again?' one of the guests asks, dragging my attention away from Alexander.

'Noelle,' I say. 'Noelle Jones.'

This guest tips their champagne flute towards me and everyone around the table, bar Alexander, quickly follows suit. 'Now, why do I feel like this isn't going to be the last time I hear your name?'

'She'll have her own restaurant by this time next year,' someone chimes in.

I laugh awkwardly and try to squash down the sudden and strange feeling of failure that starts to well up inside me. 'Maybe not by next year, but yes, I suppose that's the dream.'

Gareth claps his hands suddenly, apparently eager to move

on from any conversation about me leaving The Avalon anytime soon. 'Shall we move on to dessert?'

The guests all cheer and coo as the wait staff start setting down the puddings, flambéing them one by one. I try to focus on the warm, golden flames dancing around the table and the look of pure joy on the guests' faces, but something snatches my attention away.

Out of the corner of my eye, I swear I see Alexander lift his head to shoot me a curious glance, but when I look back in his direction, he's back to glaring at his plate again.

★ ★ ★

FROM: rreynolds@hoxtech.com
TO: noelle.jones@gmail.com
DATE: 25 December 05.45am
SUBJECT: Business query

Dear Noelle,

I hope this email finds you well.

My name is Roland Reynolds and I'm sending this email on behalf of Alexander Hoxton, CEO and founder of HoxTech. He recently attended a meal you prepared and was thoroughly impressed with the quality of your work.

We would like to enquire as to whether you have any experience working as a personal chef, or if this is something you might be interested in looking into? Mr Hoxton is greatly interested in hiring your services and would like to discuss the matter further with you at a time of your convenience.

Please let me know your availability, and I hope you are enjoying your Christmas.

Kind regards,
Roland Reynolds
Executive Assistant

CHAPTER ONE

Noelle

December 21st, Two Years Later

'But it's Christmas!' Eve's whine comes through my phone speakers with perfect clarity. I don't need to glance at the screen to know she's giving me her best pout right now.

'It's December 21st,' I deadpan.

'You know what I mean.'

I let my concentration slide away from the road ahead just long enough to confirm that, *yes,* my twin sister is holding her phone camera to her face, batting her long lashes and giving me puppy dog eyes that would put a cocker spaniel to shame. It's the kind of look that makes people melt like butter in the palm of her hand, and Eve has never had any trouble getting exactly what she wants.

From everyone except me.

'I'll be there tomorrow,' I remind her. 'Pretty sure you can survive without me for one day.'

Eve huffs out a frustrated breath. 'Fine. But when you get here and Mum and Aunt Valerie are at each other's throats, I will be accepting no blame whatsoever.'

'You're not completely alone,' I point out. 'Nathan can help.'

'It's not the same,' Eve says with a dismissive eye-roll. 'He's still new to all of this, and he doesn't get it the way we do.'

She's got a point there. Our annual Christmas family reunion at my grandmother's home is quite possibly my favourite time of the year, but even I don't mind admitting that it can be a fraught affair. My family is full of big personalities and trying to keep the peace long enough for the Christmas spirit to settle in, and for everyone – namely, our mother and her older sister – to forget their many, many issues with each other is a tough job. Eve and I have been playing referee to their relationship each Christmas for as long as I can remember and that kind of dynamic just isn't something you want to throw at a newcomer.

'They never get really bad until day three, anyway,' I say, trying to ease some of the guilt I'm suddenly feeling. 'You'll be fine.'

'Or,' Eve says with a pointed wiggle of her brows. 'You

could just ask your sexy boss to give you some time off. Appeal to his inner Christmas spirit or something.'

I bite back a snort of laughter and force a neutral facial expression. 'He's not my boss. He's a client. And stop calling him that.'

'That's how you described him to me!'

That's true.

Two years ago, when I first started working for Alexander Hoxton, his looks were just about the only thing I could think about and I'm woman enough to admit that I once allowed myself the occasional fleeting fantasy of something more.

Because Alexander Hoxton is the kind of man women daydream about. He's the person you conjure up as the placeholder in your mind when you're reading a romance novel or spending some quality time with your favourite toy late at night. The type of guy who looks like he's just stepped right off the pages of *Vogue* and straight into your life.

Then he opens his mouth and the daydream is shattered.

To start with, he was late for our interview. *10am sharp*, his assistant had made sure to include at the bottom of my confirmation email. *Hoxton values punctuality.*

You'd think a person who values punctuality wouldn't leave an interviewee sitting on one of the uncomfortable plastic seats in his grey and sterile office lobby for forty-five minutes.

And yet.

Instead of apologising when he finally deigned to saunter

in and summon me into his office, looking like he'd just strolled off a runway, he simply dropped into his chair and fixed me with a distant and unimpressed look in lieu of a proper greeting.

The urge to remind him that he was one who was interested in my services, and I hadn't come crawling to him, was overwhelming. It was like he'd forgotten all about his meal at The Avalon and thought I was some random person who'd managed to con her way into his office somehow. It was jarring to say the least.

But I smiled brightly, stuck my hand out to remind him that at least one of us was a professional, and tried to get us back on the right track. 'It's a pleasure to see you again, Mr Hoxton. I hope you had a lovely Christmas break.'

I still haven't decided whether it was the manic smile on my face or the fact that I'd leaned over his desk, inching into his personal space to shove my hand out directly in front of him, but his façade cracked just a tiny bit then. He looked genuinely startled for a moment before his features smoothed out again into that mask of carefully constructed disinterest, and he gingerly shook my hand.

'Ms Jones,' he said with a sharp nod before he dropped my hand.

I remember waiting awkwardly to see if he'd elaborate – perhaps ask about how my Christmas was – but only silence followed.

The rest of the interview went well enough. I took him through my sample menus, dutifully reeled off my culinary résumé, and then sat back and waited for him to do his part and ask me some questions. But only one question came, eventually.

'Ms Jones, I'm a busy man.'

I remember biting the inside of my cheek to stop a laugh from slipping out. *I'm a busy man*. No shit, Sherlock.

'I don't have time for culinary . . . theatrics or pretentious menus.' He waved a dismissive hand over the sample menus I'd laid out in front of him and I swear a small part of me nearly shrivelled up and died.

Culinary theatrics.

Pretentious menus.

Ouch.

'Your meal last Christ—' He grimaced as if tasting something vile on the tip of his tongue, and then shook his head. 'Your meal last year showcased your talents well, but I really don't need that every day. I just want someone who can whip up something that's nutritious, tastes good, and isn't going to make extra work for me every day. Bonus points if you can tidy up after yourself and know what discretion means.' For the first time since I'd walked into his sterile office, he met my gaze with something other than thinly veiled boredom with a dash of contempt, and asked, 'Can you do that, or should I continue to look elsewhere?'

I should've laughed in his face.

Should've jumped straight out of my seat and stormed right out of there. Because who the hell talks to someone like that without expecting an immediate fist in the face? Alexander Hoxton, that's who.

But I knew in my heart of hearts that I couldn't return to The Avalon after an opportunity like this. I couldn't get a job at any restaurant after this. As much as I still hate to admit it to this day, getting that email from Hoxton's assistant on Christmas Day was the best gift anyone could have ever given me. For the first time since I allowed myself to dream of a culinary career, I felt like I had an actual plan that would allow me to get to my end goal: a restaurant of my own. I'd never be able to save up enough working for someone else but, as a personal chef, I could make my own hours, charge my own rates and specifically seek out the ridiculously rich as clients. I'd be doing something I love and finally, finally, be earning what I deserve for it.

And it all started with him.

That's why, two years on from quite possibly the worst interview I've ever had, with a roster of other clients to cater for, Alexander Hoxton is still one of them.

His only redeeming quality – aside from being a literal Adonis – is the fact that he only really communicates via email, and even those are a rarity. I've taken to leaving sticky notes around his kitchen if I need to ask something of him and, since the day he hired me, I don't think we've shared more than ten actual words between us.

It's a strange working dynamic for sure, but it works for us and I'd like to keep it that way. Eve, as the main recipient of all my Hoxton-related complaints, knows this just as well as I do, so I can't exactly blame her for being confused as to why I've chosen him over driving to Nan's house together like we'd planned.

'First off, I'd be surprised if Hoxton even knows the meaning of Christmas spirit,' I say, glancing away from the phone screen as I turn down a familiar side road. The large houses on either side of the street are decked out in glittering lights and artful decorations that send a warm jolt of Christmas joy shooting through me.

You just don't get this kind of festive fun in the city where we're all crammed into dull, grey tower blocks and nobody wants to make eye contact with their neighbours. The houses out here, in Hoxton's rich Surrey suburb, are like something out of a film. Almost every home is covered in twinkling lights and more than a handful have doused their sprawling front lawns in fake snow.

'And secondly,' I continue, a wry smile playing on my lips as I crawl past an elegant reindeer sculpture outside a particularly grand house, 'you remember how much he's paying me for tonight, don't you?'

'Money isn't everything, Noelle,' Eve says loftily, but I can hear the grin in her voice.

I suppose that's one more good thing about Hoxton: he pays ridiculously well. So well, I thought there had been a mistake the first time he paid one of my invoices and added a tip so large, I was convinced my bank would shut down my account on suspicion of fraud. I still haven't quite managed to shake that fear every time he pays me.

The tech company Hoxton founded, almost a decade ago, has a reputation for paying some of the highest salaries in the field and it seems that this admittedly admirable generosity filters down to his other expenditures too.

He's never had a problem with my fee. Has never tried to arbitrarily haggle it down a few hundred pounds like some of the other clients I've amassed over the last two years. And he always throws a good tip my way – though this, I suspect, is less from genuine satisfaction with my work or delight with me as human being, given that we never speak, and more just a habit he's picked up over the years for all his auxiliary staff. Either way, I can't complain. As much as Hoxton irritates me, I'll take his well-paying, moody ass over the clients who smile in my face when I'm in their homes but are always late paying my invoices.

'Money isn't everything,' I concede, 'but if you want me to come on your hen party trip to Cancun next year, I need to take this job.'

Eve giggles with familiar wedding-related excitement. From the corner of my eye, I watch as she holds her hand in front of her and admires the rock Nathan proposed to her with six months ago. It's so big, the glare from it is almost blinding. 'You're right. Get the bag, girl. We've got first-class flights to pay for!'

My laughter mixes in with hers. In typical Eve fashion, she and Nathan are going all out for their wedding and, as the maid of honour, I've got to be there every step of the way. Not that I'm complaining. I'm exactly three minutes and forty-two seconds older than Eve, and I take my 'big sister' role seriously. If there's anything I can do to put a smile on her face, I'll do it. And besides, you'll never catch me complaining about a trip to Cancun, of all places.

It does, however, mean that I've had to pack out my business calendar with bookings recently in order to pay for all the festivities. Celebratory drinks. Multiple dress fittings. A bridal shower and a seven-day hen party in Cancun that I've been tasked with planning ... It all adds up and I'm determined not to dip into my 'start my own restaurant' savings to make it happen. That's why accepting Hoxton's last-minute request for tonight was a no-brainer.

Half a day of work, doing what I love to do, and my first-class return flight to Cancun will be almost entirely paid for.

I don't often give Hoxton praise, but today I find myself grateful to him.

Just a teeny bit.

'Oh shit,' Eve breathes.

I briefly glance away from the road and at my phone screen, but Eve isn't looking at me. Something off camera has caught her attention and she's got a serene, almost child-like smile on her face. 'What is it?'

'It's snowing.' She tilts her camera towards her window and I get a brief glimpse of bright white snow falling from the sky. 'I hope it settles. We haven't had proper snow for Christmas in years.'

'No snow over here,' I say. It's definitely cold enough, but the sky is still a clear, icy blue.

'It'll come,' Eve says with an assured nod. 'I think I heard something on the news about a storm today.'

'As long as it's not too heavy. I still have to drive up to Nan's tomorrow.' I turn down yet another familiar street, and all the houses here are also decked out in Christmas cheer.

Except one.

Alexander Hoxton's home sits right at the far end of his swanky cul-de-sac without so much as a single fairy light wrapped around the black metal gates that cordon off his home from the rest of the world. 'What were we saying about Christmas spirit?' I mutter as the gates open after automatically recognising my licence plate, and I let my car crawl into his sprawling driveway.

Roland, Hoxton's assistant, is already striding out of the front door as I park up. I don't think I've ever met anyone as efficient as Roland. It makes working for Hoxton that much easier, knowing I can go through Roland for most things and avoid his prickly boss.

'Gotta go,' I say to Eve, giving her a quick wave before I cut the call and fix a friendly and genuine smile onto my face. I like Roland. He's exceptionally good at his job and we seem to have developed an unspoken understanding when it comes to Hoxton.

'Noelle!' he says cheerfully. He's dressed smartly in his usual work attire, but there's an extra addition to it today – a festive tie. There's a cheerful Rudolph drawing painted across the front of it and, every few seconds, his red nose lights up and flashes. Roland catches my gaze lingering on the tie, and his smile curves into something a little more reminiscent of a smirk. 'I'm glad someone appreciates my attempt at injecting some festive cheer into this place.'

Translation? Hoxton's not a fan of the tie.

Surprise, surprise.

'I love it,' I say with a wink before grabbing my bag from the passenger seat and following him into the house. 'You should add it to your regular wardrobe.'

Roland huffs out a quiet laugh. 'And be on the hook for causing an aneurysm? I don't think so.'

The inside of Hoxton's house should be impressive. It's a

sprawling mansion with acres on either side of it, providing an apparently much-needed distance from his neighbours. It could probably fit my tiny flat inside it several times over, but I've been here so many times that the awe factor is lost on me. Today, however, it just feels bleak.

It's all sharp angles and hard edges with dark, oaky walls and not a trace of Christmas cheer. It was like this last year too, so I hadn't been expecting much of an improvement today but . . .

'Did I misread the email?' I ask, still following Roland through the winding halls. Roland guides me every time I come here. I'm pretty sure Hoxton makes him do it; not out of concern that I'll get lost but to keep his privacy intact, as if he's afraid I might go snooping and uncover some sordid secret or other. 'Is he still hosting a Christmas meal tonight?'

I wouldn't be surprised if I did misread it. Once thing I've learned since working for him is that Alexander Hoxton and Christmas are two things that don't go together. Lack of Christmas décor aside, on my first Christmas working for Hoxton, I'd expected him to request a flurry of seasonally appropriate meals for me to prepare to tide him over for the holiday season, just like my other clients had. I was prepared to make festive sausage rolls, turkey-stuffed sandwiches, honey-roasted vegetables and desserts soaked in cinnamon, but Hoxton rejected every single idea in one brief email.

FROM: hoxton@hoxtech.com
TO: noelle.jones@gmail.com
SUBJECT: RE: Christmas recipe ideas!

No to all below suggestions. No need for
'Christmas' theme. Your standard meals will be fine.

Roland hums in acknowledgment. 'That's right. It was a last-minute decision and, truth be told, it came out of nowhere. Terrible timing, if I'm being honest,' Roland murmurs, cutting his eyes ever so slightly. 'It's not like I'm about to head off on a twenty-hour flight to Australia to spend Christmas with my boyfriend's family for the first time, or anything like that.'

I glance sideways and raise a brow. Roland immediately offers me a sheepish grin.

'Sorry, like I said. This came out of nowhere and I'm already ridiculously stressed.' He pulls at the sleeve of his blazer. 'He could've at least given us more than forty-eight hours' notice.'

I nod in sympathetic solidarity. Roland is usually so calm and composed but, now that I'm really looking at him, I suppose he does look a little frazzled.

'I hope my shopping list didn't give you too much grief,' I say.

Roland waves an airy hand. 'You were the least of my

problems, trust me on that. Getting the rest of the Board to agree to attend on such short notice . . .' Roland trails off and exhales a deep, long-suffering sigh.

I don't typically make it my business to poke into the affairs of my clients, but there's something behind Roland's sigh that has my curiosity piqued. 'They don't get along?'

Roland hesitates. 'For the most part,' he says carefully before pursing his lips into a thin line. 'But that's neither here nor there. Let's focus on the now. On this dinner.'

I frown as we walk past the dining room. Like the rest of the house, there's not so much as a single candle on the large wooden table in the centre of the room. 'It's really not very Christmassy in here though, is it? Is he sending someone to come in and decorate?'

He's cutting it very fine if he is.

Roland pulls a face. 'I did suggest it, but he insisted that you'd be more than enough.'

A twisted jolt of pride shoots through me. I think that's the closest I've ever got to receiving genuine praise from Hoxton, even if it was second-hand.

'Still,' I continue. 'It's not just about the food, you know? It's in the atmosphere. Where are the party hats and the Christmas crackers?' I poke my head into the living room as we pass it. 'Does he even have a tree?'

Roland barks out a laugh, presumably at the thought of Hoxton wearing a party hat, and then quickly tries to muffle it. 'I offered to run out and get him one this morning, and he acted like I'd threatened to set the whole place on fire.'

We come to a halt outside the kitchen door – my office for the evening – and Roland fixes me with an apologetic grimace. 'Listen, Noelle. The holidays aren't always a great time when it comes to Alex.'

As far as I can tell, there's never a good time when it comes to Hoxton, but I keep those thoughts to myself. Roland and I have a decent-enough relationship, but it's obvious he feels a kind of protectiveness over Hoxton. He's been his assistant for close to a decade now and while Roland has no problem rolling his eyes or laughing with me at some of Hoxton's more irritating habits, I have no doubt where his loyalties truly lie.

'Just do what you do best and then head home and enjoy the holidays. Don't let him get you down.'

'That was always the plan,' I say with an easy grin. Get in. Make some money. Get out. Simple.

Roland surveys me for a few long seconds. I get the distinct impression that there's something else on the tip of his tongue, but then he shakes his head and throws open the kitchen door.

If there's one thing I truly love about Hoxton's otherwise sterile home, it's his kitchen. It's the only room in the whole place that feels like it has any character to it. There's a large skylight that bathes the room in natural light, and the walls are covered in rustic bricking that makes the entire room feel warm and cosy, despite the soft layer of fluffy white snow blanketing the skylight right now.

The centrepiece, though, is the cream Aga oven that sits against one of the walls, emanating a constant, gentle warmth that I felt in my very bones as soon as I stepped over the threshold of the house.

There's a spacious wooden farm table in the middle of the kitchen and, to my dismay, Hoxton is currently sitting at it, tapping away on his laptop. He's dressed as he usually is on the rare occasions I do see him, in a crisp white shirt, tailored trousers, and a pair of comfortable-looking slippers. I don't think I've ever seen Hoxton wear anything that couldn't be described as business-ready, like he's always anticipating jumping into a meeting. Eve once joked that he probably wears a three-piece suit to bed.

He looks up as I enter the room, his dark eyes appraising me with cool detachment. His hair is styled to perfection and his jawline, tight as his gaze roves over me, could cut steel. 'Ms Jones,' he says, his voice deep and wholly disinterested.

That's the only acknowledgment I get from him. He doesn't wait for me to return the greeting before his attention is back on his screen and he's furiously tapping away.

'Mr Hoxton,' I say anyway, my voice just as cool as his.

Roland clears his throat. 'Noelle, all the ingredients you ordered are packed away. I'm leaving in an hour but let me know if you need anything else before then and I'll run out and get it for you.'

It takes me five minutes to scan the cupboards and fridge to make sure everything I ordered for the night is there. Once I'm satisfied, I give Roland a nod and he disappears to finish the rest of his tasks before he needs to leave for the evening.

And then it's just me and Hoxton.

Alone in the kitchen.

He doesn't say a word, so I don't either. I've long since learned that Hoxton isn't one for small talk, and I'm not desperate to make it with him either. I hum quietly to myself as I reach into my bag and pull out the apron I've chosen specially for tonight.

A friend bought it for me last Christmas as part of a Secret Santa gift swap and I've been waiting all year to bring it out again. It's one of those ridiculously cheesy Christmas aprons, with a dancing Santa Claus and reindeer littering the edges.

It's bright.

Very bright.

Definitely not my usual workwear, but it's Christmas. Can you blame me?

Hoxton apparently can.

I'm not sure when he stopped staring at his laptop but when I look up, he's glaring at me.

His jaw ticks.

I raise a brow. *Say something if you're bad.*

Another tick.

I bite the inside of my cheek to stop myself from laughing.

Another tick.

Is this what Roland meant when he said he didn't want to be blamed for causing an aneurysm? Because, right now, Hoxton looks like he's halfway there.

'Can I help you?' I ask innocently, breaking the charged silence that's fallen over us.

In true Hoxton fashion, he doesn't say a word. Just pushes himself up from the table, collects his laptop, and then strides right out of the kitchen.

Despite everything, I can't help but laugh.

Good riddance.

CHAPTER TWO

Alex

I can hear the faint sound of Christmas music coming from the kitchen.

I can't make out the lyrics properly from here, but I'm pretty sure it's a modern spin on one of the many, *many*, festive jingles that have been playing on repeat at the office since December 1st darkened my calendar.

I don't understand how it doesn't drive more people insane.

My home, up until now, has been a refuge. A safe space. The one place where I haven't had to worry about plastering on a fake smile – or grimace if you listen to the way Roland describes it – whenever people gush endlessly about Christmas and the festive season, like it's any different from any other day of the year.

Roland's hideous tie, I could handle. But this?

Through the walls I listen as Noelle attempts to hit a particularly high note. She fails miserably, but that doesn't discourage her, and she continues to belt out the lyrics to the song crackling from her phone speaker.

What is it about Christmas that makes even reasonable people unbearable?

Roland with his tie.

Noelle with her apron and apparently never-ending medley of Christmas songs.

And Luca and this nonsense about hosting a Christmas meal with my Board of Directors.

It's my own fault really.

Tensions have been high between me and my Board for a few months now and I had, perhaps foolishly, assumed they would just continue to simmer under the surface as they always do. They've not liked the direction I've been taking the company in over the last year. Never mind that we've seen record profits over the last quarter, the consensus seems to be that we could always be making more money. Corners could be cut. Production could take place overseas. Salaries could be lower.

Their pockets could be a little fatter.

I've largely ignored their complaints, but I can't ignore the growing sense of mutiny that ripples under the surface of every meeting we've had recently. If I'm not careful, I might just find myself in trouble.

Luca, my friend since our university days and the only member of the Board I can actually tolerate, was the one to suggest tonight.

This Christmas meal.

Just the thought of it makes me roll my eyes, but Luca insisted it would be a necessary step in mending the fractured relationship.

'They don't like you,' Luca said bluntly over drinks one evening. 'And they don't think you're taking the company in the right direction, so they're already disinclined to agree with anything you suggest.'

'I hardly think one meal is going to change that.'

'No,' Luca conceded, 'but it's a gesture of peace. A way for you to show that you're not as much of a prick as they think you are.'

They're not the first to make such an assessment about me, and they most definitely won't be the last. Being liked isn't something I usually expend a lot of effort caring about, but I've worked too hard to lose everything now. If suffering through a Christmas meal with my Board is what I need to do to keep the company I founded running smoothly, then so be it.

Though to say I'm anxious about tonight would be an understatement.

I don't like people in my space. Never have and I doubt I ever will.

I was the fourth child in a family of seven unruly kids, and personal space was always something I lacked. Now that I've finally got it, I'm reluctant to let it go.

It's just one evening, I tell myself as I try to refocus on the email I've reread about fifty times already. One evening, then they'll be gone and I can go back to pretending Christmas doesn't exist.

Though the forces that be aren't making that easy.

'*On the second day of Christmas, my baby gave to me . . .*' Noelle's still off-key voice floats through the walls as clearly as if she were standing right beside me.

How is it possible for someone to be so bad at something, yet still clearly derive so much pleasure from it?

It feels odd having her in the house right now. We've stuck to a fairly rigid schedule over the last two years and having her walk into the kitchen earlier caught me off guard. I usually try to keep out of her way while she's here, leaving Roland to show her around and assist her if necessary, but hiring Noelle has undoubtedly been one of the best decisions of my life.

When I'd first started toying with the idea of hiring a personal chef, the goal was to find someone to streamline some of the more tedious and time-consuming aspects of my life. Without needing to spend hours in the kitchen each day, I could dedicate that time to sourcing new investors or creating new products.

I'd have settled for someone who knew how to throw together a half-decent Bolognese sauce, but Noelle has been a revelation.

I don't think I even knew that food could taste this good, but Noelle makes it look easy. Effortless, even. She comes in once a week, commandeers my kitchen with all the precision and prowess of a seasoned pro, and makes a week's worth of meals that only need heating up or light preparation before they're ready for me to devour.

And these aren't your typical plastic containers filled with rice, plain chicken and frozen vegetables. She makes simple dishes somehow worthy of a Michelin star like it's easy. I don't think she's ever made a dish I haven't enjoyed, and I find myself looking forward to Monday evenings when I can raid my kitchen and discover the meals she's left for me.

Her dishes nearly always come accompanied with a hurriedly scrawled Post-it note with a quick explanation of the dish and why she loves it:

Mr H
It's flu season and this is my tried and tested way
for staving off the cold. It's a family recipe.
(If you still get sick, I take no responsibility ;))
Noelle

Mr H
Happy Jamaican Independence Day! This
is the national dish 'ackee and saltfish' –
try it for breakfast tomorrow.
Enjoy!
Noelle

Mr H
Roland mentioned that your business trip to
Italy was cancelled at the last-minute. Not a
substitute for the real thing, but here's some
homemade gnocchi with pancetta and sage butter.
It's one of my fave dishes!
Noelle

I've kept every single one of them, and I'm not entirely
sure why. There's a strange energy between us. Her Post-it
notes are polite enough, but I can see the way she stiffens
slightly, the strain in her smile, on the rare occasions we're
face to face.

Noelle doesn't like me and it's my fault entirely. I tend to
have this kind of effect on people. It's probably why Luca
is the only friend I've managed to hold onto for more than
a few years. Unless we're counting Roland, and I'm fairly
certain he only sticks around for the pay cheque.

One of these days, I'll do something about it. Maybe once

I've retired and don't have to worry about backstabbing Board members and pleasing investors all day long.

'*Doesn't it feel like Christmas?*'

Right. And this Christmas meal too.

I try and tune out the rest of Noelle's singing, but it's like my ears have attuned to her voice with irritating clarity.

I knew I should've gone into the office today, but the closer we get to December 25th, the more unbearable my workplace has become. It seems like every other day another department is having their annual Christmas party, and the office halls are filled with my workers wearing hideous Christmas-themed clothing, or swapping gifts with one another. I just know the current weather we're experiencing would only encourage their nonsense, and there's only so much madness I can be expected to endure.

I let out a deep sigh and close my laptop. It's time to face the music. I make my way back to the kitchen and find Noelle humming along to the Christmas music blaring from her speakers as she deftly chops some vegetables. Her hands are moving at lightning speed, with skill that must have taken years to develop. I've always been appreciative of people who dedicate the time to truly honing their craft, and Noelle is no exception. I feel a wave of admiration for her, but it quickly disappears as I hone in on her attire once again.

She's still wearing the apron.

41

Bright red with flashing lights, a dancing Santa Claus and sparkling, galloping reindeers along the edge.

It's an abomination.

It should be illegal.

Noelle glances up as I enter and gives me a smirk that tells me my current train of thought is pasted plainly across my face.

'Mr Hoxton.' She gives me a polite nod, the corners of her lips twitching slightly, before she turns her attention back to the chopping board in front of her.

She's not looking at me, but I nod back anyway. Even with the garish apron, Noelle is the kind of woman you don't want to take your eyes off. The kind of woman you can't take your eyes off. Her hair falls just beyond her waist in thin, wispy braids, and her soft brown eyes catch the warm light in the room and almost sparkle as she works.

I stand there for a moment and watch Noelle in her element. I don't often get to witness it, but it's something to marvel at every time. Noelle moves with a gracefulness that's almost hypnotic. She's completely absorbed in what she's doing, a concentrated expression twisting her plump brown lips as she slices some carrots into long, thin strips.

It's almost a shame to interrupt, but I feel like I need to say something.

I clear my throat. 'Ms Jones?'

She sets her knife down before cocking her head to the side in silent question.

After two years, I'm not entirely sure why we're not on a first-name basis yet. Roland started calling me Alex during his first month, and I don't think there's anyone else I refer to by surname only. I'm suppose I'm taking my cues from her. She's never once deviated from the polite 'Mr Hoxton' she uttered during our first disastrous meeting.

It's a moment I replay in my head every so often and it always makes me cringe and one I've been meaning to apologise. But after two years I still haven't quite figured out a way to say, '*Sorry, you caught me at a bad time. One of our major investors had just pulled out and I was fighting bad press about the launch of one of our latest products,*' that doesn't come across as a pathetic excuse for my poor attitude that day – or the countless days that have since followed it.

It always feels like there's something going wrong.

Failed deals, underperforming products, client fatigue, bitter Board members, unhappy investors and the endless cycle of trying to keep afloat in an increasingly cut-throat market. Take tonight, for example, and this ridiculous Christmas farce. Any hope of a good mood went out the window as soon as Luca suggested the idea.

'Did you need something?' Noelle asks, snapping me out of the increasingly dour train of thought I'd been slipping into. She's staring at me and her body language is perfectly clear. Her brows are raised, her shoulders are stiff and her jaw is tight. This may be my home, but the kitchen belongs to her, and I'm nothing but an intruder right now.

I shake my head, not even sure what I wanted to say in the first place. 'Just coming to get some water.'

'Right.' She shrugs and immediately gets back to work as if I'm not even there.

I grab a cool bottle from the fridge just as Noelle goes to inspect whatever is the cause of the delicious smell wafting from the oven.

Against my better judgment, I make one last attempt at conversation. 'What's on the menu tonight?'

Noelle glances over at me with a guarded look in her eye, and then she gives me a teasing smile, as if she's been expecting this question all along. 'Something Christmassy.'

The words feel like a slap to the face. Not overtly hostile or even unfriendly, but enough to signal that my presence isn't wanted here at all.

I already knew that, of course, but it still stings just the same.

With nothing else to say, and Noelle showing no interest in elaborating, I nod and leave without another word.

CHAPTER THREE

Noelle

I'm putting the finishing touches on the appetiser – a sweet and indulgent cranberry honey baked brie – when I hear the sound of the gates bordering Hoxton's home creaking open.

From the window, I watch as a sleek black car rolls into Hoxton's driveway, disturbing the fluffy blanket of fresh white snow. The door opens and out steps an equally sleek and dashing-looking gentleman. Hoxton comes striding out of the front door with remarkable speed and an unexpected pang of irritation shoots through me.

Not once over the course of the last two years has Hoxton ever come out to greet me directly. I suppose he saves that honour for men dressed in stylish grey suits who stand with all the confidence of someone who knows he's important.

And the man I'm watching him greet right now definitely fits that description.

I watch as Hoxton claps his guest on the shoulder and pulls him into a stiff hug, like the action isn't something he's quite used to just yet and he's forcing it a little. The man breaks out into a wide grin, his shoulders shaking slightly as he says something I can't hear. Whatever it is, it makes Hoxton's lips turn down at the corners into a familiar scowl.

There we go.

That's the man I know. Grumpy. Brusque. Borderline rude.

Much better.

I lose sight of them as they head inside the house, so I turn my attention back to the meal. Without tooting my own horn too much, I'm pretty excited about tonight. I've worked on several Christmas menus for clients this holiday season, but Hoxton was the last client I'd expected to get a request from. I'd be lying if I didn't admit that I've put a teensy bit more effort into Hoxton's menu than I usually do.

I'm serving a feast that incorporates traditional Christmas flavours with a modern twist: alongside the brie, I've prepared rosemary and garlic pork loin, honey-roasted Brussels sprouts, cheesy potatoes au gratin, and a phenomenal cranberry pear tart. To top it all off, I've got some Christmas cookies and I've also made my favourite dessert as a festive extra – a spiced rum pumpkin cake that's been a family recipe for decades. My grandmother taught me how to make it as a child, and I've spent years perfecting my own unique twist on it, adding an almost scientific blend of cinnamon and star anise to the rum mixture.

It's actually the first time I've made it for a client, and I feel a twinge of anxiety at the thought of serving it to Hoxton of all people.

The door to the kitchen suddenly swings open and I tense, expecting to see Hoxton's scowling form emerging from the doorway.

But it's not him.

'Ah, here's the kitchen.' The guest who just arrived beams at me as he leans against the nearest wall. He's got a mess of floppy brown hair and a boyish charm to his features that immediately coaxes out a smile of my own. 'You must be Noelle.'

I nod in response, not entirely sure what to make of his sudden appearance in my kitchen. I can't tell whether it's the way he carries himself or the curious way he's currently peering around the kitchen, but there's something refreshingly carefree about this man.

Something that suggests he doesn't take life as seriously as Hoxton does.

'And you are . . .' I trail off, waiting for him to fill in the blank.

'Luca.' He grins at me, his dark eyes sparkling with

something I can't quite place. 'Luca Fenchurch. It's great to finally meet the famous Ms Noelle Jones.'

My brows shoot up in surprise before I can temper my reaction. 'Famous?'

Luca laughs lightly. 'The way Alex talks about you? I feel like I'm in the presence of a celebrity right now.'

That's difficult to believe but I play along, assuming Luca is just trying to butter me up in an attempt to get a sneak peek at dinner. 'And what exactly has Mr Hoxton been saying?'

He shrugs, that easy grin still on his face. 'Something, something, "culinary genius". Something, something, "would put Gordon Ramsay to shame". The usual, you know?' He leans over the farm table and reaches out for the bowl of crackers I'd set out to snack on while I work.

My cheeks warm at the unexpected compliment. I've never been one to shy away from praise, but this is the second time today I've had positive feedback from Hoxton – and neither have come from the man himself. I'm not sure what to make of that, so I push the conversation onto something other than myself. 'How do you know Hoxton again?'

Luca pops a cracker into his mouth and chews thoughtfully for a few seconds. 'We're friends.'

I barely manage to muffle my snort and Luca is polite enough to pretend like he doesn't hear it. Hoxton and the word *friends* just don't seem to compute in my mind.

'And we work together,' he continues, correctly deciphering the sceptical look on my face. 'At HoxTech. I'm on the Board.'

That makes a lot more sense. I can't imagine anyone tolerating Hoxton's icy personality for long enough to genuinely call him a friend without needing some financial incentive to do so.

The door to the kitchen swings open once again and Hoxton appears.

Speak of the devil . . .

Hoxton pauses for a moment, his gaze flitting from Luca to me before his features settle into his signature scowl. 'I thought you were going to use the bathroom.' His tone is almost accusatory. 'You've been in here the whole time?'

'Got lost,' Luca says cheerfully. He's apparently immune to Hoxton's mannerisms, because his grin doesn't fade at all under the scrutiny of Hoxton's glare. In fact, I'm pretty sure it widens. 'And I was just introducing myself to the lovely Ms Jones.'

The way he says my name is loaded with something unspoken. It reminds me of the way Eve and I speak to each other when we're trying to gossip in front of other people.

Hell, maybe Hoxton and Luca *are* friends.

I don't know who I feel more sorry for. Luca, for having to deal with the constant rain cloud that is Alexander Hoxton, or Hoxton himself for having to cope with someone who seems to be his opposite in every way.

I catch Hoxton's eye for a brief second. His gaze roves over me before settling on my apron. 'You do have something to change into, don't you?'

I force my features into a quizzical frown. 'Change? Why would I change?'

The muscle in Hoxton's jaw is surely working overtime right now, and I have to bite the inside of my cheek to stop myself from breaking. Out of the corner of my eye, I see that Luca's struggling as well.

Hoxton runs a tired hand over his face. 'The apron. It's not exactly appropriate, is it?'

I quirk a brow. 'It's Christmas.'

'It's December 21st.'

'It's a Christmas meal. I don't think anyone will complain if I serve them with a little festive cheer.'

'It'll be good to have something,' Luca chimes in. He looks like he's about one more sentence away from bursting into hysterical laughter. 'The apron gets my vote.'

I raise a hand. 'Mine too.'

'Oof. Sorry, Alex.' Luca gives Hoxton a faux-sympathetic pat on the shoulder. 'Looks like you've been outvoted.'

For the second time tonight, Hoxton looks close to having an aneurysm. He glares at Luca, then glares at me, then shoots one last glare in Luca's direction, before he turns and storms out of the kitchen without so much as a backwards glance.

As soon as he's gone, Luca bursts out laughing and I can't help but join him.

Maybe antagonising the client I already have a tenuous working relationship with isn't the smartest idea I've ever had, but what the hell.

It's Christmas.

★ ★ ★

I quickly learn that Luca is the exception. Hoxton isn't anywhere near as friendly with the other members of his Board as he is with Luca.

I watch as they all arrive, their fancy cars looking even smarter next to my old banger in the driveway. Even with the ever-increasing intensity of the snowfall, Hoxton comes out to personally greet them all, just like he did with Luca. But, unlike with Luca, there are no smiles or hugs, stiff or otherwise, as they climb out of their cars and stumble on the slippery driveway. He shakes hands with three of them: a tall, snooty-looking woman with greying hair piled high into a bun atop her head, a man in a tailored suit who seems to be permanently attached to his phone, and a younger woman with a hard-edged look in her eyes. Hoxton simply nods curtly at the fourth guest and, even from the kitchen, I can feel the tension between them sizzling in the air.

I feel an irritating twinge of sympathy towards Hoxton as

I watch him lead his guests into the house, his lips thinned into a grim line. As much as I can't stand the man, it's obvious that he's not on great terms with his Board – Luca excluded – and would rather not have them in his home. Though, to be fair, it's pretty clear that they'd all rather be anywhere but here too. When I enter the dining room, balancing a tray of champagne flutes in my hands, the first thing I notice is just how quiet it is.

There's no polite conversation. No small talk being exchanged. Even Luca's smile has dimmed. The wind howling outside and the muffled sound of my Christmas tunes still playing in the kitchen is louder than anything happening in the dining room right now.

It is, quite frankly, incredibly depressing. Hoxton's dining room is a dark and rarely used area of his home at the best of times, and the lack of any decoration, Christmas or otherwise, doesn't help to set the mood.

Hoxton's eyes find mine as soon as I step into the room, and I take a little bit of perverse pleasure in watching them narrow as he realises that I'm still wearing the apron. He can't say anything now though, not in front of everyone. So he settles for just glaring at me. I respond by fixing a bright smile onto my face as I flit around the table and hand his guests their drinks.

'Oh, I love your apron,' the tall woman with grey hair coos as I set her glass down in front of her. 'It's delightful!'

The man seated next to her looks up from his phone just long enough to give me an appreciative nod. 'Very festive.'

At the head of the table, Hoxton exhales deeply. I can feel his annoyance radiating off him in waves, but I refuse to let it ruin my mood. This is supposed to be a Christmas celebration, after all.

'I'm glad you like it,' I say to the woman, flashing her another smile before moving on to the next guest. 'Can I interest anyone in some appetisers?'

The mood around the room immediately lifts at the mention of food, and I launch into my menu for the evening. By the time I'm finished explaining the dishes and answering any questions they have about allergies and intolerances, everyone looks a little less like they'd rather be anywhere else but here.

Everyone except Hoxton.

I can only describe the look on his face as a potent mix of being incredibly bored and incredibly annoyed. I can't tell who the current recipient of his ire is, though. Me? Or his Board?

Probably both, if I'm being honest.

I've never noticed this before – never had the opportunity, given our extremely limited face-to-face time – but Hoxton is terrible at masking his emotions. Surely it has to be obvious to everyone in the room that the man is clinging onto a thread right now. Maybe they're just used to this kind of behaviour from Hoxton. It's easy enough to picture him sitting in the cold and sterile HoxTech offices, glaring down at anyone foolish enough to make eye contact with him, and any sympathy I felt for the man earlier evaporates in an instant.

At least everyone else is talking now. The glasses of bubbly pinched between their fingertips have apparently loosened their tongues enough that they now actually re-semble a somewhat cordial group of co-workers.

'Got any Christmas plans, Therese?' Luca asks, shifting in his seat to turn to the woman with the sharp eyes.

Therese nods. The champagne has helped to temper the hard-edged glint in her eyes and she gives Luca a polite, if slightly strained, smile. 'We're heading to Courchevel in two days,' she says, with the faintest hint of a French accent. 'Should be fun, though I haven't skied in years so I'm ex-pecting to come back with a few bumps and bruises.'

'I bet it's like riding a bike,' Luca says. 'Your body's proba-bly got it all down in muscle memory. But, you know what?' He shifts slightly in his seat and nods in Hoxton's direction, a wide grin on his face. 'Alex is a great skier. You should ask him for some tips.'

Everyone turns to Hoxton, who looks very much like he would like to ram his glass down Luca's throat. Luca remains happily oblivious.

'Oh.' Therese clears her throat. 'I didn't know.'

There's a painfully awkward beat of silence.

'Yes,' Hoxton says, much too delayed.

Another awkward beat.

'Though I prefer snowboarding,' Hoxton continues, apparently realising that the ball is still in his court. 'Have you—' He clears his throat and shoots Luca a sideways glare. 'Have you ever tried it?'

Therese's eyes brighten a smidge. 'I haven't, but my husband – Henri, you remember?'

The look on Hoxton's face tells me that he absolutely does not remember this Henri, but he gives her a sharp nod anyway.

'Yes, well, Henri adores snowboarding. Really, I didn't know you were such a fan. At the summer gala next year, I'll have ...'

Her voice trails off as I disappear into the corridor and start hurrying back to the kitchen to grab the appetisers. When I return, balancing a large wooden cutting board with several loaves of perfectly sliced and crusty French bread dotted around the two mini cast-iron skillets of brie in my hands, the room is even livelier than before.

Therese has stopped interrogating Hoxton about his snowboarding skills and is now in the middle of an animated discussion with Luca, the tall, grey-haired woman and the man with his phone glued to him.

'You think Christmas is expensive now,' the older woman

chortles. 'Wait until you have grandchildren, Brian. It's all "latest iPhone" this, "designer clothes" that. And not a *please* or *thank you* in sight! Back in my day, I was happy to get a doll for Christmas, and now I've got my granddaughter sending me something called a *Sephora Wishlist* that I've got to make heads and tails of.'

Brian laughs. 'Thanks for the heads-up, Meryl. But my little ones are still young enough that a few cuddly toys will suffice. It's my wife who insists on making it all a big deal.'

'Oh, but think about the memories,' Therese sighs, almost dreamily. 'Most of my favourite childhood memories have something to do with Christmas, and it's all because my mother took the time to make it special.'

'Agreed,' Luca says with a faraway kind of smile. 'My mum used to put baby powder on the floor by the tree and make my dad walk up and down with his boots on so we'd think that it was Santa.'

I can't help but grin as I approach the table and set the appetisers down in the middle. I always love hearing about different families' Christmas traditions and I'm itching to jump into the conversation and share the story of how my mother would stand outside the bedroom I shared with Eve, with a tape recorder playing the sound of reindeer stomping on the roof.

Or about the Christmas when my father went outside for a few minutes and then came rushing back in hollering,

'*Santa must've dropped this last night!*' before brandishing a bell-laden collar with the name 'RUDOLPH' printed across the front.

And don't even get me started on the Christmases spent at Gran's house, where all the children are tasked with bringing something unique to decorate the tree with, resulting in a seven-foot evergreen covered in some of the most bizarre, technically non-Christmassy ornaments you've ever seen.

But I don't share any of that. I'm here to serve, not to eavesdrop on their conversation and share my own Christmas anecdotes. And besides, something else has caught my attention.

At the furthest end of the table, Hoxton is sat with a stony expression on his face. Beside him, the last member of the Board is speaking. This is the one Hoxton barely greeted on arrival and it seems like the tension between them hasn't eased at all.

'And have you given much thought to our discussion last week about outsourcing some of the support centre staff?'

Hoxton grits his teeth. 'No.'

The man huffs. 'I thought we agreed that it was an immediate concern, and that—'

'You decided that it was an immediate concern, Wilbur,' Hoxton says, his voice icy. 'As I told you, the contract we have in place doesn't expire for another two years. No sense in worrying about it now.'

.'But if they're in breach of contract, we can terminate our arrangement with them and opt for a centre that doesn't, shall we say, dent our end-of-year financials as much as this one currently does.'

'Unfortunately, they're not in breach of contract,' Hoxton says in clipped tones. It should be obvious that he wants this conversation to end, but Wilbur ploughs on.

'We may have to get a little creative, yes,' Wilbur says with a gruff cough. 'But, and at the end of the day here, Alexander, I'm just trying to think of our bottom line. We have shareholders to keep happy. Remember that.'

Damn. I know I call Hoxton a grinch, but he's not the one trying to conjure up reasons to fire an entire support centre of staff just before Christmas.

I clear my throat, sparing Wilbur the full force of the fury that's clearly about to come out of Hoxton's mouth. 'Ladies and gentleman ... for your appetiser tonight, we have a sweet cranberry honey baked brie with French bread freshly made this morning from the fabulous Maison Badeaux.'

Therese claps her hands in delight, clearly having heard of the famous French bakery that currently has the city in a chokehold. An understandable chokehold, if you ask me. Maison Badeaux can do no wrong, and they're my supplier of choice when it comes to baked goods these days.

I take a step back from the table. 'Please enjoy.'

'It smells divine,' Meryl says, reaching forward to grab a

slice of French bread to dip into the brie. 'Mmm, and tastes even better.'

That's all the invitation anyone needs. I'm beaming as I watch them all reach forward and help themselves to a bit of bread and brie, taking in the way their eyes roll back slightly with identical hums of pleasure slipping from their lips.

My gaze flickers across the room and lands on Hoxton. That's when it hits me suddenly. I've never actually seen Hoxton eat one of my meals. I've spent the last two years assuming that he enjoys them but, for all I know, he could be palming everything off on Roland every night.

I can't take my eyes off him as he slowly reaches forward and plucks a piece of bread off the board. He seems to sense that I'm watching and looks up, his dark eyes meeting my curious gaze. And he holds it there. Doesn't so much as blink as he dips the bread into the brie and then brings it up to his lips.

He savours the taste in his mouth, his eyelids flickering in that tell-tale manner that lets on more than he's willing to admit. I'm sure the grin on my face is more smug than anything else as I turn away from Hoxton and head for the kitchen again.

I think that was my third Hoxton compliment of the day.

It must be a Christmas miracle.

CHAPTER FOUR

Alex

The Board won't stop raving about Noelle.

It started with the brie, with Brian declaring it – a wisp of cheese dripping from his chin – to be phenomenal. Everyone else murmured in agreement, mouths full with cheese and bread, and the sentiment has steadily continued throughout the night. Our main for the evening, a perfectly crispy on the outside, juicy on the inside pork loin served alongside surprisingly flavoursome Brussels sprouts and a creamy gratin, just about makes them lose their minds. Every word that comes out of their mouths is praise for Noelle and the admittedly delicious feast she's prepared for us.

Just as I knew she would.

'This is it,' Luca groans dramatically, shovelling gratin

into his mouth. 'I've reached the peak my palate will ever again experience. It's all downhill from here.'

Therese nods enthusiastically as she spears a Brussels sprout onto her fork. 'She's got the magic touch. How else can you explain Brussels sprouts tasting like this?'

'Do you think she'll share her recipes?' Brian asks, going for his second serving of pork loin. 'Or is she available for hire?'

'I bet she's in high demand,' Meryl says, daintily dabbing at the sides of her mouth with a napkin. 'Where did you find her, Alex?'

'She's his personal chef,' Luca says cheerfully. 'Whenever you're at the office, have you never noticed Alex doesn't eat at the staff canteen and always brings his own food in? This is why.'

I scowl at Luca from across the table.

'A personal chef?' Wilbur murmurs beside me. It's the first thing he's said in quite a while, too preoccupied with devouring the meal on his plate. I suppose I should thank Noelle for that. Anything that can render Wilbur mute and save me from his constant scheming is nothing short of a miracle in my book. 'You know, I've been considering hiring one for a while now. Do you know if she has any openings for new clients?'

'No,' I say, quicker and sharper than I'd intended. 'She's fully booked.'

'A pity,' Wilbur says. 'She's quite talented.'

I don't need Wilbur of all people to tell me that. There's a reason I've held onto Noelle for as long as I have, and I don't intend on sharing her with the rest of them. Wilbur opens his mouth but whatever is on the tip of his tongue is cut off by the return of Noelle, pushing a small cart into the room.

'Dessert, anyone?' Her voice is almost like a song as she darts around the table and places small plates in front of us. 'First we have—'

'First?' Meryl cuts in, eyes wide.

Noelle nods, an almost sly grin tugging at her lips. 'I've got two and a half desserts for you tonight.'

'I don't usually have a sweet tooth,' Meryl says. 'But if your desserts are anything like the rest of the meal, you might find me slipping some into my handbag to take home.'

Noelle beams and I realise, with a jolt, that this is the first time I've seen her smile like this.

It's a lovely smile.

Wide and bright.

The kind that takes over her whole face and lights up her eyes.

'You flatter me,' she says demurely.

'Trust us, it's well deserved,' Brian says.

'Thank you. So, first up we have a rich cranberry pear tart with a buttery walnut shortbread crust.'

Everyone *oohs* – literally – as Noelle sets the circular pan in the middle of the table and we get our first glimpse of our first dessert for the evening. Thick pear slices are artfully laid out with glistening cranberries sprinkled around the top.

'You made this yourself?' Therese asks, mouth slightly agape as she stares at the dessert. 'Today?'

Noelle nods and Therese shakes her head in disbelief.

'You are simply magnificent.'

Noelle ducks her head, her smile turning slightly bashful. 'You haven't even tried it yet.' She hands out forks to everyone and then gestures for us to dig in. As predicted, the dessert is—

'Phenomenal,' says Brian again, and I'm starting to worry that it's the only descriptor he knows.

'Delectable,' Therese purrs.

'Outstanding,' Meryl mumbles through a mouthful of buttery crust.

'Heavenly,' Wilbur says, and I'm pretty certain that's the highest compliment I've ever heard him give anything.

'Fucking amazing,' Luca finishes off as he practically licks his plate clean. 'Noelle, you should open up your own restaurant.'

It's a blink-and-you'll-miss-it kind of movement, but Noelle hesitates suddenly. Her beaming smile falters slightly before she shrugs and says, 'Maybe one day. It's not really my focus right now, though. I actually really enjoy working more intimately with my clients.'

She glances over at me and, if I'm not mistaken, her lip twitches slightly. 'It's just so nice to get feedback directly, like you've all been giving me today. Nothing beats that.'

Sarcasm is dripping from her every word, but nobody else seems to catch it. They all erupt into murmurs of fervent agreement, and Noelle's smile blooms into something wonderous.

'Didn't you say something about another dessert?' I ask, my voice cutting across their delighted murmurs like a whip. A small part of me hates how brusque I know I sound, but I push aside the feeling without a second thought – I've got good at that over the years. Besides, this evening has gone on long enough already.

There's no need to keep stretching things out.

Noelle's smile stiffens into something a little more forced as she turns to look at me. Now that's what I'm used to. Barely concealed contempt flashes across her face, and I do my best to ignore the spark of shame that alights inside me.

'Right. Dessert number two,' she says curtly, turning back to the cart she pushed into the room. 'This is a true Jones family Christmas tradition.' She brandishes a two-tier cake and places it on the table with a flourish. It's covered in intricate icing swirls, and delicate sugar snowflakes cascading down the side.

'Spiced rum pumpkin cake,' Noelle announces proudly.

'It's an old family recipe with a few tweaks from me. My grandmother makes it every year for our annual family reunion and it's reached a point where it just doesn't feel like Christmas if I don't get a slice of this.'

And what would be so wrong about that? It's just another day in the calendar, and I've never understood what's so special about it. What is it about December 25th that turns people into sickeningly twee versions of themselves?

I poke at my slice of cake as Noelle sets it down in front of me. It takes me all of five seconds to discover that it's just as delicious as the rest of her meal. I take a bite and the flavours explode in my mouth, a moist, perfect blend of spices and sweetness that warms me from the inside out. I glance around the table to see everyone else nodding in approval, their eyes closed in bliss as they savour each mouthful.

'Noelle, this is incredible,' Meryl exclaims between bites. 'You should seriously consider selling this cake. People would queue down the street for a taste.'

Noelle smiles at the compliment, her eyes meeting mine for a brief moment before she turns her attention back to the group. 'Thank you. I'm glad you're all enjoying it.'

Even Wilbur, usually so reserved in his praise, nods in approval.

Noelle watches us, her gaze lingering on each of our faces as we indulge in her desserts. There's a quiet satisfaction in her eyes, a sense of fulfilment that I can't help but envy. She seems truly content, as if our enjoyment of her food is the only thing she needs right now.

'Didn't you say something about two and a half desserts?' Luca says as he finishes his plate, scraping up the last of the crumbs to the point where his plate looks spotlessly clean once he's finished.

Noelle grins. 'This one, I can't take the credit for entirely.' Her eyes twinkle mischievously as she turns back to the cart. She lifts a beautifully decorated tin and delicately pries it open to reveal an array of Christmas cookies, each one more intricately designed than the last. The sweet scent of cinnamon and nutmeg fills the air. 'These are also from Maison Badeaux,' Noelle explains, her voice filled with excitement. 'I thought it would be a nice touch to end the night by sharing them with all of you.'

The group murmurs appreciatively, their faces lighting up at the sight of the treats.

She flits around the table, placing a cookie in front of each of my guests.

And then she gets to me.

I expect her to place the cookie on the napkin in front of me, but she freezes, hands hovering uncertainly over the box.

'Have we run out?' Therese asks, craning her head around to see what the hold-up is.

'No,' Noelle says, her voice coming out like a croak. 'I

ordered the right amount. It's just ... well, I didn't think about the designs when I was handing them out, and ...' She holds up the last cookie in the box and gives me an apologetic grimace.

The cookie is a miniature masterpiece of mischief; the Grinch's scowling face etched onto its surface with uncanny accuracy. Green icing curls around its edges like a malicious grin, and even the tiny red Santa hat perched atop its head seems to exude child-friendly malevolence.

My jaw tightens as Luca bursts into loud, raucous laughter, and the rest of my Board follow his example, even Wilbur. Fucking *Wilbur.*

'You hit the nail on the head with that one, Noelle,' Luca laughs.

I feel a flush of embarrassment rise to my cheeks as Noelle looks at me with an awkward mix of apology and amusement. The room is filled with laughter, but all I can focus on is the Grinch cookie sitting in front of me, its mocking expression seemingly taunting me.

I push the cookie back towards Noelle, my irritation bubbling underneath the surface. 'I appreciate the gesture, but I think I'm full,' I say curtly.

Noelle's expression falls, a potent mix of regret and concern flashing in her eyes. She opens her mouth to apologise, but I turn away and she clamps her mouth shut before she can utter a word.

The laughter around the table slowly dies down, replaced by an awkward tension that hangs in the air like a heavy fog. I can feel the eyes of my Board on me, all of them judging my reaction to an admittedly harmless joke, so I force a tight smile and they all heave quiet sighs of relief.

As soon as their attention is no longer on me, I discreetly check my watch and bite back a groan.

How much longer do I have to endure this charade? The seconds tick by slowly, each one an eternity as I count down the moments until I can finally escape this suffocating room and any mention of Christmas.

CHAPTER FIVE

Noelle

'Please tell me your sexy boss had a sudden change of heart, sent you home about four hours ago, and you're currently in the process of making your way to Gran's a day early to surprise everyone. Please.'

'Client,' I murmur, almost on autopilot at this point. 'And stop calling him that.' I pause my loading of Hoxton's fancy dishwasher and glance over at my phone propped up on the countertop. For the second time today, Eve's pouting face fills my screen. 'What's wrong?'

'I swear to God, Noelle,' Eve whimpers, a slightly frantic expression flitting across her face. 'I'm genuinely on the brink. We had maybe half an hour of peace after Aunt Valerie arrived – I think the snow distracted everyone for a bit – but it's been non-stop since then.'

I slam the dishwasher door shut and turn to give my sister both my full attention and a sympathetic grin. I can hear the faint sound of reggae and loud voices in the background. 'Then I've got some bad news for you there.'

Eve lets out a loud and overly dramatic groan. 'There's only so much I can take, and I've already temporarily tapped out for the evening. Poor Nathan's down there all by himself trying to stop them from verbally abusing each other every five minutes. I don't know how much longer he'll last before he realises he's in over his head and takes back the ring.'

I resist the urge to roll my eyes. 'Stop being dramatic.'

'I'm not!' She squints at me and then points a perfectly manicured finger at her phone screen. 'Do you see what you've done? My wedding is on the line, Noelle. I need you to hurry up.'

This time I do roll my eyes. It's not like I'm not trying to hurry – like I particularly want to spend any more time in Hoxton's home than I already have to – but clean-up is just as important as the meal itself. And the last thing I want to do is give Hoxton even more of a reason to turn that icy glare in my direction.

'I've got a couple more things to finish off here and then I'm heading home.'

Eve blinks at me with wide, hopeful eyes. 'Or – and hear me out. You could drive through the night and get here by . . .' She glances briefly at, I assume, the clock in the top corner of her screen. '3am.'

My only response is a derisive snort.

'Fine,' Eve huffs, finally accepting that she's beaten. 'I guess I'll just suffer then.'

'Sounds good to me.'

She glares at me for a long second and then shrugs, any trace of frustration wiped from her face. Despite all her dramatics, Eve never really means it. I've long since known that my twin is the kind of person who just always needs a healthy injection of drama in their life. 'How's your night been, anyway?' she asks. 'Did Sexy Boss – sorry, Sexy Client – burst into flames at the sight of your apron?'

'Almost,' I laugh as I make my way around the kitchen, wiping down the countertops as I go. 'But it was fine. Bit weird at the start, but everyone got into the spirit by the end.'

Well. Mostly everyone.

When I returned to the dining room at the end of the night to start collecting their dishes, Hoxton was still proudly wearing his signature scowl, still apparently reeling from the unfortunate Grinch cookie – which I ended up eating myself, and it was phenomenal.

It didn't matter that someone – Luca, I suspect – had taken out their phone and was blaring Christmas music from it, and that everyone else was singing along to the familiar tunes with a grin on their face and rosy cheeks. Hoxton didn't so much as twitch in his seat, a faraway look in his eyes as his lips turned even further downwards into a frown.

'At least you survived,' Eve says with a smirk. 'And maybe Sexy Client will thaw out a bit by the new year. Who knows, maybe he'll even crack a smile next time you see him.'

'You've really got to stop with the name.'

Eve shrugs. 'I'll stop when he stops looking like that.'

It really is quite unfair.

Even the perpetual grimace plastered across his face does irritatingly little to distract from the fact that Hoxton is stupidly, unfairly, attractive. Thankfully, his personality is enough of a deterrent and stops me from losing myself in wildly inappropriate daydreams involving Hoxton, myself, and the wooden farm table I'm leaning against right now.

For the most part.

I clear my throat. 'I do need to go, though. I've got to finish up here so I can head home before the snow gets any heavier.'

At the mention of snow, Eve perks up a little more. 'Oh yeah. How is it down there for you? It's coming down pretty hard up here. Uncle Morris was talking about heading outside later and building a snowman with the kids.'

I peer out of the nearest window. A thick white layer covers my car and the rest of Hoxton's drive. I squint into the distance. I can just about make out the shape of Hoxton's neighbours' homes through the flurry of snow that's rapidly falling from the dark night sky. 'It's definitely coming down pretty steadily,' I say, watching as a few more icy flakes float past the window. 'But nothing too crazy yet. I don't think it'll slow me down too much on the drive home.'

Eve nods. 'Just make sure you drive safely, okay? Let me know when you get home and when you head out tomorrow morning.'

'Got it,' I say, giving her a mock salute. 'No driving into ditches.'

'Ha ha,' Eve deadpans, giving me an uncharacteristically serious look. 'I need you here. Christmas isn't Christmas without you.'

For a second, she's almost got me, and I briefly consider throwing caution to the wind and making the four-hour drive to Gran's in the dead of night. But then I hear the slightly muffled sound of familiar arguing coming from somewhere in the distance behind Eve. 'You just want me to deal with Mum and Aunt Valerie for you.'

Eve breaks out into a sheepish grin. 'That too. But, also, the Christmas thing. Mostly the Christmas thing.'

I know exactly what she means. The tiny amount of Christmas cheer I've managed to sneak into Hoxton's home tonight hasn't been enough to change the gloomy atmosphere that hangs over this place like an everlasting rain cloud.

Definitely not the Christmas vibe.

I can't wait to drop down onto Gran's soft, squishy sofa, and inhale the warm scent of freshly baked cookies and cake wafting in from the kitchen as I watch my little cousins add their latest monstrosities to the tree. Even the threat of Mum and Aunt Valerie being at each other's throats isn't enough to sour the image in my mind. In fact, their arguing is practically part of the fabric of Christmas at this point.

'I'll see you tomorrow.' I cut the call, drop my phone into my bag, and survey the rest of the kitchen. There are still pots and pans piled high in the sink, empty wrappers, boxes and containers strewn across the island, and a bag of food scraps I'll need to take out to the bins before I go.

Thirty minutes. I'll give myself thirty minutes and then ...

And then what?

I'm suddenly acutely aware that Hoxton is in the house with me.

That we're the only two people in the house right now.

And this has never happened before.

In the two years I've been working for Hoxton, I'd say we've both been in the house at the same time a grand total of maybe five times. And never alone. Roland is always here with me, pottering around in the background and acting as a helpful buffer between me and Hoxton. He's the one who leads me through the house, forcing me to stick to the pre-approved route that doesn't allow for any detours or good-natured snooping. Two years in, and I only vaguely know the layout of the downstairs. The upper floor of Hoxton's home remains a mystery – one that I doubt I'll ever solve.

I jump as the kitchen door suddenly creaks open and Hoxton's head pokes through the gap. I watch as he scans the room before his gaze settles on me and his brows furrow.

'You're still here?' His frown deepens as he steps fully into the kitchen.

A flash of irritation shoots through me and I gesture silently to the pots still in the sink and other bits and pieces I need to finish off. I turn back to the sink to resume washing up, assuming he'll leave and head back to whatever dark and joyless corner of his home he came from, but instead of the door slamming shut behind him, I hear his footsteps shuffling closer.

I hear the creak of wood as he leans against the island and then clears his throat. 'What I mean to say is – you can go.'

I drop the pot I'm holding into the soapy water and glance over my shoulder. Why do I feel like I'm about to walk into a trap? 'I need to finish cleaning. It's part of the job.'

'You're mostly done,' he says gruffly, avoiding any eye contact with me. 'I can finish up here.'

I swallow down a scoff. For some reason, I just can't imagine Hoxton with his sleeves rolled up to his elbows, standing over the sink and scrubbing away at these dishes. Surely he's the type of guy to let it sit and soak until his cleaning staff turn up, and I'm not going to give them any extra work if I can help it.

'It's fine,' I say. 'It'll only take me another half hour or so, and then I'll be out of your hair.'

Thank God.

Hoxton's gaze flickers towards the window. I follow his line of sight and feel a slight twinge of alarm when I notice how frosted the glass has become in the time since I last glanced out of it. The twinkling lights from his neighbours' homes are blurry now, and I can barely see the outline of my car in the drive.

'Are you sure? It's getting pretty—'

'I'll be fine,' I say again, a little firmer this time. How much worse could it really get in another half hour? And besides, Hoxton is already in a sour mood thanks to the Christmas-ness of this evening; I don't need to give him another reason to criticise me and my work.

Hoxton opens his mouth, looks like he wants to argue, then clamps it shut and shrugs. He pushes himself off the counter without another word and leaves me blissfully alone once again.

I won't lie though; the increasing intensity of the snow-storm has got me a tiny bit rattled. The last thing I want is to get stuck on the side of the motorway or, even worse, stuck here with Hoxton. Just the thought of it sends a shudder wracking through me. With that thought motivating me,

I get the rest of the kitchen done in record time – eighteen minutes to be exact – and try very hard to ignore the increasing howling of the wind outside.

Once I'm officially finished, I heft my bag onto my shoulder, grab the bin bags to toss on my way out, and frown. Typically, once I'm done, I'll let Roland know and he'll lead me to the front door and that's it. Even on the rare occasions that Hoxton is home while I'm busy working my magic in his kitchen, he's never come to see me off himself and I've certainly never had any desire – or chance, with Roland around – to pop my head into his office and say goodbye.

But it feels weird leaving without a word tonight. Rude, almost. Which is just laughable considering how Hoxton pretty much owns the trademark on rudeness. I shouldn't care. I shouldn't give a damn about being rude to the man who glowers at me as if I'm responsible for every wrong in his life, who doesn't bother to even wave a hand in greeting when I enter his home.

But I do.

Hoxton may have been raised in a cave, but I most definitely wasn't.

I stride over to the kitchen door and tug it open, stepping over the threshold before I can talk myself out of it.

I don't get very far.

Mostly because I immediately hit a wall. It's somehow equal parts hard and soft, and there's a warmth emanating from it that floods my senses. And it's moving. Something that feels oddly like an arm wraps itself around my waist and steadies me as I stumble backwards.

I glance up.

Not a wall.

A *Hoxton*.

A Hoxton with one arm wrapped loosely around my waist to steady me, his chest pressed up against mine, and a look on his face I don't recognise. It's not his standard scowl, but it's not anything I could describe as being even remotely close to a smile either.

His brows are furrowed, his cheeks slightly red, and his lips are parted in what I think is surprise. I watch as his dark eyes drop a fraction, roving over my body before flitting up to meet mine again. His lips twitch into an almost smile.

'Oh, shit, sorry,' I mutter, dropping my gaze as I leap out of his touch and back at least five steps. 'I didn't realise ... didn't hear you coming.'

Hoxton clears his throat, and his cheeks darken a little more. 'I was coming to ...' He trails off and clears his throat again. 'To check how things were going.'

I raise a brow – we haven't even got close to the thirty minutes we agreed on – and gesture around his now-pristine kitchen. The urge to respond with a snarky '*Yeah? Well, clean-up takes a while*' is on the tip of my tongue, but I swallow it down because I know what he's getting at.

Hoxton clearly wants me out of here.

Me and him both.

Though I doubt his reasoning has anything to do with the intensifying storm. Still, no sense in delaying what we both want.

'Sorry,' I mutter, clinging on tighter to my bag. 'I was just about to leave.'

He opens his mouth like he wants to say something, but he just shakes his head and steps aside for me to pass him. 'Right.'

The walk from the kitchen to the front door is a painfully awkward and silent one. I find myself desperately missing Roland and the easy way conversation just seems to roll off him. Every so often, Hoxton clears his throat and I stiffen at the thought of him trying to make small talk with me, but nothing ever comes. Thankfully. When we reach the door, he pulls it open for me and an icy wall of cold air hits us immediately.

Hoxton glares up at the sky and I dip my head to hide my eye-roll. Of course the sight of snow would piss him off. Could he be any more of a stereotypical Grinch?

'Looks like we're in for a white Christmas,' I mutter, reaching out to let a few cold snowflakes land on my hand. They settle against my skin for a brief moment and then melt. 'Isn't that lucky?'

Hoxton scoffs. 'What's lucky about it?'

I shrug. 'You know – snow on Christmas? There's just something magical about it.'

Another scoff. 'Temperatures have dropped below freezing and it's relatively humid. Nothing magical about it. Just basic thermodynamics.'

An irrational twinge of anger shoots through me. What is his problem? Would it really be so hard to just smile and nod and marvel at the beautiful snowflakes falling silently down on us? If he wants to be a miserable asshole, that's fine, but there's no need to drag the rest of us down with him.

'To each his own.' I clear my throat and shift my bag higher onto my shoulder. I take a step off the porch and, without glancing back, say coolly, 'Have a lovely Christmas.'

I don't get any kind of response. Just the sound of the front door closing before I even reach my car.

NOELLE

Never in my life have I met such a Grinch.

EVE

LOL
What's SC done now?

NOELLE

SC?

EVE

Sexy Client

NOELLE

Nothing in particular. Just seems determined to sap all of my Christmas joy.
But it's whatever. Finished now. Omw home.

EVE

WOOO!!
Drive safe xoxo

I would love to drive safe.

I would love to drive at all, actually.

But I can't.

Because my car splutters to life, the engine roaring, heat blasting at maximum to try to inject some warmth into my rapidly freezing bones, and then just as I'm about to pull away and leave Hoxton's miserable home in the dust, my car goes ahead and dies.

Dies.

The pathetic sound it makes as it shuts down is drowned out by my shriek of frustration.

This cannot be happening.

I try again, praying to any deity that so happens to be listening – even Santa gets a shoutout – but to no avail. My car gives me one last feeble groan and then shuts down completely. I stare, unblinking, out the window as the snow quickly piles up on my windscreen. Within a few minutes, I'm left shivering as I stare out at a white expanse. The air in my car is icy, so cold I can see my breath frosting out in front of me with each frustrated whimper.

I can't stay in here, that much is clear. I'll freeze to death within the hour and my hands, stuffed deep into the pockets of my jacket, are already well on their way to becoming numb. Just the thought of freeing them from the relative warmth inside my pockets to grab my phone and book an Uber is enough to make me want to weep.

The solution is obvious. If I'm being honest, it's been obvious for the last five minutes but I've been stubbornly avoiding that particular reality, hoping that perhaps my incessant pleading will somehow cajole my car into pulling itself together.

No such luck.

'This,' I grit out as I slide out of my car, slam the door, and start stomping back across Hoxton's drive, 'is the worst Christmas ever.'

In the back of my mind, I hear Eve's smug cackle. *You said it was December 21st.*

In the five minutes I've been sat in my car, desperately willing it to gain sentience and a sense of empathy, the snow has picked up more than I could have imagined. It flurries around me in mini cyclones, the icy wind whipping against my cheeks painfully as I make my way back up the snow-covered pathway to Hoxton's dark home.

I peer around as I trudge through the blizzard. Hoxton's neighbours, the homes I'd admired as I crawled up the street hours ago, somehow seem much further away than before. They're nothing more than tiny blips on the horizon, houses covered in a sheet of untouched white snow. Apparently, I'm the only one stupid enough to be out in the blizzard right now and I can just about make out tiny white and gold lights twinkling in the distance, the only sign that there is in fact any life beyond Hoxton's iron gates.

I ring the bell and then pound three times, as hard as I can, against his door. To his credit, Hoxton doesn't make me wait long and I have to wonder if he's been peering out of a window watching and snickering because this is exactly what he was warning me against.

Hoxton opens the door a few seconds after my last knock, a quizzical, almost wary, look on his face.

'My car won't start,' I manage to get out, teeth chattering. 'Can I—'

He doesn't wait for me to finish my sentence. Just steps aside and quickly ushers me in, taking care to close the door firmly behind me once my feet are planted on his mat. A rare feeling of gratitude towards him washes over me.

'I see the Christmas magic is working,' Hoxton says, with what I'm pretty sure is a hint of amusement.

Any sense of gratitude melts along with the snow I'm currently stomping off my shoes.

Asshole.

I glare up at him. 'If the whole tech giant thing doesn't work out, I don't think I'd recommend a career in comedy for you.'

His eyes widen and – *shit*. Probably not the smartest choice of words. I'm usually good at holding my tongue around Hoxton, but the combination of being freezing cold and desperate for my warm bed to drop into isn't a good one and I can't bring myself to care that I've just insulted my best paying client.

I'm not entirely sure he cares either. He doesn't look angry or like he's two seconds away from opening the door and flinging me out into the cold again. He looks almost chagrined.

'Sorry.' The word comes out gruffly, almost too quiet for me to hear, and he dips his gaze. 'I wasn't trying to make a joke.'

'Could've fooled me.'

He opens his mouth like he wants to respond but then snaps it shut again, and I can literally see his jaw working overtime as he grits his teeth.

I swear, this man is one more jaw tick away from a mouth ulcer.

'Look,' I sigh and run a stressed hand through my braids. They're cold to the touch and slightly damp with melted snow. 'Just give me ten minutes to order an Uber and then I'll be out of your hair.'

Hoxton nods stiffly. 'Take all the time you need.'

If that had come from anyone else, I'd have no doubt in my mind that they were being genuine, but the words ring false as they fall from Hoxton's lips.

Take all the time you need.

Translation?

Hurry up and get the hell out.

He turns abruptly on his heel and starts making his way down the corridor. It's only when he glances over his shoulder and quirks a brow at my still-shivering form in the lobby that I realise he wants me to follow.

At first, I think he's guiding me back towards the kitchen, the only place in his home where I feel even a modicum of comfort and ease, but he doesn't take the right turning for it and instead directs me to a room I've only ever seen in passing.

His living room.

The second I step over the threshold, the scent of vanilla hits me. There are two large candles lit on the dark oakwood coffee table, bathing the room in a yellowy glow. The news is playing on mute on the large flatscreen TV on the wall, a ruffled blanket is slipping off his slightly uncomfortable-looking sleek black leather sofa, and there's a dog-eared book balancing precariously on the dark wooden armrest.

I wouldn't call Hoxton's living room cosy by any definition of the word, but I realise that this is the first time I've seen any room in his house that looks even vaguely lived-in. It's still too dark and sleek for my personal taste – and the distinct lack of any Christmas décor feels like a targeted attack against me personally – but I can see the appeal. It's easy to imagine Hoxton sprawled out on his sofa, the dark blanket draped over him, getting lost in a book under the candlelight.

I inch further into the room and promptly choke on the laugh that threatens to come out of my throat. I don't know what I'd been expecting to see on the front cover of Hoxton's late-night read – maybe something like *48 Laws of Power* or *The Art of War* – but the words *The Return of Krampus,* accompanied by a truly gruesome depiction of a horned creature wearing a torn Santa hat with blood dripping down its mouth, is definitely not it.

'Are you—' I turn to face Hoxton, eyes wide in disbelief. 'Are you seriously reading a Christmas horror?'

Hoxton snatches the book up and turns it over, as if that's going to do anything. The dark flush is back on his cheeks again. 'It's a classic,' he says, almost defensively.

'No,' I laugh, shaking my head. '*A Christmas Carol* is a classic. *How The Grinch Stole Christmas* is a classic. That is—' I gesture at the book in his hands and huff out another quiet laugh. 'That is actually very on-brand for you, I guess.'

'And what's that supposed to mean?' Hoxton asks as he strides across the room and slots *The Return of Krampus* back into its space on his bookshelf. I'm suddenly filled with the urge to follow him and take a peek at the rest of his library. See if his shelves are filled from top to bottom with Christmas hating books, or if *The Return of Krampus* is a one-off.

But I don't.

The look on his face tells me that Hoxton is very much regretting inviting me into his home and unless I want to find myself out in the blistering cold for the second time tonight, I'd better not push him.

'Nothing,' I say innocently, fishing through my bag to grab my phone. 'Just an observation.'

I ignore the suspicious look he shoots me and fire up the Uber app.

**THERE ARE CURRENTLY NO CARS
AVAILABLE IN YOUR AREA.**

The words jump out at me from the screen, dancing in my vision. Taunting me. I close the app and restart it. **There are currently no cars available in your area.** Refresh. **There are currently no cars available in your area.** Refresh. Refresh. Ref—

'I don't think there are any cars available in the area.'

Hoxton is looming over me, an expression on his face that seems to be a mixture of amusement and exasperation. I hadn't even heard him approach.

'Really?' I ask weakly. I'm still staring at the screen, desperately refreshing the app every few seconds. 'What makes you say that?'

He stares at me critically for a second or two and then taps my phone gently. 'It says right—'

'I was joking,' I bite out. 'It was a joke.'

'Hm.' His lips twist into another one of those almost smiles he's apparently become fond of. 'Seems like a career in comedy isn't on the cards for you, either.'

'Seems like it,' I mutter absentmindedly, my fingers already tapping away at my phone to try to find the local taxi service number. That ends up being as fruitless as my attempts to book an Uber. When I eventually do get through to the operator at the taxi company, the only response I get is a sharp bark of laughter followed by a 'Have you taken a look outside lately, love?'

At that point, I do look outside. The snow, which was already achingly cold and furious just ten minutes ago, has whipped itself up into even more of a frenzy. I can barely see a metre out in front of the window, and the night sky is more white than black at this point.

'Nobody's coming out tonight,' the operator says with a yawn. 'I'd advise you to stay where you are and give us a call in the morning, and we'll see what we can do. Wouldn't get your hopes up, though.'

'But I can't—'

The operator hangs up without even waiting to hear what it is I can't do.

'That didn't sound like it went very well.'

'Didn't it?' I ask, voice rising in slight hysteria as I turn to find Hoxton sitting on the sofa, frowning at me.

'No,' he says slowly. Calmly. A lot calmer than I currently feel right now. 'It didn't.'

'Thank you for such an astute observation,' I say, slumping down onto the other end of the sofa. For all its sleekness, Hoxton's sofa is surprisingly comfortable. 'I never would've figured it out without you.'

'Glad to be of service.'

'Can you just—' I wave a hand in his general direction. 'Can you just not for two minutes?'

'Not what?'

Not be you, I think. But instead, I drop my head into my palms and hiss out, 'Just be quiet. I need to think.' Except, that's a lie. I don't need to think. I already know exactly what I need to do right now. I just don't want to do it.

I desperately, desperately, don't want to do it.

My phone vibrates suddenly in my hand, and I allow myself the brief, slightly unhinged delusion that it's the taxi company operator calling back to apologise and to tell me he's about to send someone to come and collect me.

EVE

Holy shit where are you right now?
This storm just got real bad real quick. If you're driving PLEASE stop and wait somewhere safe until it calms down.

And, as if I needed any further confirmation that I am currently in deep, *deep* shit, Eve sends a short video through. She's standing on Gran's porch, and it looks like she's in the eye of a storm. Snow whirls in every direction, howling and screaming as the wind lashes around her. She lets out a loud shriek as a particularly powerful gust batters against her and she turns and runs inside, slamming the door behind her as she goes.

EVE

Scary shit, right?
Where are you? Please tell me
you're holed up in a Tesco or
something.

NOELLE

That would be the dream
right now.

EVE

???????

NOELLE

SC's house

EVE

HUH?

My phone vibrates in rapid succession and I get a flurry of increasingly nonsensical messages from Eve, but I push her out of my mind and shoot Hoxton what I hope is a friendly, endearing kind of smile.

I'm not sure that I succeed because he looks vaguely alarmed.

'Is everything all right?' he asks uncertainly.

'Just peachy,' I say brightly. 'There is, however, one teeny tiny thing.'

Hoxton hesitates. 'Go on ...'

'I'm not sure if you've noticed, but we seem to currently be in the middle of quite a dangerous storm.'

His lip twitches. 'I had noticed.'

I grip the fabric of my coat and squeeze tightly. 'Then maybe you've also noticed that, with my car not working, and the lack of Uber and taxi services in the area, I don't currently have a way of getting home. Which is great because I am supposed to be going to my gran's for Christmas tomorrow . . .'

The thought of not making it to Gran's causes a knot to form in my throat suddenly.

Hoxton's entire face drops, like he's finally realised where I'm going with this. As if this hasn't been the only logical conclusion for the last ten minutes.

'I—' He swallows. 'I hadn't noticed that.'

'So,' I start, 'and this is just a suggestion, but—'

Hoxton doesn't wait to hear whatever my suggestion might be. Instead, he abruptly stands up from his sofa, reaches for his own phone resting on the coffee table, and begins pacing his living room.

'What're you—'

Hoxton holds a finger up to silence me and it takes every ounce of my self-control not to reach for one of the cushions on his sofa and fling it in his direction.

He's the only thing currently standing between you and that blizzard, I remind myself as my fingers inch towards the nearest cushion.

'I need a car,' Hoxton says suddenly, omitting any kind of greeting to the person he's currently on the phone to. I can't hear what the person on the other end says but, in response, Hoxton's brows furrow deeply in the middle. 'I'll triple your fee.' Another deep furrow, this time accompanied by a scowl. 'Fine. Consider it quadrupled. Though this is price-gouging, and I will be— Hello? Hello?' Hoxton stares at his phone, eyes wide in disbelief. 'I think he just hung up on me.'

From the way he says it, I don't think anyone has ever hung up on Alexander Hoxton before.

'Listen, I appreciate the effort, but—'

He holds up another silencing finger and I grip the nearest cushion.

Stop it, Noelle! Or do you want *to freeze to death?*

'I need a car sent over in the next twenty minutes,' Hoxton says to the next person he tries. Their response is muffled slightly, but I do manage to hear what is clearly a snort of laughter before, once again, Hoxton is left staring at his phone in disbelief. *'Again?'*

This time, I don't bother interrupting. I leave him to it as he punches in another number, and turn my attention to the large television on the wall. The news is still playing on mute but there's a banner beneath the presenter that reads: **MET OFFICE ISSUES RED WARNING DUE TO BLIZZARD.**

Shit.

Why does it feel like I'm not going to be able to get out of here anytime soon? Though I suppose I should be looking on the bright side in that it's a good thing my car broke down in Hoxton's drive. Just the idea of being stuck on the side of the motorway while the blizzard rages around me and

I freeze to death in my car is enough to make me give silent thanks to Hoxton and his blissfully warm home.

Over the next fifteen minutes I alternate between watching the muted TV, where they're cutting between choppy video clips of the blizzard currently battering the country, and sneaking glances at Hoxton. His attempts to try to get me a car out of here haven't gone anywhere, and it's clear he's becoming increasingly irritated with each abruptly ended call.

If my situation weren't so dire, I might laugh. Someone as rich as he is probably isn't used to being told no, and I don't imagine there are many things he's come across that he can't throw a fat wad of cash at to make disappear. Unfortunately for the both of us, a blizzard that brings the entire country to a standstill seems to be one of those rare occasions.

I'm not sure how many frustrated calls Hoxton makes – I lose count after the sixth one – but he eventually puts down his phone and sinks into his sofa with an expression on his face that suggests one of his nearest and dearest has just died.

'No luck?' I ask innocently.

Hoxton narrows his eyes at me. 'Evidently not.'

'Well, thanks for trying.' I clear my throat and try to inject as much faux cheer into my voice as I possibly can, given the circumstances. Like we're two friends having a perfectly normal conversation and the sense of dread I feel pooling in the pit of my stomach simply isn't there. 'And I'm glad we're both finally on the same page about the reality of our current situation.'

Hoxton looks at me like I've just slapped him across the face. '*Our?*'

'Yes, *our*,' I say firmly. 'And I hope you know that I would never, ever, in a million years, ask this of you under any other circumstance unless it was a true emergency.'

His face goes pale, and his voice comes out in a dry rasp. 'Ask what?'

I shift awkwardly on the sofa. For some reason, I suddenly feel like a kid trying to figure out the best way to ask their parents for a ridiculously expensive gift for Christmas. 'Could I ... perhaps ... if you wouldn't mind ... and I promise I'll keep out of your way ... but if you could find it in your heart ...'

'Noelle.'

I freeze. I think that's the first time Hoxton has ever said my name. And he had to go ahead and say it like that.

Noelle.

It sounds like a plea. I try very, very hard not to think about other situations where my name might sound like that falling off his lips.

'Could I please stay the night?' I whisper. 'And I'll be gone as soon as the storm passes. First thing in the morning.'

I should email Roland and let him know that he had nothing to worry about on the aneurysm front. Because

Roland's tie wasn't enough to send Hoxton over the edge, and neither was my apron. But this? Me asking if I could possibly stay overnight? This just might do it.

The colour, previously drained from Hoxton's face, is back again. His cheeks are a dark red, bordering on purple, and his mouth opens and closes several times in quick succession before he manages to choke out, 'Stay? You want to stay? Here?'

'I don't want to,' I correct him, probably much quicker than I should. The way he said my name is still echoing in my mind. 'I'd rather be in my own bed, thank you very much. But that's not an option right now, is it? Unless you particularly want to be responsible for poor Roland stumbling on my frozen remains in your drive come January?'

'No,' he says gruffly. 'Of course not.'

'So . . . so can I can stay?'

He gives me a stiff nod. 'Just one night.'

Relief floods through me. 'That's all I need.'

Hopefully.

CHAPTER SIX

Noelle

It's not like I'm expecting a full-blown tour of the mysterious upper level of Hoxton's home, but he marches me through the upper corridors like we're on a secret military base. If I so much as turn my head in another direction, Hoxton not-so-subtly redirects me back to where he's pointing.

'This is the guest room,' Hoxton says bluntly, throwing open a door at the end of the corridor, past several firmly closed doors. 'It's an en-suite, so . . .'

He trails off, but the meaning is clear: don't go wandering around his home under the guise of '*just trying to find the bathroom*'.

It's not like he has anything to worry about there. Between working all evening and the stress of the last hour or so, there's nothing I want more than to flop face down into the bed and immediately render myself unconscious for no less than ten hours. Twelve, if I'm lucky.

'The heater controls are on the wall over there,' Hoxton says, nodding to a white control panel on the wall nearest the bed. 'Feel free to change the temperature to your liking.'

That was already a given. As soon as he's gone, I plan on cranking the temperature up as high as it can go because this room is freezing. It's not untidy, not dirty or anything like that, but everything about the room feels stale. Unused. Untouched. Like someone – Roland maybe? – set it up months ago and nobody has stepped inside it since. There's a bed against one wall, a chest of drawers against another, a built-in wardrobe to my left, and that's about it. There are no photos on the wall, no pieces of art, no kitschy décor people typically use to decorate their guest rooms and give them a sense of personality and life. Even the sheets on the bed are bland. Just plain white without even a simple pattern on them.

I get the distinct feeling that Hoxton probably doesn't get many guests.

I also get the feeling that this probably doesn't bother him at all.

'Thanks again,' I say as I inch further into the room. 'I know this isn't an ideal situation, but I really appreciate it.'

'It's fine,' Hoxton says in a tone that suggests it's absolutely not fine, but he's aware that he's bound by social constructs to say that it is. 'Sleep well and drive safely in the morning.'

Translation?

You'd better not be here when I wake up.

I'm getting pretty good at deciphering the hidden meaning in Hoxton's words. Maybe I'll put my findings into a book one day.

'Thank you,' I say again.

Hoxton nods, hovers for a beat too long and then disappears out into the hall, gently closing my door behind me.

As soon as I hear his footsteps disappear down the hall, presumably to his own room or back downstairs to finish *The Return of Krampus*, I march over to the control board by the bed and turn the heating up to the highest it can possibly go. The vents kick in almost immediately, sending a blast of welcome warm air straight into the room.

Perfect.

Once I'm satisfied the room is going to heat up to a decent temperature in the next ten minutes or so, I make my way to the bathroom. Just like the rest of the room, it's perfectly serviceable, but also nondescript. You can tell that the cleaner whom I assume Hoxton employs doesn't skip this room, but I also get the sense that it hasn't been used as an actual room in forever. I half-heartedly wonder why he even bothers with having a guest room. *Singular.* There are plenty of rooms in Hoxton's home, but it hasn't escaped me that he was very explicit about this being the only guest room. I wonder what he's using the other rooms for, since it's certainly not for entertaining.

Gran would have a heart attack if she ever found out one single man was living in a house this big. The whole reason my family are even able to have the giant Christmas spectacle we throw every year is because of her and her home. It's a gorgeous, eight-bedroom country manor she managed to snag at an auction for repossessed homes years ago, and spent the better part of a decade renovating. When Grandad passed, there was a lot of talk about Gran selling up and downsizing because everyone thought she'd be lonely in that big old house. Those conversations lasted for all five minutes before Gran shut them down.

'A family needs its heart. And that's what this house is. If I sell, where would we all spend Christmas? Where would we be a family?'

I can practically hear her voice in my head, sharp as ever, the words delivered with that no-nonsense tone she's always had. It's hard to argue with logic like that and I don't think any of us really wanted to see her sell. The house is as much a part of her as anything else. It's her sanctuary, her pride, the place where all the chaos of our family can come together every holiday.

Not that Hoxton would understand. Given how cold and sterile his home feels, I doubt he'd understand the idea of a place being the 'heart' of something. He'd probably scoff at the thought of it and dismiss it as sentimental nonsense, but not me.

Eve always says I get my love of cooking from Gran. Not directly – though Gran can throw it down in the kitchen like nobody's business – but how she sees her home is exactly how I see food. It's the heart of everything and brings people together like nothing else. Sometimes it feels like a superpower, being able to pull together a dish the way I do, and I don't take it lightly. There's nothing I love more than cooking for people. Except, maybe Christmas.

The thought of missing Christmas jolts me back to reality and I step inside the shower. It's gleaming like it's brand new, and I don't hesitate to turn the tap to the hottest it can possibly get, strip down, and jump in.

The warm water seeps into my bones and helps to work out the knot of anxiety and stress I've felt building inside me. It's exactly what I need right now, and I give myself the luxury of twenty minutes of peace and warmth as I stand under the powerful spray and force myself to forget all about the ridiculous situation I've somehow managed to find myself in.

It's not until I step out of the bathroom and back into the bedroom, a slightly scratchy towel wrapped around me, that I realise something.

I have nothing to change into.

Shit.

I glance at my pile of discarded clothes by the door to the en-suite. The idea of forcing myself back into my slightly damp work clothes – a not entirely comfortable pair of black trousers and a fitted black turtleneck – isn't high up on my list of things I desperately want to do right now.

I briefly entertain the idea of crawling into bed and under the duvet in nothing but my birthday suit but, for some reason, the heat coming out of the vents above isn't as powerful as it was twenty minutes ago and I can already feel a creeping chill spreading throughout the room.

I need something to wear. Ideally something I haven't spent the last twelve hours in and that doesn't smell vaguely of pork loin and cheese. I briefly consider striding down the hall to ask Hoxton if there's any chance I could borrow something for the evening, but I shut down that idea as quickly as it comes.

I've asked Hoxton for enough already and I'm not keen on seeing what his limit is. For some reason, I think opening his bedroom door to find me standing there in a towel asking if he happens to have a spare pair of boxers might just be it.

Spare pair of boxers.

Spare clothes.

And where might Hoxton keep those?

I whirl around and tug open the drawer nearest to me. Surely these can't just be for show? The first drawer is filled with linen sheets, all the same white as the ones on the bed, and so are the next three I rifle through. Just sheets and pillowcases galore. Some are still in their original plastic packaging, further reinforcing the belief that Hoxton probably hasn't had a guest stay over in months at best.

The last two drawers prove more fruitful. I find a stack of old clothes folded at the bottom. One drawer is filled with old sweatshirts with a university logo embroidered across the front and the other, blissfully, has several pairs of dark sweatpants stuffed into it. It occurs to me suddenly that everything looks a size or two too small for Hoxton. These are probably old clothes from several years ago, long relegated to an unused drawer in an unused room. I doubt he even remembers they're in here.

I have to tell myself this so as to assuage the slight twinge of guilt – and creepiness – I feel as I hurriedly pull one of his sweatshirts over my head and then dive into a pair of sweatpants. For having sat dormant at the bottom of a drawer for God knows how long, they're surprisingly comfortable. The cotton is still soft and, as I make my way towards the bed, I get a waft of something familiar.

Vanilla tinged with ... something. Something warm. Something inviting. Something I want to stay wrapped up in for a little longer.

Something nice.

Whatever it is, I don't have time to dwell on it. My eyelids are becoming heavier with each passing second and a wall of tiredness hits me as soon as I crawl under the sheets. I curl around myself, causing another wave of that something nice to caress my senses, and let my eyelids flutter shut.

Only to snap them open a second later.

The steady stream of heat blasting from the vent above has dwindled into a pathetic huff every so often and the chill that was steadily creeping up on me has turned into a full-blown arctic tundra.

'For fuck's sake,' I murmur, twisting my body around so I can stab at the control panel again. The screen lights up as soon as my fingers make contact, and I frown. According to the panel, everything should be working as it's supposed to. The temperature is as high as it's going to get and everything looks right.

So why am I shivering?

I turn the panel off and then on again, which is pretty much the extent of my tech prowess.

Unsurprisingly, nothing happens. In fact, I'm pretty sure it gets a little colder.

I swallow down the scream of frustration that bubbles up my throat. Did I do something wrong? Accidentally overtake an old lady on the motorway? Not give up a seat to someone who needed it on the tube? Maybe it was that snail I accidentally stepped on a few weeks ago? Because the only explanation for my absolutely abysmal string of bad luck right now is that I'm currently undergoing some kind of karmic retribution for some heinous act or other.

I give the control panel one last try and can't even bring myself to groan when, once again, absolutely nothing happens. Although I suppose that's not entirely true. I actually think the room gets about a half degree colder, which, given the fact that my breath is now forming in front of me in tiny little clouds, is pretty damn cold.

I reach for my phone – 2.28am. Definitely too late – early? – to bother Hoxton right now.

The only thing left to do is wrap myself up as tightly as I can in the blankets and pray that my tiredness will win against chill and I'll fall asleep before I freeze to death.

God. I sound just as dramatic as Eve right now.

Speaking of . . . I reach for my phone and send one last message before my thumbs go totally numb:

NOELLE

Worst. Christmas. Ever.

EVE

It's December 22nd ;)

CHAPTER SEVEN

Alex

December 22nd

The sound of wind battering my windows snaps me out of a surprisingly deep slumber.

I frown as I sit up and the events of last night start flooding my mind with irritating clarity. The meal – the bloody Christmas meal – and the Board infiltrating my home, me scowling at Luca from across the table when he decided to play a seemingly never-ending medley of Christmas music, Noelle and her apron and those damn gingerbread cookies, and—

Noelle.

I shoot up in bed as my thoughts focus in with laser precision on my personal chef. My personal chef who didn't leave last night. I jump out of bed and peer out of the nearest window. The glass is mostly frosted over, but I can still make out a swirling sea of white in the distance. Snowflakes dance in the air, and a thick blanket of snow covers everything for miles in every direction. I scan my drive quickly, not that it does any good. The snow is whipping itself up into a flurry and I can barely see a few metres ahead.

What I can see is untouched white snow. There's not a tyre track in sight.

She must've left at the crack of dawn for the snow to have covered any trace of the tracks by now. Was she able to fix whatever it was that was wrong with her car, or did she somehow manage to cajole a mechanic into coming out in the early hours of the morning to tow her away?

Neither option is preferable right now. It's clear that nobody should be out on the road in this. As if to prove my point, a particularly violent gust of icy wind lashes at a tree and, with a loud crack, a thick branch snaps off and careens to the floor in a cloud of white powder.

I suppose I could've been nicer about it all, I reason to myself as I pull on a pair of sweats and a T-shirt. Last night, I mean. I didn't have to make my discomfort so obvious that Noelle would rush out in the middle of a storm just because I'd only promised her one night of haven in my home. I could have – how does Luca put it? Right, that's it. I could've been less of a miserable prick and told her that she was, of course, free to stay as long as she needed and that her safety was my priority. Like a perfectly rational human being would have said.

Well, no. A perfectly rational human being would've thanked her for her hard work last night. Would've told her that, hideous apron aside, she did a brilliant job and I value and appreciate the time and effort she puts into her work for me. Would've done anything but lightly antagonise the woman who is single-handedly responsible for 80 per cent of my Board members no longer thinking I'm – to use Luca's verbiage one last time – a miserable prick.

Therese has already emailed enquiring whether Noelle would be willing to cater our annual summer gala for investors and signed said email with a cheerful, '*Can't wait to hit the slopes—you'll have to join us next year!*' and I think I've somehow managed to agree to sponsor one of Brian's kids for some charitable event or other.

I do have to admit it – Luca was right. The evening did exactly what he'd suggested it would – Grinch cookie aside – and I'd categorise the atmosphere amongst myself and my Board as tentatively jovial. Not including Wilbur, of course, who spent most of the evening sharing his vaguely mutinous schemes but, for a first attempt, I'd say things went well. I'm no longer dreading our first Board meeting in January.

I wish I could say the same for my first interaction with Noelle in the new year.

I briefly consider emailing her to check that she's got home safely, but I dismiss the idea as quickly as it comes. A vision of Noelle and her barely concealed disdain towards me last night jumps to the forefront of my mind. The way her eyes would narrow ever so slightly whenever she thought I wasn't looking, the tension that coiled between us as she lapped up the praise and attention from the rest of my Board.

No, I'm fairly certain the last thing Noelle wants right now is to see an email from me lighting up her phone screen. Not least because of the fact that it's almost Christmas, and that might not mean much to me but I know Noelle is eager to get into the Christmas spirit, whatever the hell that means. All I know is, the sight of my name flashing across her screen might cause a panic-induced heart attack.

I do my best to shake off the lingering guilt I'm feeling and make my way downstairs. I should be used to the silence, but today it reverberates through the house like a drumbeat with each step I take. An irritating reminder of the consequences of my stubborn actions.

The kitchen door is slightly ajar and I nudge it open, intent on grabbing a slice of toast before I migrate to my office and get a head start on some of the Q2 forecasts for next year.

And then I freeze.

Noelle is sitting at my kitchen table, tension carving deep

lines on her forehead as she cradles a bowl of cereal, spooning it into her mouth with mechanical movements while her other hand swipes across her phone screen.

It's . . . it's jarring to see her sitting here, like a scene from a domestic dream I would never admit to having. She's wearing some of my old university tracksuit bottoms rolled up at the ankles, and a hoodie that's much too big for her, sleeves bunched up at her elbows but still swallowing her hands. I watch as she lifts a hand and tucks a stray braid behind her ear, a soft sigh falling from her pursed lips. The unexpected wave of attraction hits me like a sucker punch to the chest and—

Noelle glances up. 'Oh . . .' She inclines her head in my direction. It's a shadow of a nod more than anything else. 'Morning.'

Morning, she says.

Good morning, I should respond.

That's the correct response. The polite response. I know it is. But instead, my voice gruffer than I intended, all I say is, 'What're you doing here?'

Her brows lift momentarily in displeasure before she schools her expression into something more neutral. 'Have you looked outside lately? No way I could drive back in this.' Her words hang between us, an explanation offered up with a shrug of resignation. 'The Met Office is saying we should stay put if we can. We're officially snowed-in.'

'But your car . . .' I start, glancing out the nearest window.

'It's still out there,' she says with a sigh. 'Somewhere under that new glacier in your drive.'

I press closer to the glass and squint past the frosty veil. She's right. There it is – a barely distinguishable shape beneath a shroud of white. Her car has been disguised as just another mound in the winter wasteland that my drive has become overnight. I step away from the window and, despite my best efforts, I can't help but linger on Noelle for a little longer. I realise the sweats are too big for her too, the waistband rolled several times around her waist. The grey fabric simultaneously swallows her up and accentuates her soft curves in a way I desperately, desperately, need to avoid dwelling on.

'And this?' I ask, gesturing vaguely in her direction. 'You're wearing—'

She glances down as if she's forgotten what's currently clinging to her skin. As if just the sight of her in my old clothes isn't currently driving me mad. 'Oh. Right. The heater in the guest room gave up on me halfway through the night. It was either this or freeze to death.' She shrugs with a carefully feigned nonchalance, but I catch a fleeting glimpse of something that looks suspiciously like vulnerability before she busies herself with another spoonful of Cheerios.

'You should've said something,' I say, even as I know exactly why she wouldn't. 'I could've fixed it or found you some extra blankets.'

She sets her spoon down, her brows creasing as she chews on her bottom lip, like she can see through me perfectly. After a second or two, she mutters, 'I still would've needed clothes.'

Still would've needed – what?

'What I mean—' My voice gets stuck in my throat, and I have to hastily clear it. 'What happened to the clothes you were wearing last night?'

Noelle arches a brow. There's a slight flush to her cheeks I can't quite account for. 'They got damp last night in the snow. I didn't want to put them back on after I showered, so . . .' She trails off and shrugs. 'And I didn't want to bother you, so . . .'

My chest almost tightens at her words.

Bother.

I study her for a long moment, watching the way her eyes dart away from me, the slight tension in her shoulders, the stiffness to her jaw.

Bother.

I'm suddenly struck by the inexplicable urge to assure her that she could never be any kind of inconvenience to me – the exact opposite is true when it comes to her, if we're being honest – but the words lodge in my throat, leaving a silence that hangs awkwardly between us.

I take a step closer to the table and clear my throat. 'I wanted to say . . .' I start. My words hang, suspended in the chilly air. 'You're know you're not . . . I mean, you couldn't be . . .'

Her hazel eyes meet mine and I'm sure I spy a flicker of curiosity dancing across them. I feel the confession swelling in my chest, ready to finally bridge this forced gap between us. But then it sticks, stubborn in my throat, and all that escapes is, 'What's for breakfast?'

A sudden burst of laughter erupts from her and cuts through the tension. I've never heard her laugh like this before. I'm painfully familiar with the dry scoff, complete with an eye-roll, she's thrown my way a few times, and even the nervous giggle she let out at dinner last night, but this? This feels different.

It resonates somewhere deep within me, warming me from the inside like a sip of aged whiskey.

'Breakfast?' she echoes, leaning back on her stool with a smirk. 'I'm off duty. If you want something you'll have to figure it out yourself. Or ...' She cocks her head to the side and shoots me a daring look. Like she's begging me to challenge her. 'You've got my bank details.'

It's not a quite a laugh that splutters out of my throat, but it's close. 'Are you implying that I need to pay you to cook for me?'

'That is the basis of our entire relationship, yes.'

'While you're staying at my home for free?' I finish.

Her lips twitch but she manages to keep the moderately unimpressed expression fixed across her face. 'Are you implying that if I don't make you three square meals a day, you'll kick me out and leave me to freeze to death out there?'

There's a playful glint in her eye and it hits me, a second delayed, that she's toying with me. Teasing me, even. Like we're old friends and this kind of easy back and forth is commonplace between us. I'm not sure how to respond, but it feels like she's thrown me a ball and is tentatively watching to see if I'll toss it back her way.

I open my mouth, ready to respond. Ready to finally chip away at this wall between us and take the first step towards a new kind of relationship with Noelle. But then my watch vibrates and I instinctively glance down. The word **URGENT** jumps out at me from the small email preview on the tiny screen and I let out a groan. HoxTech is branching into the phone market in the new year for the first time, and every step of the way has been met with problem after problem.

'Are you kidding me?' I murmur under my breath as I scan through the email as it scrolls up my watch face. There's been a leak, and a tech blogger somewhere in America is gleefully tweeting out sneak peeks of the phone. An irritating problem, but nothing too dissimilar from the ones I've dealt with over the years.

'Sorry,' Noelle says suddenly, her voice several degrees cooler than it was before.

I glance up to find her scraping back her stool, any trace of a smirk wiped completely from her face.

Now this?

This is familiar territory. She's looking at me with thinly veiled dislike, and it's obvious she can't wait to put several feet between us again.

'Sorry?' I repeat, confused and half distracted by the flurry of emails I can see coming through via my watch. 'What're you—'

'I promised I'd keep out of your way, and . . .' She smiles, but it doesn't reach her eyes. 'Here I am. In your way. Give me two minutes to wash up here and then I promise you won't see me again.'

I'm not entirely sure how we got here, but she doesn't give me a chance to question the sudden change. Doesn't even take the two minutes she asked for before she's striding out of the kitchen, head held high and without a backwards glance in my direction.

I'm not sure why, but I get the distinct feeling that I've messed up.

CHAPTER EIGHT

Noelle

'It could be worse.'

'How?' I groan as I kick the bedroom door shut behind me and drop down onto my bed with the kind of dramatic flourish you'd expect from a teenager. 'Please tell me how exactly it could be worse.'

Eve chews thoughtfully on a slice of toast before shrugging. 'You could be stuck on the side of the road.' She pauses and shoots me a pointed look. 'You know, freezing to death.'

'Don't tempt me with a good time,' I mutter, trying desperately to ignore the fact that she does have a good point. On paper, being holed up in Hoxton's home while we wait for the storm to pass is definitely the best-case scenario here. But in reality ...

'It's just so awkward,' I continue with a grimace. Every

attempt I've made to bridge the gap between us and soften some of the tension in the air has been met with a blank stare, like he's committed to keeping me at arm's length. I'd be offended by it if I hadn't seen, first hand, that this is just how he treats most people. But still, we're shacked up together for at least another twenty-four hours; according to the Met Office alert still running across every banner on every news channel, people are 'strongly advised' to stay at home. The least Hoxton could do is be a little more hospitable. Crack a smile. Laugh at one of my jokes. Do absolutely anything other than commit to the whole 'miserable prick' persona he's insisted on adopting.

'I thought we were getting somewhere this morning, but even that ended in him rolling his eyes and muttering under his breath when I tried to make a joke.'

'Maybe it wasn't a very funny joke.'

If looks could kill, Eve would be a dead woman right now. 'Whose side are you on?'

'Yours,' she laughs. 'Always yours. You know that. I'm just saying, things could be worse. Have you seen the news, or even scrolled through any socials today?'

I wince, knowing that once again, she does have a point. A quick doomscroll through my various social media feeds while I was eating breakfast confirmed that, overnight, chaos has unfolded all across the country. Every other post seemed to be a report of massive traffic pile-ups, power outages and people, weighed down with Christmas shopping, stuck on crowded trains. And that's not to mention the videos people have posted of the wind battering their gardens, sending trampolines flying and tree branches falling to the ground.

A sudden gust of wind rattles the windows loud enough for Eve to hear through the phone and we exchange a nervous glance. The storm shows absolutely no sign of letting up anytime soon. But while being stuck in Hoxton's home seems like a luxury compared to the havoc outside, the thought of spending another day trapped inside with just him for company feels suffocating.

'Have you seen the tree yet?' Eve asks suddenly, her eyes lighting up. It's an obvious change of topic, but I'm grateful for it. I need something to take my mind off the increasingly gloomy train of thought I've headed into. Eve doesn't wait for me to answer before she's leaping up and tearing across Gran's house. I get brief glimpses of bleary-eyed cousins and aunts and uncles as she dashes through the halls. 'They put the finishing touches on it last night, and . . . Voila!' She steadies her camera in front of her and I get my first glimpse of this year's tree.

At seven foot high, it stands tall and proud in the corner of the living room. Its branches are practically bowing under the weight of an endless stream of Christmas decorations and sparkling fairy lights. Every bit of tension and irritation I've been carrying since I woke this morning melts away as I spot some of decorations clearly added by the younger members of our family. There's a plastic dinosaur perched precariously on one branch, wearing a tiny Santa hat, a sock puppet with mismatched googly eyes peeking out from behind a cluster of tinsel, and right at the very top of the tree in place of the traditional star or angel, is a pine cone absolutely dripping in glitter.

In the background I spot a gaggle of my baby cousins running through the hall, quickly followed by Gran hollering half-heartedly after to them, 'Slow down before you break something!'

'Oh Noelle,' Eve breathes suddenly. 'Don't cry.'

'I'm not crying,' I sniff, blinking away the tears before they can spill. 'I'm just . . . it's just, what if I don't make it to you guys for Christmas?'

It sounds ridiculous to admit it out loud – childish even – but that question has been festering in the back of my mind since last night. What if I don't make it home? Christmas has always been a huge deal in my family. We've never been the type of family to come together during the summer for barbecues and games at the park, and we're far too spread out across the country for the majority of us to turn up at birthdays or christenings or any other special occasions with any kind of regularity. Christmas is all we have. The one time of the year everyone has unanimously agreed to set aside for family, and I love it.

I love catching up with my cousins and sitting by the fireplace listening to and sharing a year's worth of drama. I love waking up on Christmas morning to the smell of cinnamon and spices wafting through the house and watching all the little cousins tear into their gifts with megawatt grins on their faces. Even Mum and Aunt Valerie's eternal feud has carved itself into the backbone of Christmas, and the thought of missing it is genuinely enough to make my vision blur.

'You will,' Eve says firmly, even as the wind howls in the background. 'Trust me, by tomorrow morning this storm will have broken and you'll be on your way.'

'And if it doesn't?' I ask, brow raised because someone has to be a realist right now. It feels weird being on this side of things. Our relationship for the last twenty-odd years has been reassuringly steady: Eve is the resident drama queen and I'm the constant voice of reason, steadfastly reassuring and logical.

Eve shoots me a weak grin. 'Like I said, there are worse things than being cooped up with your sexy boss.'

'Client.' I roll my eyes. 'And in any other situation, sure. But it's Christmas—'

'It's December 22nd,' Eve mutters.

'And he,' I continue, pointedly raising my voice and ignoring her smirk, 'is quite possibly the most miserable person I have ever had the displeasure of meeting. Saint Nick himself couldn't coax any Christmas joy out of that man.'

'Maybe that's what you're here for,' Eve says sagely, wiggling her brows just a little *too* suggestively for my liking. 'Let some of your festive spirit rub off on him.'

'And how am I supposed to do that?'

She shrugs. 'Get creative.'

Despite everything, that gets a snort out of me. 'He's got a cinnamon scented stick up his ass when it comes to Christmas. I swear, I just want to wipe that smirk off his face.'

Memories of last night flood my mind. Hoxton glaring daggers at me from the head of the table, his eyes zeroing in on my apron and the plate of Christmas cookies in my hands. The way he refused to even crack a smile when the others were belting out Christmas tunes. The barely concealed sneer when I dared mention it being a white Christmas. Just the thought of it twists my lips into a frown.

'Put Hoxton and the Grinch in a room, and even the Grinch would say he's doing too much.'

Eve's loud cackle in response is drowned out by the sound of something thudding. For a moment, I think it's the storm outside upending another branch or sending a rock hurling across Hoxton's drive, but then I hear it again.

It's a little muffled this time – hesitant, even.

'I'll call you back,' I murmur to Eve, hang up the call before she has the chance to protest, and pad to the door. Just as I wrap my fingers around the door handle, I hear it for the third and final time. As I feared, someone is knocking on my door. And, unless things are about to take a very dire turn, there's only one person it could be.

'Yes?' I ask as I yank open the door and find Hoxton looming over me once again. I notice several things right away: there's a slight flush to his cheeks, his eyes refuse to meet mine and – and this is definitely the most pressing issue right now – he's got a pile of clothes neatly folded in his arms.

Before I have the chance to question it, Hoxton shoves the pile straight into my chest. 'Here,' he says gruffly, still determinedly staring anywhere but at me.

I stumble backwards slightly under the new weight in my arms. A quick once-over shows that he's handed me a pile of cosy-looking sweats, all in varying shades of black, blue and grey. I shift onto one foot and the movement is enough to jostle the pile and a familiar, vanilla-tinged and oddly comforting scent wafts towards me. The urge to lean forward, bury my face in the fabric, and take a deep, *deep* inhale creeps up on me with surprising fierceness.

'Thought you might need these,' Hoxton says, his voice breaking the sudden silence that has blanketed itself over us. His usual stoic façade is in place, but there's a softness in his eyes that definitely wasn't there before. 'The ones you're wearing have been in that drawer for God knows how long. They should be clean, but I—' He shrugs, still refusing to meet my eye. 'I thought these might be more comfortable.' Every word that falls from his lips sounds stiff, almost robotic. Like he's following a badly written script and he's afraid to go off page.

A hot flash of panic suddenly shoots through me as I realise that Hoxton probably – most definitely – heard the tail end of my call with Eve.

Put Hoxton and the Grinch in a room together, and even the Grinch would say he's doing too much.

Hot shame crawls up my body. Oh God.

But he doesn't look mad, offended or even mildly irritated. The look on his face is more akin to the one last night, when I flung open the kitchen door and barrelled straight into his chest. He looks almost . . . shy?

I choke down the snort that threatens to bubble out of my throat, dismissing that thought as quickly as it came. Hoxton and shy are two words that just don't mix.

'Thank you,' I say as I step back into the room to drop the clothes onto the bed. I glance over my shoulder and find he's still lingering in the doorway, like he's not sure if he should come in or not.

A flash of something that looks like panic but couldn't possibly be darts over his features, before he seemingly makes a decision and remains awkwardly in the hall. I watch, amused as he rolls back onto his heels and stuffs his hands into his trouser pockets. If it weren't for the violent whooshing of the storm outside, I'm pretty sure I'd be able to hear the gears turning in his head.

'This is your house,' I say, more to break the silence than anything else.

He shoots me a quizzical look.

'And, as far as I know, you're not a vampire.'

The look intensifies.

I laugh, and the sound surprises me. It's a genuine one, not the dry huff of irritation I've come to associate with being in Hoxton's presence. 'You can come in,' I clarify, deciding to throw him a bone. 'If you want to, I mean. You don't have to just wait out there.'

His brows shoot into his hairline and, for a moment, I'm sure he's going to deny wanting to come in at all, but then he clears his throat and takes exactly one step over the threshold into my room. His gaze roves over my still-unmade bed, the pile of damp clothes I unceremoniously dumped in the corner of the room last night, before coming up to finally – *finally* – meet my eye. 'Glad to see you're making yourself at home.'

I narrow my eyes at him, not entirely sure how to interpret his words. Twenty-four hours ago, and I definitely would've seen them as a slight. Would've described the slight curl to his lips as nothing but a downright sneer. But now I think I see a faint shadow of amusement there, and I definitely don't sense any hostility.

I think, once again, that Hoxton is doing his best attempt at a joke. My mind flashes back to this morning in the kitchen, when we'd been getting along decently before I said something to turn his mood upside down. I'm still not entirely sure what I did or why it bothered him so much but it's clear this – the clothes, the almost smile – is his way of making amends. A peace offering of sorts.

I suppose I can meet him halfway.

'You mean you don't provide a maid service?' I ask, cocking my head to the side in faux shock. I stick out a hand and start listing things off using my fingers. 'So that's no maid and the heater's out. I think you should probably add the hospitality industry to the list of things you should avoid if you ever go broke.'

A hint of a smile tugs at the corners of his mouth, but he doesn't quite laugh. Though I think it's close. 'No danger of that.'

'Mm,' I hum. 'Well, aren't you lucky.'

We lapse into a silence but it's not uncomfortable or tinged with any of the tension from before. For the first time in the two years that I've known him, the air between us feels light and breezy.

Hoxton opens his mouth, then closes it, opens it again and eventually huffs out a gruff, 'I'll take a look at the heater, by the way.'

I raise a brow and he mirrors my expression.

'What?' he asks.

'Nothing,' I say quickly. Apparently too quickly, from the way his eyes narrow. 'You just . . . you don't really seem like an "I'll take a look" kind of guy. You know, the type to roll your sleeves up and get dirty?'

His lips thin into an unimpressed line. 'And what type do I seem like instead?'

Hoxton seems like the 'I've got a guy' type of guy. The kind of person with a never-ending list of people he can call and throw money at, at a whim, to sort out whatever problem it is he's got. But I can't say that, can I? So instead, I shrug and try to imagine Hoxton on his hands and knees, wearing one of his expensive suits, trying to figure out the plumbing, and this image alone is enough to bring on the threat of laughter. 'The type of guy to pay people to do stuff like this for you?'

'We're in the middle of a snowstorm, Noelle.'

I flick back through my memories of the last twenty-four hours, trying to pinpoint exactly when he dropped the *Ms Jones* he's steadfastly used for the last two years, and why it doesn't bother me at all.

'And I'm very capable of getting my hands dirty.'

It's an innocent-enough phrase, but the way he says it? His voice has dropped to an almost purr and his eyes are hooded with something I can't place. Something *hot*.

I take a jerky step backwards, the back of my knees hitting the edge of the bed.

'Really?'

He takes a step closer to me and I know I'm not imagining it now. His eyes *are* slightly darker.

He nods. 'I've never had any complaints before.'

I suddenly can't help but wonder if the guest room is for *special* guests. Hoxton doesn't seem the type to cuddle with a partner after the act, but I also can't see him throwing them out at 3am.

Stop it, Noelle, I mentally scold myself. *He's still staring at you.*

I swallow. Something in the atmosphere between us has changed. We're on new ground now.

A branch suddenly slams against the window, sending a shower of snow careening down to the ground with a loud *thud* and we both jump apart. I hadn't even realised we'd moved so close.

Hoxton blinks several times, like he's snapping himself out of a trance, and I realise, belatedly, that my lips have parted and my chest is heaving.

He takes another step backwards, clearing his throat as he goes. 'I'll come back and take a look at it later.'

'Right. Yeah. Later.'

He looks at me one last time before turning on his heel. I expect him to disappear out into the dark corridor without a second glance, but he hesitates in the doorway and turns around. 'The Grinch gets a bad rep.'

I look up so fast, I'm surprised I don't get whiplash. Hoxton is standing in the doorway, one hand on the frame, glancing back at me with a look I can't quite place. Any trace of heat or want from a few seconds ago is long gone, replaced by something that looks almost sad.

Ah, shit. 'You heard that?'

He nods.

Double shit. 'Listen, I didn't—'

'Have a nice day, Noelle,' Hoxton says before he disappears out into the hall.

★ ★ ★

The idea of a misunderstood Grinch haunts me for the rest of the day. Along with the memory of Hoxton's crestfallen face as he stood in the doorway.

'I can't be the first person to call him that,' I mumble to myself as I deftly tilt the wok, watching as the chicken begins to sizzle and brown amongst the vegetables already cooking inside it. My stir-fry isn't a particularly complex meal, but it's delicious and has become a fast favourite amongst my friends over the years. 'He has to know how he comes across.'

The Grinch gets a bad rep.

I groan as I start turning the noodles, making sure everything is mixed and cooked. I have no doubt in my mind that Hoxton knows *exactly* how he comes across; I just think I might be the first person to say it to his face.

Well. Not to his face. He *was* eavesdropping after all. But still.

The Grinch gets a bad rep.

I *get a bad rep.*

That's what he wanted to say, I'm sure of it.

I take the wok off the stove and start separating the contents into two bowls. Hoxton's face – that sad little grimace, the self-depreciating way he turned and disappeared – I can't get it out of my mind.

He looked almost *hurt*. Like the idea of me comparing him to the Grinch of all things cut him to his core.

'I'm a nice person,' I reassure myself as I balance both bowls in my hands and make my way towards the living room. I'm wearing my Christmas-themed apron and my car boot is filled with presents for the family I should be with right now. I'm not the problem here. Hoxton is. And yet, I can't help the guilt I'm currently feeling.

It's empty in here, but I set both bowls on the coffee table and then stomp upstairs, making as much noise as physically possible so I can't be accused of snooping around. I've not seen Hoxton since he left my room this afternoon, and the only proof I have that he hasn't abandoned me and run off into the snowstorm has been the occasional cough or the sound of his footsteps creaking against the hardwood flooring throughout the day. I've alternated between darting from my bedroom to the kitchen, taking solace downstairs whenever the cold in my room got too much.

The upper-floor landing is dark, but there's a light coming from a closed door several rooms away from me and I hover outside it for a few seconds. Something gnaws at my stomach and I recognise the feeling as guilt. I shake my head, lift my chin, and steel my shoulders.

Now it's my turn for a peace offering.

I wrap my knuckles on the door three times and then listen out. I hear the sound of his chair creaking and then—

'Come in?'

It sounds more like a question than anything else and, despite everything, I can't help but huff out a quiet laugh. I doubt he's ever had to utter those words in his own empty home before.

Hoxton's office is just like his living room: dark and sleek with a large oak desk cutting across the middle of the room. He's sat behind the desk in an impossibly expensive leather chair, an orange lamp beside him bathing him in a warm glow. Behind him, there's a window, and the snow is falling into little tornado-like flurries.

I open my mouth to speak but then he leans backwards in his chair and I get a proper glimpse of him in the soft amber light. His sleeves are rolled up to his elbows, revealing tanned muscular arms. I can see the subtle definition of his biceps and the veins that trace the length of his forearms.

It's not the first time I've noticed how strong Hoxton is, but there's something about the low light, the way it wraps around him like it's a part of him, which makes it impossible to look away.

For a moment, I'm just standing there, frozen in the doorway. His sharp jawline catches the light, and there's something almost dangerous in the way he sits so still, his posture like a predator at rest. I should say something – anything – but my mind goes blank. All I can think about is how ... *attractive* he looks. It's not just the way his body fills out his sweatshirt, or the way his strong hands rest on the arms of his chair, but the entire aura around him.

The light catches in his eyes as he glances up at me, and I snap out of my trance, blinking rapidly. He raises an eyebrow, and I'm painfully aware that I've been standing here like an idiot.

'I made dinner,' I say quickly, before he can put a voice to the clear apprehension that's painted across his face.

He looks vaguely amused. 'I thought you were off duty?'

I purse my lips and swallow down the snarky response that immediately comes to sit on my tongue. *Peace offering*, I remind myself, gritting my teeth and forcing a probably deranged smile. *This is a peace offering.*

'I made too much,' I say with an airy shrug, like a professional chef getting her portion-sizing wrong is a perfectly normal everyday occurrence.

It's clear Hoxton doesn't buy it and I expect him to pull me up on it. But he doesn't. Instead, he mirrors my shrug and pushes himself away from his desk, shutting his laptop as he goes. 'Thank you.'

I shrug again. 'Like I said, I made too much. Don't get used to it.'

He hums as he passes me, his chest brushing against mine in the kind of way that sends a deep warmth shooting through me. 'Isn't that lucky?'

'Very.'

When we reach the living room, instead of making a beeline for the sofa and the bowls on the coffee table, Hoxton fumbles around in a drawer and plucks out a lighter. I sink into the sofa and watch as he switches off the overhead light and methodically lights several candles dotted around the room. The action blankets us in that same warm glow Hoxton had in his office and it's cosy. Intimate even.

He doesn't move to turn on the television and I don't reach for the remote either. It's just the two of us, our shadows flickering in the candlelight.

Hoxton settles down next to me on the sofa, close enough that his legs bump against mine. The borrowed sweats I'm wearing are soft and thick, but I still feel a lick of heat start to bloom where we touch.

We eat in silence, the only sounds filling the room the

quiet clinking of our chopsticks against the bowls and oc-casional howl of the wind.

I use this as another opportunity to observe, stealing glances at Hoxton as he eats, noticing the way his brow is slightly furrowed in concentration, how he chews thought-fully before swallowing. His usual demeanour seems softer somehow, more vulnerable in the flickering candlelight. His features are softened, the shadows playing on his face, making him look less guarded than usual. I study him and commit to memory the way his eyes crinkle slightly at the corners when he smiles after swallowing down a mouthful or how his long fingers wrap around the chopsticks with practised ease.

Hoxton, noticeably less distracted than I am, finishes the last bite in his bowl several minutes before me and sets it down, a satisfied look crossing his features.

'Thank you,' he says, his voice soft. 'You really didn't have to cook. And—' He clears his throat before turning his body towards me, his gaze steady. 'The food was delicious. As usual.'

I freeze, chopsticks still in hand, my heart pounding in my ears. For a moment, I can't find my voice. I don't think Hoxton has ever given me a compliment directly to my face before. Every bit of praise I've ever received from the man has come second-hand, mostly from Roland passing on a paraphrased message.

'Uh . . . thank you,' I manage to stammer out, feeling heat rush to my cheeks. I dip my head and focus on finishing the last few bites in my bowl, suddenly desperate to avoid his intense gaze. 'Just think of it as a peace offering for the whole Grinch thing.'

Hoxton chuckles and I look up just in time to watch his eyes crinkle in the corners and a tiny dimple form just above his left cheek. I'm really starting to like that sound, as rare as it is. Every time it slips from his lips, I want to bury it deep in the recesses of my mind until I've committed it to memory and can play it on loop whenever I need to hear it.

'The biscuit or earlier today?'

I feel my cheeks warm. 'How about both?'

He laughs again and I can't help but savour the sound.

'Consider your offering accepted,' Hoxton says. 'Are we even now?'

I nod in agreement, silently grateful for the ease that has quickly settled between us again. The awkwardness is gone, and it's like we're two friends enjoying a meal together.

Almost.

The wind is still howling and I let my gaze linger on the winter wonderland outside the nearest window.

'It really doesn't feel like Christmas,' I murmur, more to myself than anything.

'That's because it's December 22nd.'

I laugh. 'You know what I mean.'

He leans back into the sofa and shrugs. 'I don't think I do. Christmas has never been more than just another day to me.'

I can't help but frown. 'Even when you were a kid?'

Hoxton's face tightens ever so slightly. 'Particularly then. So . . .' He nudges my leg with his thigh and I pretend like the touch doesn't set every nerve ending alight. 'Enlighten me. What does a Christmas look like for Noelle Jones?'

He's really got to stop saying my name like that. It's starting to do something to me.

I shift slightly on the sofa, all too aware of how close we are. 'Normally, right about now, I'd be heading over to my grandmother's house to spend Christmas with my family.' I shift on my seat until I'm facing him, one leg tucked under the other. 'I always finish my Christmas shopping by December 1st and that means I can spend the week eating good food and making memories.' Just the thought of it brings a smile to my face. 'What would *you* normally be doing right now?'

Hoxton frowns. 'How do you mean?'

I gesture around the sparse living room. 'Obviously you weren't planning on staying here.'

The corner of his mouth twitches up slightly, like he's just heard a joke but I'm not privy to it. 'Obviously?'

I nod and scooch a little closer, closing what little gap there is between us. 'I know Christmas isn't your thing . . .'

He exhales deeply through his nostrils and I laugh.

'Okay, yes, understatement of the year,' I concede. 'But seriously? If aliens invaded right now and knocked on your door, they'd never even know it was Christmas.'

'I'm not seeing the problem,' Hoxton says dryly.

I swat his arm gently and roll my eyes. 'You weren't really planning on spending the holidays here, were you?'

Hoxton's face remains a blank canvas.

'Seriously?' I ask. 'Here, alone? Without so much as a fairy light or even a little bit of tinsel to inject any Christmas joy into your life?'

'Christmas joy is overrated, forced and also—' Hoxton leans in and drops his voice to a conspiratorial whisper. 'Not a real thing.'

I reel back and pretend to clutch at my chest. 'Spoken like a true Grinch.'

Hoxton throws his head back and laughs. A real, shoulder-shaking laugh. It rapidly climbs up my list of favourite sounds and nestles itself right at the top. 'If you say so.'

'You really were just planning on staying here over the holidays?' I ask. 'Alone? What about your family? You guys don't do anything?'

Hoxton's smile falters. '*They* usually do something,' he says slowly, and it's clear he's choosing his next words carefully. 'I believe my mother is hosting this year.'

'And what?' I ask, trying to wrap my head around a

family dynamic so clearly different to my own. 'You weren't invited?'

I know I'm not one to talk, considering I've spent the last two years complaining to Eve about what an asshole Hoxton is, but I didn't think he was *that* bad. I feel a small spark of anger light up inside me on his behalf, but it snuffs itself out almost immediately when Hoxton turns a wry grin on me.

'Of course I was invited,' he says. 'I choose not to go.'

Choose. Not chose. *Choose*. This is a conscious decision he makes every year, not just this once. The idea of missing even one Christmas with my family is enough to make me tear up. How many Christmases has Hoxton deliberately skipped out on over the years? And *why*?

I can't help but ask. 'Why not?' I know that I'm prying, that I'm getting far too close and any semblance of professionalism or keeping an appropriate distance from my client has disappeared out the window and into the storm about ten minutes ago, but I can't help myself.

Hoxton shrugs. I can tell it's supposed to be nonchalant, light and airy, but it comes out stiff and forced. 'I'm not fond of Christmas.'

I want to push, to get to the bottom of whatever it is that's caused this hatred of Christmas, but it's clear Hoxton is reaching his limit with me and my questions, and I don't want to ruin whatever this is between us right now. Though, to be fair, I think I already have.

His shoulders tense imperceptibly, his jaw clenching slightly as he avoids my gaze. The casual air that once enveloped us now feels strained and the weight of his unspoken words hangs heavily between us. Hoxton's once-relaxed posture stiffens visibly, his shoulders tensing imperceptibly as he shifts slightly in his seat. Two minutes ago, his gaze was warm and inviting, but now it's turned distant.

I offer Hoxton a gentle smile before shifting back slightly, putting some distance between us.

I'm not going to push. He can have his secrets.

I clear my throat awkwardly. Hoxton's distant gaze lingers on me for a moment longer before he blinks, as if he's coming back to reality.

'Well,' I start, my voice sounding too loud in the now-quiet room. 'I should probably let you get some rest. It's been a long day.'

Hoxton nods, his expression unreadable as he rises from his seat. He reaches for the bowls, but I stick a hand out to stop him.

'I've got it, don't worry about it.'

He hesitates but then nods as he moves towards the door. 'I fixed the heater in your room, by the way. Just needed a system reset.'

Relief floods through me and I manage a small, genuine smile in return. 'Thank you.'

He gives me a half-shrug, as if to say, '*it's no big deal*', the same way I did with the dinner, and then disappears down into the hall, leaving me alone in the dimly lit living room.

I sit there for a while, enveloped in the silence that now seems suffocating without his presence. Only once I'm sure he's upstairs and in his room do I let my head loll back against the headrest and allow a low groan to slip from my lips.

Why does it feel like we've taken one step forward today, and at least three back?

CHAPTER NINE

Noelle

I jolt awake, my teeth chattering in rhythm with the shiver that courses through my body. My toes are numb, my fingers are almost there, and my entire body has that weird stinging sensation you feel when you get too cold.

'You've *got* to be kidding me,' I whimper to myself as I sit upright and glare into the darkness around me. My room, once again, is an icebox. My teeth are quite literally chattering, and my breath is forming into tiny little puffs of mist in front of me with each frustrated exhale. With nothing to fight off the cold, my room has been turned into an arctic wasteland.

'What happened to "I fixed the heater in your room"?' I grumble as I pull my duvet tight around my shoulders like a makeshift cape. But it's no use – the cold has seeped into my bones. '*System reset,* my ass.'

The quick fix Hoxton promised earlier echoes mockingly in my head as my toes grow numb with each passing second. I glance to my left where the thermostat sits on the wall. Its screen is flashing a bright, angry red and I resist the urge to smack it as hard as I can. No sense actually breaking the damn thing now, is there?

Another shiver racks through me and I let out an unholy groan before burying my face in the duvet. I genuinely don't think I've ever been this cold before.

I can't stay here like this.

The thought hits me like a truck because where else am I supposed to go? Besides, I know the moment I leave the bed, the cold will creep in fully, settling over me like an oppressive blanket. But the idea of staying here, shivering and helpless, isn't much better. I close my eyes for a moment, taking a shaky breath, and force myself out of bed. The duvet slides off my shoulders a little, and I wince at the shock of air that hits the few pieces of exposed skin. My feet feel like they've been dipped in ice water as they touch the floor and I scramble towards the door, my mind racing with curses aimed at Hoxton.

He's the one who assured me the heater was fixed. And yet, here I am, about to go full-on polar bear just to make it through the night. I can just picture him in his nice warm bedroom, sleeping without a care in the world while I freeze to death in here.

Maybe our conversation last night got to him more than I

thought, and this is just my punishment for daring to broach the topic of Christmas in his home.

Letting your personal chef freeze to death in your home simply because she asked about your Christmas plans definitely seems like overkill. Though I wouldn't put it past Hoxton. Or maybe that's just the brain freeze talking. Because this cold is most definitely affecting my brainpower right now.

I need to get out of this room.

I wrench the door open and peer out into the dark hall. As usual, all the other doors are closed and there's no light to be seen under Hoxton's office door whatsoever. Which means that he's in his room, and I have no idea which one that might be.

Hoxton's thinly veiled warning to not to go snooping around his home echoes in my mind; I have to admit, I'm intrigued. What is it he's so desperate to hide? Is he just insanely private or does he have a *Fifty Shades*-esque sex dungeon hidden behind one of these doors?

My curiosity is officially piqued.

I reach for the door directly opposite mine and step inside, bracing myself for the worst. But instead of blistering cold, I'm met with a strange stillness. The room isn't freezing, but it's not like I'm rushing to describe it as *warm* either. Still, definitely an improvement on my room.

I flick the nearest light switch and my eyes adjust quickly to the dim lighting as I glance around the room.

To my surprise, it's a home gym, though not one I would've ever expected to find in a place like this. The floors are polished wood, gleaming faintly in the low light. Several sleek machines sit along the walls: ellipticals, a treadmill, and some free weights stacked neatly in one corner.

I step further in, my bare feet padding silently against the cool floor, relieved that at least the temperature here isn't actively trying to kill me. The gym smells faintly of rubber and wood polish: clean, almost antiseptic, and eerily untouched. There's a large mirror on one wall, stretching from floor to ceiling, and in its reflection, I see myself: dishevelled from sleep, braids gathering in a knot at my waist, wrapped in a duvet cape.

I turn toward the far corner of the room where a row of neatly stacked yoga mats rests against the wall. If worse comes to worst, I guess I could hole up in here for the night, stretched out on one of those mats.

Though I really hope it doesn't get to that.

I glance around, wondering if there's any hint of Hoxton's personal touch here. Maybe a towel draped over one of the machines, a forgotten protein shake bottle . . . anything that might tell me he actually uses the place. But the room seems pristine, almost clinical. Not a single speck of dust, and certainly no trace of Hoxton's presence. Which is ridiculous, because the man can't look the way he does and *not* regularly work out. Can he?

I run a hand over the smooth surface of one of the weight machines, a heavy piece of equipment made of polished steel and leather. For a moment, the soft click of metal echoes through the room as I shift it, and I pull my hand back, startled by the sound.

It's so quiet, so *still*, that the tiniest noise feels amplified.

A pang of irritation flickers in me. The small, rational part of me knows that this isn't Hoxton's fault. That this is just an unfortunate side-effect of the blizzard still battering us from all angles, but *still*. What exactly is Hoxton's deal? I can't understand how a guy who owns a house this big – this *cold* – could have a home gym like this and still let someone freeze to death in their own room.

The air around me seems to grow heavier with the thought of Hoxton, and I feel my frustration bubbling back up. Maybe it's the cold that's making me angry, or maybe I'm just fed up with everything about being trapped in this house. I don't know. But I definitely don't want to sit around in here any longer.

I back out of the home gym, careful not to leave any trace of my snooping, and try the next door to the right. I knock a few times and then wait, conscious that this might be Hoxton's bedroom. When I get no response, I tentatively push open the door and flick on the light. It's a bathroom. But it's not a bathroom I ever would've expected to see in Hoxton's home.

With the massive clawfoot bathtub dominating the centre of the room, I can't help but feel that this is the kind of bathroom that wouldn't look out of place in a kitschy country hotel. The tub is a gleaming white, impossibly inviting, and its curved shaped is more decadent than any tub I've seen in my life. This is the first room I've seen that doesn't have the same hardwood flooring as the rest of the house. Instead, it's made of sleek black tiles that contrast sharply with the soft, warm light emanating from the lights dotted around the walls. There's even a huge, framed mirror hanging above a marble countertop that's packed neatly with expensive-looking toiletries.

The only thing that doesn't quite fit is the stillness of the room; seemingly everything in this house bar his office and kitchen feels untouched. Almost frozen in time. The towels hanging on the towel rack are too neat, too perfectly folded. The bottles of shampoo and soap are labelled in elegant fonts, but there's not a single fingerprint on them. I think about my own tiny bathroom back home. There's just enough room for a small shower and all my toiletries are haphazardly stuffed in a basket on the floor. There are at least three half-empty shampoo bottles in the basket, along with no less than twelve various cosmetic tubs that are almost certainly out of date by now. Hoxton might just have a heart attack if he saw the way I lived.

I wonder how else we're different.

My curiosity gets the better of me, and I cross the room, my bare feet leaving faint impressions on the cool tile floor as I move past the tub. I can't help myself; this feels like an opportunity too good to waste.

I glance at the shelves above the bathtub, half expecting to find some basic bath products – something utilitarian and manly, something that makes sense for someone who likely has no time for anything as indulgent as a hot soak after a hard day at work. But what I actually find makes me pause.

Bath bombs.

A collection of them.

Rows of neatly organised, colourful bombs in all shapes and sizes lined up in perfect formation.

For the most part, the labels are from Lush, and each one promises something different. There are lavender bombs to soothe, rose ones to relax, and a whole stack of citrus ones to energise, more than I can even count right now. My fingers hover over the colourful bombs. I can't believe he has so many, and I can't help but smile a little. Hoxton, of all people, has a small *arsenal* of bath bombs in his ridiculously decadent bathroom. It's the last thing I expected to find in this sterile house. But here they are, rows of soothing, fragrant little balls and squares, and even an animal-shaped one or two. Their brightly coloured wrappings feel almost too cheerful for this kind of surrounding.

I take one out, a delicate pastel pink one wrapped in a paper that promises 'relaxation' in bold black letters and I press it lightly between my fingers. It's soft, delicate. It doesn't feel like it's been used. None of them do. I peer around some more and try to see if there are any half-opened bath bombs, but they're all neatly packed away as if he just brought them home from the store and hasn't touched them since.

What is he waiting for?

A moment of peace and quiet that never comes? Are these rows and rows of bath bombs just wishful thinking on his behalf, or maybe they're a gift? That makes a little more sense. Maybe he's got a headstrong aunt somewhere who sends him the same birthday gift year on year and Hoxton doesn't have the heart to simply throw them out.

Yeah, that's it. That's got to be it. Because why else would someone like him – someone so impeccably sharp, cold, and distant – have so many bloody bath bombs? It's almost ... *humanising.*

I snort quietly to myself, realising I'm actually starting to understand Hoxton a little bit better, even if it's just based on the fact that he apparently has a secret soft spot for bath bombs. It's not a side of him I'd have expected to see, considering how private and guarded he is about everything else.

But then, I catch myself.

What the hell am I doing?

The second the thought crosses my mind, I quickly stuff the bath bomb back into its place, pretending like I wasn't just having a small existential crisis over the fact that Hoxton maybe has something resembling self-care in his life. But the discovery doesn't feel like something I can just ignore.

I move on, trying to pretend like I'm not already a little too invested in the mystery that is Alexander Hoxton. I don't know why, but something about this room feels like an inadvertent invitation. Like Hoxton never meant for anyone to see this side of him, but I've somehow stumbled into it anyway. He's always so composed, so businesslike, it's strange to see these small human moments sprinkled around his house like breadcrumbs; like *he* might need to relax, to unwind, to indulge in little luxuries at some point.

If he'll ever let himself.

I stand up straight, take a last, lingering look at the claw-foot tub and then turn to leave. When I step out into the hall again, it feels noticeably colder than before. Like the paralysing chill from my room has seeped out and is steadily infecting the rest of the house.

Damn it.

I glance down the hall at the door right at the end. That's got to be his room, right? I shuffle towards it, duvet still wrapped tightly around me like some marshmallow-esque gown, and rap my knuckles against the door to the rhythm of '*Your heater sucks, and so does my mood.*'

I wait a beat, my hand hovering over the doorknob. A small part of me actually hopes this *isn't* his room and I'll get another opportunity to snoop around and learn something new about my unwilling host. But then the door swings open, revealing a yawning Hoxton looking as dishevelled as a man worth millions can possibly look at one in the morning. So, not really dishevelled at all, but his dark hair is sticking up in every direction, and his eyes – usually dark and piercing – seem softer and clouded with sleep.

He stares at me, unblinking, for a few seconds and then asks, 'Is something wrong?' His voice is rough with sleep and, despite my annoyance at this whole ridiculous situation, I can't help but find the groggy tone irritatingly attractive.

'Add "heater repair" to the list of fields you probably shouldn't go into anytime soon,' I say, injecting as much humour as I can into my tone, despite the fact that I'm rapidly losing feeling in my toes. When Hoxton continues to stare at me, dumbfounded, I add, 'My room's turned into a walk-in freezer.'

He stands there for a moment, blinking the sleep from his eyes like he's batting away snowflakes caught on his long lashes. 'Come again?'

Now it's my turn to blink at him. Because those are most definitely two words I don't want to hear from him when he currently looks and sounds like *that*.

Something warm and tight coils in the pit of my stomach

as my mind starts unhelpfully racing with thoughts of scenarios where he might repeat those two words to me.

'Noelle?'

The use of my name snaps me back to reality and I pray to whichever deity is currently looking out for me – apparently, none – that my cheeks aren't as red as they feel.

'The heater you allegedly fixed earlier today stopped working,' I say, tugging the duvet around myself a little tighter. 'I don't mean to be the bearer of bad news but I can't sleep in there.'

Hoxton rubs at the back of his neck and squints down the dark hall, as if the act of focusing might somehow repair the broken heater telepathically. 'That's . . . that's unfortunate,' he says after a moment or two, the edges of sleep still clinging to his voice in that distractingly attractive way.

'Very,' I say. 'Is there another room I can sleep in? Another guest room? Or I guess I could take the sofa.'

Hoxton shakes his head. 'I only have the one guest room.'

A house this big and only two of the rooms are capable of housing someone for the night? Insane.

'Okay . . .' I say slowly. The yoga mats in the gym are starting to look worryingly enticing. 'I guess . . . the sofa, then?'

I grimace as I remember the abomination in his living room. I'm sure it cost thousands upon thousands of pounds, but I'd pick my cheap and fluffy IKEA sofa over his rigid leather one any day. Needs must, though.

Hoxton steps fully into the doorway. His gaze drops to my bare feet, which are still most definitely freezing from the icy hallway floors. His eyes flicker up to meet mine and a faint frown creases his forehead.

'I'm not sure the living room will be much of an improvement on your room,' he says, voice still rough. 'And it won't exactly be comfortable.'

I raise an eyebrow at him, my mind already working through various snarky responses. Something like '*better than freezing to death in there!*' But something in his tone makes me hesitate. It's like he's trying to be . . . considerate? Which feels weird coming from him. Very weird. But then again, it is Hoxton, and apparently nothing he does is ever quite what it seems.

'Well, I'm not exactly spoiled for choice here,' I say, forcing a half-smile, though I don't know why I'm even trying to lighten the mood. The situation's ridiculous. And, most importantly, not my fault. I'm a guest here. Technically. Where is his sense of hospitality? 'So, what do you suggest I do? Just camp out in the gym? Use one of those yoga mats?'

Hoxton looks momentarily startled and I cringe inwardly. *Damn it.* Wasn't planning on admitting to snooping around. I watch as his gaze flicks between my still-shivering form and the hallway beyond. Then he sighs and rubs the back of his neck again. 'I suppose . . . I mean, it's only fair – you can stay here for the night.' And then he steps aside and gestures into his room.

I blink, stunned by the offer. I mean, I *heard* him, but it takes a moment for the words to fully register. I probably look as surprised as I feel, because Hoxton doesn't strike me as the type to invite *anyone* into his personal space – I'm still running with the theory that any 'late-night' visitors take the guest room.

But here he is, suppressing a yawn as he waits for me to enter the most personal room in his house.

Another chill suddenly hits the both of us and Hoxton visibly shudders. I wasn't imagining things. It *is* getting colder in here. He raises a silent brow at me and I nod stiffly, not needing to be told twice.

I shuffle past him, duvet still wrapped tightly around myself, and immediately feel every muscle in my body begin to relax. The warmth from Hoxton's room floods every single one of my senses, and it's all I can do not to moan in pleasure. It's like stepping into a different world entirely – one that doesn't feel as cold and clinical as the rest of the house. The room is spacious, minimalist and undeniably *his*. Everything is dark wood, clean lines and sharp angles, just like his living room, but there's something about it that feels more comfortable than the rest of the house.

I let out a quiet sigh of relief, my impromptu duvet cocoon still wrapped around me like a safety net. But then, it hits me.

I glance around, and the realisation slams into me a split second before I can stop it.

Wait.

This isn't just any old room in Hoxton's home ... This is his *bedroom*.

There's a bed. A massive king-sized bed covered in a thick, incredibly warm-looking duvet, and a surprising number of plush pillows.

The silence in the room suddenly becomes deafening, the only sound the soft hum of the heating system, as I realise that *we're going to have to share it.*

A sudden flush crawls up my neck, heat rushing to my face as the awkwardness settles in. Hoxton's offer is kind, sure. But has he considered the implication of what he's offering here? Has he even thought about the fact that this is *his bed*? I've been invited into his most private space, the one place in this house that doesn't belong to the meticulous, businesslike persona he puts on for everyone else.

And I'm expected to *sleep* in it?

With *him*?!

Roland was wrong. Hoxton's at no risk from an aneurysm, but I definitely am right now.

'Um ...' I say, forcing myself to break the silence, but the words stick in my throat and it comes out sounding like a gargled cough. 'So ... the bed?'

Hoxton is standing at the foot of the bed, looking at me

expectantly as if this whole exchange is entirely normal. He runs a hand through his messy hair again, clearly still in that sleep-drunk haze. 'Yeah, you can have the bed. I'll sleep on the sofa.'

There's a beat of silence.

I blink. 'Wait, no. I didn't mean it like that. I just … uh … wasn't expecting … well …'

My gaze flicks towards the bed, then back to Hoxton, who's looking at me as if he's already made some kind of logical decision.

He shrugs, completely unfazed by my hesitation. 'It's fine. I'm sure the sofa's comfortable enough for one night.'

'It's not fine,' I say, stubbornly. 'If it's too cold and uncomfortable for me, it's going to be too cold and uncomfortable for you.'

Hoxton takes in a deep, long-suffering breath. 'There's no other alternative, Noelle.'

'There is.'

'Then enlighten me.'

I look pointedly between him, the bed, and back to him again. It takes a second or two, but then I see realisation dawning behind his eyes.

'Oh. You want …' We stare at each other in silence for a few long seconds before he lets out a heavy sigh that seems to carry the weight of the world. His jaw clenches once, twice, a third time. 'Look,' he says with another long-suffering sigh, like I'm the absolute bane of his existence. To be fair, at this point, I probably am. 'I suppose ... I mean ... We're both adults, right?'

'Right.'

'So, we can share the bed without any—'

'Without it being weird,' I finish for him. 'Exactly.'

Hoxton nods hesitantly. 'Just ... You just stay on your side, and I'll stay on mine.'

I swallow down a snort. That's exactly what Eve and I would say to each other when we went on holiday and had to share a hotel bed as children. 'Nothing to worry about there, trust me.'

I think I hear Hoxton chuckle, but I'm too busy striding across the room and making my way towards his bed to care. I don't think I've ever been more thankful for a bed in my life. The promise of warmth is too much and I practically dive onto Hoxton's giant, cloud-like bed without a second thought.

Hoxton's duvet is heavy and luxurious, trapping the heat underneath like a personal cocoon designed to combat the North Pole itself. As soon as my head hits the equally soft and warm pillow, a long, involuntary groan escapes me. The sound is horrendously inappropriate, but I can't quite bring myself to care.

'This,' I mutter, wiggling around under the blankets. 'This is *heaven*.'

'Mm.'

I peek out from beneath the duvet. Hoxton is lingering by the foot of the bed, a look I can't quite place sparkling in his eyes. For the first time since invading Hoxton's personal space, I let myself take a good look at him.

Sorry, Eve, I think, taking in the plain white T-shirt and baggy grey pyjama bottoms he's wearing. *Not a suit.* I try not to focus on the fact that his trousers hang low on his hips and how the shirt clings to his chest like a delightful second skin, showing off every crest and peak of his muscles.

Delicious is the first word that jumps into my mind and I immediately turn over.

'Better?' Hoxton asks eventually.

'Like you wouldn't believe,' I mumble into the pillow, my words muffled.

Hoxton chuckles softly, and I feel the bed dip slightly as he crawls in beside me. For a fleeting moment, I freeze, the absurdity of the situation settling in all at once.

Me and Hoxton.

Sharing a bed.

His bed.

A nervous laugh bubbles out of my throat, but I think I successfully manage to turn it into a cough before he has the chance to comment.

'Well ...' Hoxton says, his voice clipped. He's stopped moving around now and in the darkness I can just about make out the shape of his body lying next to mine. 'Goodnight.'

I swallow. I don't think I've ever felt more awkward in my life. 'Yes. Um. Yeah. Goodnight.'

I wait for him to say something else but only silence comes. I try to ignore the inherent awkwardness clinging to us right now but, as I nestle deeper into the duvet, trying to cling onto as much warmth as I can, something feels off.

The initial blast of warmth from being in Hoxton's bed has faded, and the air around me is growing steadily colder. My heart sinks when I realise that the heat isn't radiating around me like it was when I first entered the room. It's gone, just like in my room.

At this point, I'm sure I must be a beacon for all the bad luck in the universe because this is just *ridiculous*.

I snap open my eyes and glare into the darkness. 'Hoxton?'

'Mm?'

'Is it just me, or is it getting cold in here, too?'

There's a pause, then the slight dip of the bed again, followed by the sound of padded footsteps, and then the soft beeping of several digital buttons being pressed in quick succession. No comforting hum of machinery follows, no rush of warm air – just the sound of our twin sighs filling the rapidly cooling room.

'Great,' Hoxton murmurs, and I hear the rustle of fabric as he slips back under the duvet again. 'I think the heating's conked out here as well.'

'Perfect,' I deadpan, the word heavy with sarcasm. 'Your house really knows how to welcome a guest.'

'Seems like it.' His tone matches mine entirely, dry with a hint of resignation.

I shift in the bed, trying to generate some warmth by sheer force of will. It doesn't work. The cold seeps into my bones and I can't help but shiver under the duvet. I steal a sideways glance at Hoxton lying beside me, his silhouette barely visible in the darkness. His breathing is steady, an irritating contrast to the chaotic whirlwind of thoughts racing through my mind and the storm outside.

Why does *he* get to be cool, calm and collected when it feels like there's a livewire burrowing its way under my skin right now?

The room, sadly, only gets colder.

We lie there in the dark, each lost in our own thoughts as the chill of the room turns into something almost glacial. I shiver involuntarily, pulling the duvet tighter around me in a lame attempt to conserve any lingering warmth left from before.

After what feels like an eternity, Hoxton finally breaks the silence. 'I know this isn't ideal,' he offers, his voice barely above a whisper in the darkness.

I roll my eyes, then remember he can't see the action and say, 'You think?'

He scoffs in response. 'We could—' He cuts himself off

and I'm pretty sure I hear the sound of his head shaking against his pillow, as if he's convinced himself that whatever he was about to say wasn't worth voicing aloud.

I wait a beat or two and then sigh. 'We could what?' I ask. He might've decided that it's not worth saying, but we're running low on options here.

'Nothing.' The bed creaks slightly as he shifts beside me.

As the minutes tick by, my body gradually adjusts to the temperature, or maybe I just grow numb to the cold. Either way, exhaustion starts to tug at my eyelids, pulling me towards another uncomfortable night of sleep. I can hear Hoxton's breathing evening out beside me, a steady rhythm that drags me closer to slumber. I curl around myself as best I can, desperately trying to trap even a sliver of warmth.

Just as I'm starting to teeter on the edge of dreams, a sudden jolt of movement startles me awake. Before I can fully comprehend what's happening, Hoxton's arm snakes around my waist, pulling me back against his chest. The warmth of his body is like a furnace against the icy chill of the room, searing through my layers of borrowed clothing and sending a shockwave of heat through me. I tense at the unexpected contact, feeling the solid wall of his chest against my back, his heartbeat steady and reassuring.

In that split second, every rational thought flees my mind, leaving behind a swirling mess of confusion and desire.

I should push him away, demand an explanation, assert

my personal space. But I don't. Instead, I find myself relaxing into his embrace, the tension and cold draining from my body as if it had never been there.

For a long moment, we lie there in silence, the only sound filling the room our mingled breaths and the howling wind outside. I can feel the rise and fall of his chest with each inhale and exhale, matching my own rhythm with ease.

And then, as if on cue, Hoxton murmurs softly into the darkness, 'Just for tonight.'

His words hang heavy in the air and I turn slightly in his arms to look over my shoulder at him, but it's too dark to make out his expression. Instead, I nestle back against him, letting the comforting warmth of his body lull me into a state of drowsy contentment.

As sleep finally claims me, I offer no resistance to the steady beat of Hoxton's heart against my back.

The last coherent thought I have before sleep takes its hold of me is, *Eve is going to lose her mind.*

CHAPTER TEN

Alex

December 23rd

Noelle is a deep sleeper.

Incredibly deep.

I've been awake for at least an hour, woken by the sound of the raging storm outside, but Noelle hasn't so much as stirred.

I don't think I want her to, anyway.

She turned around at some point in the night, and now she's pressed up against me, one leg draped over my waist, her hand resting just above my heart. I watch as her chest rises and falls in rhythm with each calm breath, her long braids splayed out across my pillow.

I shift slightly, not wanting to wake her, and try to ignore the flood of warmth that spreads through me as her soft breath tickles my neck.

This is most definitely not how I envisioned today starting.

She murmurs something nonsensical in her sleep before nuzzling closer to me, her hips bucking gently into mine. I freeze. I shouldn't be enjoying this, but her body slots beside mine perfectly and, for a split second, I consider playing dead – just to prolong this unexpected comfort. But then the reality of the situation settles in and I shake my head roughly, well aware that my thoughts are quickly drifting into dangerous territory.

I *absolutely* shouldn't be enjoying this. Noelle is technically my employee and we agreed last night that this was a one-time thing. *Strictly* for warmth.

One time. As in, I'm going to need to fix the heater properly today unless we want a repeat of last night.

A treacherous, unfamiliar voice whispers in the back of my mind, '*Maybe you* do *want another night with Noelle*' but I swat the thought away as quickly as it came.

Carefully, I slide my arm out from beneath her and try to pull away. She stirs immediately – a frown pinching her thick brows, lips parting in silent protest – and I freeze again, holding my breath.

Her eyes flutter open, bleary and clouded with sleep, and meet mine. It feels like the storm outside has faded away into nothing but a whisper, and the only thing I can hear is the rapid beating of my heart and that voice in the back of my mind telling me 'Get up, idiot.'

But I don't move.

I *can't.*

I'm frozen in place as she blinks the sleep away. I can practically see her brain catching up with her as her gaze focuses in on me and her mouth drops open.

'Oh,' she murmurs, brown eyes scanning the length of our bodies, still tightly wrapped around each other. '*Oh.*'

Everything seems to happen at once.

'Shit. Sorry,' Noelle says before trying to spin around and roll over to the other side of the bed. But our legs are still tangled up with each other and the movement only ends up pulling me with her. She yelps as she rolls onto her back, taking me with her.

I have to put my arm just above her head, caging her in, to stop my weight from crushing her. I'm hovering over her, our faces are only inches apart and up this close, I can see a faint pink blush spreading across the peak of her cheeks.

It would take nothing – absolutely *nothing* – for me to lean down right now, close the space between us, and press a kiss against her lips.

Which is definitely *not* a thought I should be having right now. Not with her underneath me like this, her soft curves pressing gently into me as she takes deep breath after deep breath.

I'm not sure how long we stay like that. Me, looking down into her deep brown eyes, watching as her tongue darts out every few seconds to lick at her full lips. It feels like an eternity but can't be much longer than a few seconds before she swallows thickly and shoots me a nervous grin. 'This is . . . um. Good morning.'

The sound of her voice pulls me back to reality. I'm in bed with Noelle. My personal chef. My head of HR will have a field day if she ever finds out.

I pull back, detangling myself from her, and try not to dwell too much on how I immediately miss the feel of her body pressed up against mine.

'Morning.' My voice is gruff and I'm not sure how much of that I can pin on lingering drowsiness. I slide over to my side of the bed, leaving more than an arm's length of space between us. 'Did you sleep well?'

'Yep.' Her voice is higher than usual and she's also moved to the opposite end of the bed, obviously determined to put as much space between us as possible. 'You?'

I nod.

'Great,' she says quickly. Too quickly. Her cheeks are still flushed and every few seconds she sneaks a not-so-subtle look at me before quickly glancing away. 'Just great.'

'Great,' I echo, clearing my throat even though there's nothing lodged in there.

We lapse into another silence. Noelle seems fixated on a

spot on the wall, her fingers fidgeting with the edge of the duvet. Then she sighs, lolls her head towards me, and grins.

'I think I've had one-night stands less awkward than this.'

The bluntness of her statement shocks a dry laugh out of me. 'Yeah?'

'Mhm.' Her grin widens as she reaches across the bed to poke at my side. 'Like you said last night, we're both adults. And this was . . .' She waves her hand around, fumbling for the right words to use. 'This was a necessity. Life or death, you know?'

I quirk a brow. 'Life or death?'

'Most definitely,' she laughs. 'I'm telling you, if I'd stayed in that room last night, you would've had to carve me out of a block of ice this morning.' She shifts slightly until she's facing me properly, and there's not much room between us anymore. Not that there was much in first place. 'So, let's agree to keep things moving, all right?'

'Keep things moving?' I don't think I've ever heard that phrase before.

Noelle laughs. 'Don't let it get weird. So we cuddled a little bit? Big deal.'

I don't think I've used the world *cuddled* since I was a child, but that's not the point here. The point is that we *did* cuddle and I, against all odds, actually enjoyed it. Very much so.

But it's clear that she didn't. That look of contentment

on her face as she nuzzled against my chest was all in my mind. She was just trying to keep warm. Nothing more, nothing less.

'Right,' I force out. 'No big deal.'

She lets out a happy sigh and leans back against the headboard, her eyes fluttering shut. 'Good. Glad to see we're on the same page.'

'Definitely on the same page,' I say, trying to match her nonchalance. Noelle seems to have moved on from our moment of intimacy, and I know that I should do the same. Though that seems impossible right now because my mind is playing images of Noelle resting against my chest on a loop right now, and I'm enjoying it more than I should.

As we both lie here in silence, the room gradually grows colder. Or maybe it's always been this cold, but the adrenaline rush from this morning has only just worn off. Either way, the heater must be acting up again and Noelle shivers slightly, pulling the duvet tighter around herself.

'I'll see if I can fix the heater,' I blurt out suddenly, eager for an excuse to leave the room. 'Properly this time, so we don't have to . . .' I trail off and gesture towards the empty space between us.

Noelle nods, a grateful smile playing on her lips. 'No pressure.'

No pressure, indeed.

'There are—' I clear my throat and nod to my drawers.

'You can borrow a pair of socks, by the way. Top-left drawer.'

Her eyes widen. 'Thank you.'

I nod and quickly get up from the bed, feeling her eyes on me as I make my way to the door. I hit an icy wall of cold air as soon as I step out into the hall and a sliver of panic shoots through me. It's definitely getting colder in here.

This doesn't bode well for Noelle's chances of getting out of here in time for Christmas. And we may freeze to death while we're stuck here. Not ideal.

I pad downstairs and yank open the cupboard that hosts the beast of metal and wires that is my heating system. It hums and whirs as I pull open the door and I bend down, pop open the panel and dive in. But no matter which wire I poke or which valve I twist, the thing refuses to spit out even a puff of warmth. The only response I get is the wind still howling outside, and the occasional *thud* – a new shelf of snow sliding off the roof and slamming to the ground. I'm half tempted to give the thing a kick, just to assert some dominance – I've never met a piece of technology I haven't been able to wrap my head around – but then I imagine Noelle's raised eyebrows and the hint of a smirk on those full lips.

'*Tech genius bested by inanimate object,*' I can almost hear her say, humour glinting in those expressive brown eyes. '*Social media is going to have a field day.*' And if that doesn't sting a little, poking at my pride like a fork testing the rawness of a cake.

I spend the next twenty minutes scowling at my phone as I scroll through an online manual for my heater. It's a fruitless endeavour, to say the least. I try every troubleshooting tip it offers, but the heater remains as uncooperative as ever. Maybe this is my sign that we need to get into making heaters at HoxTech, because I most definitely won't be buying from this brand again.

Defeated, I stand, brushing my hands on my pyjama trousers, and glance out the window. Icy droplets are battering the glass, the storm outside growing more furious by the minute. Just how long is this thing supposed to last?

For a brief moment, I entertain the idea of calling someone to ask for a second opinion. Roland, perhaps? Maybe Luca? I reject that idea as soon as it jumps into my mind. While Roland is contractually obliged not to spend the next few weeks mocking me for my technical inaptitude when it comes to the heating system, Luca has no such obligation.

Reaching out to Luca for help is officially out.

I pull up my message history with Roland and thumb in a quick message:

ALEX

> Roland, do I have any spare
> portable heaters in the house?
> In the loft, maybe?

As a general rule, I try not to bother Roland when he's on leave. He's spookily efficient at his job on a day-to-day basis and I know, better than anyone else, how much he deserves a true break. But this is an emergency.

Noelle is, quite literally, freezing to death here.

And so am I. Kind of.

A particularly loud gust of wind slams against my home and I can feel the cold seeping in with each passing second.

I glance back at my phone. Still no response from Roland. I suppose I can't blame him. It is the early evening in Australia, and I imagine he's enjoying quality time with his boyfriend's family. The last thing he should be doing is looking at his work phone right now. A twinge of guilt pricks at me.

ALEX

> Sorry. Ignore.

Reluctantly, once I'm sure I've exhausted every avenue the internet has available to me, and I haven't missed something ridiculously simple, I pull up my chat history with Luca.

ALEX

Any idea how to fix a heater from this brand?
IMAGE SENT

Luca's response, as always, comes in almost immediately. I swear, the man is glued to his phone.

LUCA

Not a clue. Why?

ALEX

Why do you think?

LUCA

Fair point. Have you checked
the manual? Googled?
Or even tried Reddit?

ALEX

Yes. Yes. Yes. All three have
been equally unhelpful.

LUCA

Got nothing for you then, man.
Sorry.

I roll my eyes and move to stuff my phone back into my
pocket, but then it buzzes again with another message
from Luca.

LUCA

You good, though?
Storm's hitting pretty hard.
Glad we all got out after the
dinner when we did.

ALEX

Not everyone.

LUCA

Huh?
Don't tell me ... you've been
snowed-in with Wilbur?

Wilbur actually might be an improvement right now. I can't stand the man, but at least I wouldn't be in danger of cuddling him. Besides, I'd happily let Wilbur freeze to death in my guest room.

LUCA

No. Can't be Wilbur.
One of you would be dead
by now.
It's not Noelle, is it?

I don't respond. It's best not to engage Luca sometimes.
Though, that hasn't stopped him yet.

LUCA

It is!! She's the only person
from that night – excluding
yours truly – you wouldn't have
thrown out into the blizzard
by now.

ALEX

I would most certainly leave
you out to freeze.

LUCA

Thank you for confirming it is Noelle.

Damn it.

LUCA

Poor girl.
Hope this storm breaks so she can have a real Christmas.

ALEX

A real Christmas?
December 25th doesn't cease to exist because of the weather you know?
The day will still happen no matter where she is.

LUCA

As I said: Poor girl.

A few more messages come through from Luca, but I stuff my phone back into my pocket with a scowl and steadfastly refuse to open any of them. Everything just keeps on coming back to Christmas, and the infuriating obsession people have with it.

I'm tired of it.

My mood is, admittedly, dour as I return to my room where Noelle is still cocooned in the warmth of the bed. The temptation to dive back under the sheets with her hits me like a brick as soon as I step into the room. But, as I approach, she glances up and her features twist into a frown.

'No luck?'

Should I be impressed at how easily she can read me?

I shake my head and drop down onto the edge of the bed. 'No idea what's wrong with it. It's definitely *on*, but it's not sending any heat our way.'

I brace myself for a joke or some light taunting, but it doesn't come. Instead, Noelle bites her lip and I can almost see the cogs turning behind her eyes as she tries to come up with a solution.

'I could check the loft,' I say with a half-hearted shrug. 'I may have a portable heater or two up there.'

'What's the likelihood of that?' she asks.

'Not high,' I admit. It's not like I've ever had an issue with the central heating before. 'But if I do have one, that's where it'll be.'

Noelle slumps against the headboard. 'It'll also be *really* cold up there. And if you open it up and that gets into the rest of the house . . .' She trails off and I nod. She's right. The loft will be an icebox right now, and we can't risk letting out the little warmth we do currently have by rummaging around up there.

Damn it.

'What about leaving?' I suggest.

Noelle laughs. 'That's what I've been *trying* to do, in case you hadn't noticed.'

I shake my head. 'Your car might be a piece of junk—'

'Hey!' Noelle squawks and tosses a pillow in my direction. 'She is *not* a piece of junk!'

I nod towards the window where the storm continues to rage on. 'Right now, she might as well be. But presumably my car is fine. We could try our luck at a hotel? I know there's one about a twenty-minute drive from here.'

Noelle bites her bottom lip, clearly considering the offer. After a beat or two, she shakes her head. 'What if they're closed or full? It is Christmas, after all.'

'It's December 23rd,' I mutter.

Noelle stubbornly ignores me. 'It's too dangerous out there to risk it only to get turned back. Eve will never forgive me if I freeze to death on the side of the road.' She fumbles around for her phone, taps something onto it, and then turns the screen so I can see it. 'See? We're still in a Red Alert and they're recommending we stay put.'

I exhale a deep breath. 'Back to the drawing board it is.'

I don't like this. I don't like not feeling in control of something that should be easily controllable.

'Oh!' Noelle suddenly sits upright and claps her hands together. 'We should be in the kitchen!'

'The kitchen?'

She nods enthusiastically, eyes brightening with each passing second. 'Your oven . . . You've got an Aga which is always on. We can hang out in the kitchen during the day to keep warm, and at night . . .' She trails off and suddenly looks bashful.

'We can *cuddle*?' It's a genuine question but I think she misinterprets the tone of voice for something else entirely because she visibly bristles.

'I get that it's not *ideal*,' she says stiffly. 'But it's better than freezing in our rooms.'

I quickly hold up my hands in surrender, not wanting to give her the wrong impression. The idea of spending another night with her in my arms is anything *but* something I'm not looking forward to. 'No, no, it's a great idea. It's not like I've got anything better. The Aga it is.'

Relief washes over her features, and she offers me a small smile that, thankfully, reaches her eyes. 'Great.'

We both get up from the bed, the chill in the room palpable as our feet touch the floor again. I notice she's wearing a pair of my socks now, and I can't quite account for the warmth in my chest. Noelle wraps the duvet tighter around herself, and I grab an extra blanket from the wardrobe before we make our way to the kitchen.

The moment we step into the kitchen, I can see Noelle visibly relax. This is her domain, after all. She lets out a contented sigh as she goes over to inspect the Aga. I watch as she expertly adjusts the dials and knobs – ones I haven't so much as glanced at since the day I hired her – getting the temperature just right. It's fascinating to see her in her element, taking charge with such ease.

I could watch her all day.

As the kitchen fills with warmth, I can't help but admire how Noelle's face softens in the cool light. Her eyes are sparkling with a mixture of determination and relief, and there's a fire in her that I haven't seen in a while.

She turns to me with a grin. 'There we go. That'll heat up nicely as long as we keep the door closed.'

I return the smile, feeling a warmth that has nothing to do with the Aga blooming in my chest.

★ ★ ★

I'm not a religious man, but I say a silent prayer of thanks to the owners of this home who installed, and left, the Aga before I moved in. I'd been half-heartedly considering replacing it with something more my style when I bought the property, but Roland had been aghast at the suggestion and ultimately convinced me to keep it.

The warmth of the Aga has become a silent companion in the kitchen, its steady hum a backdrop to the clattering of keys on my laptop. I've commandeered one end of the table, my laptop open in front of me with a seemingly endless stream of spreadsheets up on the screen. I'd rather be in my office, with both of my large screens, but this will have to do.

After showering and getting dressed in another pair of my sweats and a hoodie, Noelle comes back downstairs into the kitchen and spends most of the day peering through my cupboards and taking notes on her phone.

'Might as well get started on restock,' she said with a shrug when I asked her what she was doing. 'Nothing else to do.'

And that's how we spend our day. Noelle methodically going through my groceries, taking notes on her phone, and writing down recipe ideas as they come to mind. And me, hunched over my laptop, trying to make sense of the numbers swirling on my screen. It's strange how fast the time passes and how normal it feels to have Noelle in such close proximity while I work.

'You look like you're about to put a fist through your screen.'

Her voice cuts through the click-clack of my dismal dance with numbers. I look up, finding her leaning against the counter, wooden spoon in hand, her expressive eyes fixed on me with what I think is genuine curiosity.

They're the first few words we've shared in at least an hour.

'I just might.'

She gives me a small smile and tilts her head. 'Trouble in tech paradise?'

I lean back in my chair, feeling the weight of my Board's expectations pressing down on me. This isn't something I'd normally talk about with anyone aside from Luca, but I don't feel any of the apprehension and irritation I usually do when it comes to Noelle. 'The Board wants me to trim the fat. Cut corners.' My hand instinctively clenches into a fist beneath the table, my fingers desperate to wrap around the stress ball I keep at my HoxTech offices. 'But I built this company based on the idea of *quality*. Not quantity. And definitely not profit.'

That's how it started anyway. I was tired of buying products that fell apart or ultimately became obsolete after a few years. I didn't want my products to be added to the piles of mass-produced, useless garbage floating somewhere in the Pacific Ocean years down the line. So, I put my computer science degree to use, and set out to make the HT Nexa, a sleek, lightweight yet high-performance and long-lasting laptop for professionals. The kind of product that wouldn't need replacing every three to five years. The kind of product my customers could *rely* on.

Luca helped immensely with the initial networking

to ensure we got the early investors needed to make the company a runaway success, and here we are, fifteen years later. We've since branched out to other technological appliances – TVs, fridges, coffeemakers, vacuums and, most recently, phones – and I've tried to keep that same ethos running through the company.

Quality over quantity.

Quality over profit.

Unfortunately, the bigger you get, the more people you have to please, and each day it's proving harder and harder to stick to the original plan.

'But you *do* make a profit,' Noelle says, her smile dipping and replaced with a frown. 'Right?'

'We do.'

'So, what's the problem?' She comes over to my side of the table and leans against it, propping her elbows up so she can rest her chin in the palms of her hands. 'As far as I can tell, you're doing pretty well.'

I laugh quietly. 'Pretty well is an understatement.'

'So, *again*, what's the problem? Why's your Board on your back all the time?'

I blink at her and she gives me a sheepish grin.

'The energy was pretty easy to read at the dinner,' she says. 'They don't like you?'

'*That* is an understatement, and an entirely separate issue.'

Noelle waits patiently for me to continue.

'They want *more*,' I say. 'But we're already pushing our team to the limit. It's a balancing act.' I pause, not entirely sure this is interesting to her, but Noelle is looking at me with wide open eyes, like she's genuinely interested in hearing what I have to say. 'If someone's doing good work, the key to making sure that continues is to give them the space to keep doing it. Not pile more on top of them. That's when the quality drops. When corners get cut because they're more focused on meeting deadlines than delivering good work.'

'But I don't get it,' Noelle says, brows furrowing. 'If you suddenly start releasing products that drop in quality, wouldn't that mean losing all your customers?'

'You'd think so.' We've both shifted in our seats, turning so we're directly facing each other and our knees are brushing against one another. 'But we're so ahead of the market, we've probably amassed enough goodwill from our target audience that people would still continue to buy our products for a good while even if that quality slips.'

Noelle's eyes widen in understanding and she leans forward slightly, mulling over my words as she comes further into my personal space. 'It's all about brand loyalty, right? People already trust you to deliver quality, so they overlook the little hiccups? But there's a limit to how far you can push them.'

I nod, impressed by how quickly she grasps the concept. 'Exactly.'

She lets out a soft chuckle, her hand absentmindedly playing with the end of one of her long braids. 'It's the same for me. Imagine I started cutting corners and using subpar ingredients just to save some money – you'd notice right away, wouldn't you?'

'I think you'd be able to make a Michelin-star-level meal out of anything,' I say, blurting the words out before I can even think about my answer.

Noelle's mouth falls open slightly and she blinks at me. 'I—'

'But I get what you mean,' I say quickly. 'People trust the quality you deliver, and once you compromise that, it's hard to win back their trust.'

She nods slowly. Her cheeks look warm, her expression thoughtful. 'Cooking is my passion. It's not just about making food. I don't just do it for a cheque. It's about creating an experience, about sharing joy through something as simple as a meal. Cutting corners would compromise that. Would compromise *me*.'

I don't think I've ever thought about it like that. Thought about it beyond eating as necessary for survival. But when she puts it like that? My thoughts drift to the bottom drawer of the desk in my home office, filled with the little Post-it notes she leaves me with every meal.

It's about creating an experience, about sharing joy through something as simple as a meal.

'Have you ever thought about taking this—' I gesture awkwardly at her. 'And scaling up?'

She frowns. 'Ha, you mean like when you met me? I've already worked in a restaurant.'

'No, I mean starting your own.'

She dips her head slightly. 'It's definitely crossed my mind. But no, I couldn't. There are too many—'

'There's always a reason to say no to something. There were a million and one different things in my way when I was starting up HoxTech, but here we are now.'

Noelle snorts. 'Not all of us were born with a golden spoon in our mouths, you know.'

It's my turn to snort. 'I certainly wasn't.'

'What? You're not from like, some eternally rich family and you're just the latest nepo baby to get lucky?'

'No. God, no. Have you never read my bio?'

Noelle rolls her eyes, but her lips are twitching slightly. 'Someone's full of himself.'

'It's a perfectly reasonable question.' And assumption. Almost every single person I've met has read up on me, and it never occurred to me that Noelle has never deigned to do the same.

'No, your highness. I have not bothered to read your bio. Should I?' She gives me a look that's downright devilish. 'What am I going to learn? Is there a whole section about bath bombs in there?'

185

'Bath bombs . . . ?' Realisation dawns on me and Noelle holds her hands up in defence. Though she's still grinning.

'I did a *tiny* bit of snooping. Not intentional by the way – I was trying to find your room.'

'And the bathroom was the first place you looked?' I raise an unimpressed brow.

'No. Your unused gym was. The bathroom was a close second.' She wiggles her brows and nudges me with her elbow. 'What's the deal with that, by the way? Brand new gym, beautiful bathroom, all those hundreds of bath bombs?'

'There aren't *hundreds*,' I grumble, feeling my cheeks warm. 'And what do you mean, "what's the deal"?'

She shrugs lightly. 'I just mean, you've got all these things in your home and it seems like you put them there for a reason, but you don't use them.'

I try to think back to the last time I used the home gym I'd been adamant about setting up. Maybe three, four months ago? Five wouldn't even be a stretch at this point. Work has been a never-ending series of fires that I'm apparently the only person who can put out for as long as I can remember, and my daily workouts were one of the first things to go. It's part of the reason I hired Noelle in the first place. When you're looking for ways to make those twenty-four hours stretch a little longer, getting rid of time-consuming things like working out and spending hours in the kitchen every day felt like a no-brainer.

And the bathroom along with the most definitely *not* hundreds of bath bombs? It's probably been over a year since I last stepped in there. The thought is enough to bring a frown to my face.

'The gym I can get,' Noelle says, continuing on, completely oblivious to my train of thought. 'But the bathroom? It's gorgeous and, well, not trying to be rude, but not very *you*.'

Despite everything, I can't help but smirk at that. 'Not very me?'

Noelle squirms slightly in her seat. 'I just can't imagine you filling up the tub and soaking in a bath filled with soap and bombs. It's very . . . *domestic*.'

'I can't be domestic?'

She stares pointedly at my laptop and the plethora of spreadsheets currently taking up the screen. 'I don't know. Can you?'

'*Yes*,' I say stiffly, even though it's been at least a year since I last, as Noelle put it, filled up the tub and soaked in it. The en-suite attached to my bedroom has a shower and that's been more than enough for me recently. 'I just don't have the time.'

'But if you did have the time . . .' Noelle says, like she's goading me on.

'If I did,' I concede slowly, 'then yes, I'd use my gym and make full use of that bathtub upstairs.'

'And the bath bombs . . . ?'

My cheeks suddenly feel warm. 'I like them.'

She laughs, leaning in a little closer, her voice teasing. 'Oh, so you *do* have a soft side. Who would've thought? Alexander Hoxton, tech mogul, drowning in bath bombs and pretending to have no time for luxury.'

I roll my eyes, trying to suppress my own smile creeping up on me. 'I'm not pretending. I don't know. I like having those things available when I *can* take the time. It's just—' I pause, the words suddenly feeling heavier in my mouth than I'd intended. 'I don't get to take the time.'

Noelle tilts her head and her smile softens into something more understanding.

I think she's about to say something, but then she shakes her head suddenly and pushes herself up from the table. I watch as she marches towards the cutlery drawer and pulls out a large wooden spoon. Then she turns on me and says, 'You need a break.'

CHAPTER ELEVEN

Alex

Now it's my turn to stare, dumbfounded, at her.

She wags the wooden spoon in my direction, and there's a look of what I've come to recognise as faux sternness on her face. 'Come on. You've been staring at that screen all day and you're frowning so hard, I'm worried your face will get stuck that way.'

I give her a wry grin. 'My mother used to say that when I was younger.'

'Glad to hear that you've always been consistently grumpy and it's not just a *me* thing.'

I frown. 'A *you* thing?'

She shrugs and gives me a low, self-deprecating kind of laugh. 'It's not important.'

I open my mouth to argue – this is absolutely

important – but she stops me in my tracks as she strides towards the other end of the kitchen and begins throwing cupboards open and pulling out bowls.

'What's *important* is that you have some fun. Relax a little.' She glances over her shoulder and wiggles her brows. 'Get into the Christmas spirit.'

'It's December 23rd,' I parrot for the second time today.

She laughs, and it's her proper laugh this time. The sound is light and clear, like bells over the howl of the wind outside.

'Haven't we already established that, for me, Christmas and all its nonsense encompasses the entirety of December?' I ask.

Noelle ignores me. Instead, she dips into another cupboard and pulls out the monstrosity of an apron she wore the other night. 'Here. Put this on.'

I don't make a move and her smile hardens into something lethal.

'Hoxton.'

'Ms Jones.'

She arches a brow and then marches across the room to press the apron into my chest. 'We're back to *Ms Jones* now, are we?'

'Do you prefer it?'

'No,' she says without a trace of hesitation. 'I definitely prefer Noelle.'

Her voice has dropped to something that's not quite a

whisper, and her fingertips brush against me as she holds the apron against my chest.

I do too, I can't help but think.

'But, for the next . . .' She trails off and glances up at the clock on the wall. 'Hour and a half, it's not Ms Jones *or* Noelle. It's *Chef.*'

I raise an eyebrow, a smirk playing on my lips. 'Chef?'

She matches my smirk and gives the apron another sharp push into my chest. 'Exactly. Now, put this on and come and help me.'

Should I be worried about the fact that Noelle ordering me around sends a heady rush of blood straight to my dick? Potentially. I'm not used to being ordered around, but apparently I like it.

I clear my throat, shaking my head slightly to rid my mind of the flurry of increasingly inappropriate thoughts currently flooding it. 'And what exactly are we doing?'

She raises a brow expectantly.

'Chef?' I add.

Noelle beams at me and I swear the sight of her smiling widely is almost blinding. 'I already told you. You need to have some fun and relax. So, we're going to bake something.'

'Because making a tart will solve all my problems?' I ask, scepticism lacing my words.

'Maybe not,' she concedes, 'but it'll taste a lot better than eating spreadsheets for hours on end.'

I shake my head and watch as she flits towards the cup-boards, her braids swishing behind her as she pulls out all the equipment and ingredients we need. She's a force of nature, more powerful than the storm raging beyond the walls of my home, and I like it.

I like it a lot.

I stand up, drawn into her orbit as she rummages through my kitchen, and reluctantly pull the apron over my head.

'I don't have a word strong enough to describe how much I hate this,' I grumble as I take in the dancing Santa and the grinning reindeer plastered across my front. This is, quite literally, my own personal hell.

Why am I going along with this?

Noelle glances back at me, her lips stretched into that megawatt grin again.

Ah, yes. That's why.

'Yeah,' she shrugs. 'It's pretty ugly.'

'So why wear it?' Why even *own* it?'

Another shrug. 'It's Christmas.'

'That's not an answer.' And it's not Christmas, but I sense that rebuttal won't go down well a third time.

Noelle gives me a questioning look. 'Isn't it?'

'No.'

That's another thing I hate about this time of the year. People do the most outlandish, ridiculous things that go against every normal tenet of societal expectations and when you question them, they always have the same answer.

It's Christmas.

What the hell does that even mean?

December arrives and people start acting like complete and utter nutjobs, spending money they don't have and forcing themselves to spend time with friends and family they'd usually avoid at any other time in the year because, what the hell, it's *Christmas.*

Am I the only person on this planet who thinks that sounds insane?

'Well,' Noelle says, with all the air of someone who clearly doesn't care to argue. 'That's my answer. And we've still got a tart to make.'

Noelle moves around my kitchen with effortless grace, her movements precise and confident. I can't help but observe how she rummages through each cupboard and drawer with familiarity, her hands almost dancing as she works.

It's weird feeling out of place in my own kitchen, especially in this ridiculous apron, but there's something strangely comforting about being here with her.

'Have you ever baked anything before?' Noelle asks, swivelling round to face me once she's finished lining up all our ingredients on the counter. 'Like, anything ever?'

I raise an eyebrow, trying to maintain my façade of

nonchalance. 'I may have attempted a boxed cake mix once or twice.'

About twenty-five years ago and under the guidance of an aunt or older cousin. But still.

She pulls a face. 'That's *something*, I suppose.'

'And what are we making today?'

She doesn't answer right away, just waits patiently for me to add, 'Chef.'

My dick twitches again. Definitely something to look into.

'A strawberry tart,' Noelle says, once she's satisfied. She gestures towards the ingredients on the counter. 'We've got everything we need, luckily. And it's simple *and* delicious. The perfect combination. Sound good?'

'Do I have any real say in the matter?'

'Nope!' She laughs and claps her hands together, her eyes sparkling with mischief. 'Let's get started. I need you to wash these strawberries.'

'Yes, Chef,' I say dryly, grabbing the bowl she's already put out and making my way to the sink. As I rinse the strawberries under the running water, I can't help but steal glances at Noelle. She's humming a soft tune – a Christmas song, I think, her fingers expertly working the butter into the flour with all the precision of a surgeon. The warmth from the oven envelops us, and for a moment, it feels like we're in our own little world, just the two of us, shielded from the chaos outside.

When I bring the strawberries back to the counter, Noelle shows me how to slice them perfectly into two identical halves. Her brow is furrowed in concentration, and her tongue darts out to wet her lips as she brings the knife down. It's a perfectly ordinary gesture, one I'm sure I've mimicked before when I'm deep in concentration, but for some reason, it sends another heady jolt of awareness through me.

'Something wrong?' Noelle's voice startles me out of my reverie.

I clear my throat. 'No, just admiring your handiwork.'

Noelle exhales deeply and puts the knife down. 'Every time you do that, I'm not sure how to react.'

'Every time I do what?'

She hesitates, and then, 'Compliment me.'

'You're not good at taking compliments?' That's surprising. I would've thought she'd be more than used to them by now, given her line of work and how much she excels in it.

'I'm *great* at taking compliments,' she laughs. 'It the compliments from *you* that throw me a little.'

Ah.

An emotion I'm rapidly coming to recognise as shame washes through me.

'Well, get used to it. I'm changing my ways, Chef,' I reply, feeling the corners of my lips tug into a small smile, despite myself. Noelle's laughter is infectious, filling the kitchen with a warmth that goes beyond the heat from the oven.

* * *

Thirty minutes later, and I'm no longer smiling.

I'm attempting to fold the pastry, but it's not cooperating. The dough is either too stubborn or I am. At this point, I don't care to figure out which one of us is the problem, I just want this to be done.

Noelle stands across from me, her sleeves rolled up and a dusting of flour on her cheek that she's blissfully unaware of. She's trying to conceal a smile as she watches my pathetic efforts.

'You're doing great,' Noelle says. It's a blatant lie, but she says it with an encouraging grin. 'Don't let the dough get the better of you. Just imagine you're negotiating a tough deal or something like that. That dough has nothing on you.'

'Negotiations I can handle,' I mutter, giving the pastry another go. 'This, on the other hand, is pure anarchy.'

I glance over at the example she showed me earlier. It's neat and tidy, the very definition of culinary perfection. Mine, on the other hand, is a misshapen blob. And that's being generous. White pockets of flour stick to the dough where it should be a smooth, yellowy colour like hers. I'm not sure where I went wrong because I'm sure I followed her example perfectly, and she made it look so easy.

'Maybe if you didn't scowl at it so much, it would be more pliable,' Noelle says, her braids swishing as she leans in to inspect my handiwork. 'Didn't you know that food absorbs the energy of the person making it?'

'Ha, ha,' I deadpan. 'Then this tart is doomed to be as bitter as I am.' After a few more pathetic attempts, I finally getting the fold somewhat right, though it's nowhere near as neat as Noelle's.

Noelle's smile dips slightly. 'Bitter isn't always bad. There's just a time and a place for it.'

'Is this where you tell me that a bitter strawberry tart is the height of culinary perfection?'

She gives me a weak smile. 'Time and a place, remember?'

'Such as . . .'

Noelle surveys me for a few long seconds. 'It's all about balance. Bitterness in particular, I mean.' She leans in a little closer, hesitates for a moment, and then places her hand above mine. Warmth floods every single one of my senses as she threads her fingers through mine and then pushes downwards, forcing my hand to mimic the movement.

'People don't tend to like bitter foods,' she says, guiding my hands through the motion of folding out the dough. 'Kale, Brussels sprouts, any dark leafy green really. By themselves, they're usually too bitter for most people to enjoy. Combine it with something *sweet*—' She pauses for a moment, fingertips ghosting along my hands as she pulls away and gives me an encouraging nod to continue with the dough. 'And it balances out the taste.'

'That just proves my point,' I continue, already missing the feel of her hand on mine. 'Nobody wants something bitter. Not by itself anyway.'

Noelle shrugs, the corner of her mouth lifting into a small smirk. 'What about dark chocolate?'

I scowl at her. 'That's one thing.'

'Pretty much every citrus fruit out there is technically bitter. Peppermint, too. And people love that.' Something lights up behind her eyes, and her smirk widens. 'And I, for what it's worth, love my coffee *bitter*.' Her words are innocent enough, but there's something in the way she says it – *I love my coffee* bitter – that sends a wave of unmistakable, unbridled arousal shooting through me. If this were anyone else – if we were *anywhere* else – I'd take that as an invitation to cross the space between us and press my lips against hers.

But this is Noelle. My personal chef.

And we're in my home.

Trapped in my home, if we're being technical about it.

Whatever I think I'm reading from her right now, I know that I'm wrong.

Noelle laughs suddenly, the sound filling the kitchen and a cavern in my chest I hadn't realised was even there. 'And seriously, you should try smiling more often.' She looks up at me, her gaze softening slightly. 'You've got a nice one, might as well show it off.'

My heart thuds an irregular pitter patter and I try to

deflect with some humour. 'Is this a standard part of your personal chef services? Life coaching?'

'Consider it a bonus feature,' she replies, winking at me before turning back to her own perfect pastry creation.

The evening wanes, and the sickly-sweet smell of baking strawberries begins to permeate the air. Noelle's effortless skill with the rolling pin makes me painfully aware of my own clumsiness. I watch, slightly envious but mostly in awe as she lifts the pastry with such grace, it's practically pirouetting into the tart tin.

'Let me help you with that,' she offers, catching sight of my third attempt at lining my tin, which looks more like a pastry massacre than anything else at this point.

I step aside and watch as she works the dough with well-practised ease, her skilled hands moving with the kind of confidence that comes from years of dedication.

'See?' she says, finishing up with a flourish. 'You were pushing the dough too hard, and it's not about force; it's about finesse.'

'Finesse,' I echo, trying to etch the concept into my brain for next time.

'Don't worry, I wasn't expecting you to get it on your first time. I just wanted you to try. Baking is hard, and you're definitely not alone.'

'Is that supposed to make me feel better?' I quip, but even I can't deny there's something endearing about the situation. Her joy is infectious, and despite the irritation of being bested by some bloody *dough* of all things, I find myself chuckling along with her.

'Absolutely,' she beams up at me. 'It means you're human. And humans are allowed to mess up in the kitchen. It's half the fun.'

Fun isn't a word I'd normally associate with failure, but watching Noelle's brown eyes light up, I reconsider its application. There's a playful challenge in her gaze, like she's daring me to let go and just enjoy the process, no matter the outcome.

'And it *does* look good,' she says, pointing at my dough which, objectively, looks awful. 'I think I'll promote you to apprentice baker. Congrats.'

'What was I before?'

'An unpaid intern.'

I let out a squawk of indignation, but Noelle ignores it in favour of moving on to the filling. She slides both our tart shells into the oven and then gives me free rein over the blender, instructing me to blend strawberries and water until they turn into a smooth purée.

It hits me as we work, each doing our separate tasks, that we've slid into something that feels comfortable.

Natural. Like having Noelle by my side in the kitchen, just the two of us working together to make a meal, is normal. *Ordinary.*

'How's it going?' Noelle asks, peering over my shoulder. I've finished with the purée and I've moved on to steadily adding cream cheese to the mixture. She told me to keep going until *stiff peaks begin to form* and I was too stubborn to ask what the hell that even meant, so I'm stuck sneaking glances at her, hoping she'll stop me when I get it right.

'Fine?' I say eventually, once it's clear that she's not about to jump in. The word comes out sounding more like a question than any kind of assurance. The mixture looks lumpy, and I can still see noticeable strawberry chunks dotted throughout. 'Not entirely sure how I've managed to mess this up.'

Noelle rolls her eyes and detaches the stand from the mixer. 'You haven't messed anything up. It looks fine. Great, even.'

Another blatant lie. But, as if to prove her point, she starts pouring the lumpy mixture into a piping bag and then begins squeezing it out onto the tart. The strawberry cream splutters out in elegant swirls and Noelle gives me a satisfied nod before passing the bag over to me.

She made it look easy, but I quickly learn there's an art to even something as simple as squeezing out icing. 'Is it supposed to look like this?' I say, eyeing the dollops I've added to the tart uncertainly.

Noelle sucks her lips in, obviously trying to hold back peals of laughter. 'Absolutely,' she says, once she's calmed herself down, eyes still shining. 'Think of it as . . . avant-garde.'

'Avant-garde,' I repeat, feigning contemplation. 'Right. Because when people bite into this, they won't be thinking "*delicious*", they'll be thinking "*oh, what a brave exploration of form and texture*".'

I'm being sarcastic but either my intention doesn't come across or she's ignoring it because Noelle nods earnestly at me.

'Exactly! And don't compare yourself to me. Desserts are like snowflakes – no two are exactly alike, and they're all beautiful in their own way.'

'That sounds suspiciously like something you tell a child who's just failed terribly at a task and they're on the verge of tears.'

Noelle gives me a sheepish grin that tells me I'm right on the money. 'Maybe,' she admits with a shrug, her smile unwavering. 'But it's still true. Besides, taste trumps appearance. *Always.*'

My disbelief must be scattered across my face, because Noelle rolls her eyes and then dips a finger into the remnants of mixture still lining the bowl.

She coats her finger in the pink paste and then lifts it to her lips, closing her eyes as she savours the taste. There's something undeniably intimate in the act, and I shift slightly, feeling all the blood in my body head south.

She lets out a sigh of contentment and then, without hesitation, extends her finger towards me, a dollop of cream still poised on the tip.

'Try it,' she says, voice low and soft. 'Just a taste.'

I hesitate, the same hesitation that always clings to me in moments requiring unguarded spontaneity. But seeing her there, with flour on her cheek and warmth in her gaze, something shifts inside me. I don't think, I just move.

I lean in until her finger is resting lightly between my lips, and a sudden truth hits me like a bolt of lightning.

I want more than just a taste.

The realisation rolls through me, heavy and undeniable. My heart picks up its pace, thudding against my chest like it wants to break free.

I look at her finger, then into her eyes, and something between us shifts imperceptibly. Before I can stop myself, I wrap my lips around her fingertip, tasting the creamy sweetness, rich and velvety against my tongue.

We both freeze. The air between us is suddenly charged with an energy I can't describe but recognise all too well. It's the sudden silence that's loud, the way time seems to slow down, and how every moment we've shared in this kitchen tonight feels like it was leading up to this one.

Noelle's eyes widen and she snatches her finger back suddenly. I realise, at this point, that we're at a crossroads. I could pull back and pretend like this never happened, like it was a simple taste test of the strawberry cream. Like the feel of her skin on my tongue hasn't set every single one of my nerve endings on fire.

But the truth is, I don't want to pretend.

Not anymore.

I hold her gaze, searching for any sign of hesitation or uncertainty, but all I see is a flicker of something similar to longing in her eyes.

Without breaking eye contact, I reach out to cup her cheek, my thumb brushing lightly against her soft skin. Noelle leans into my touch, her eyes fluttering closed for a moment before opening again, dark and intense.

It's like the world around us fades into the background, until there's only the sound of our ragged breathing filling the space between us. And then, as if moving of its own accord, my hand slides to the nape of her neck, pulling her closer until our lips meet.

And I'll be damned. If I thought my nerve endings were on fire before, what I feel now is nothing short of an all-consuming inferno.

CHAPTER TWELVE

Noelle

Kissing Hoxton is like tasting forbidden fruit – sweet and intoxicating.

For a moment, nothing else exists but the sensation of his lips moving against mine, the warmth of his body pressing close to me. His lips are warm and soft, the taste of strawberry lingering on his tongue as he pushes against me.

My every thought goes cloudy as a rush of desire courses through me. Hoxton's hands find their way to the small of my back as I thread my fingers through his hair, pulling him even closer.

His touch is somehow gentle, urgent and electric at the same time, his fingers dipping under the hem of my borrowed sweater to trace aimless patterns on my skin. I feel his hands roam over my back, drawing me impossibly nearer to him. Our bodies mould together perfectly, fitting like two pieces of a puzzle that were always meant to be joined.

How did we get here? My mind replays the events of today, trying to find a logical link as to how I went from loathing my client to clinging onto him like he's my sole life source. Has this been building up since last night and our impromptu cuddling session? Is this the result of a day spent in casual companionship with each other? Is this *cabin fever*?

I don't know.

But I do know that I can feel my heart pounding in my chest, echoing the rhythm of Hoxton's breath against my skin. I try to ground myself and focus on the sensation of his hands, hot and steady against my back, but it's hard when the only thing I want to do right now is give in to the fire that's flooded my bloodstream.

I pull back slightly to catch my breath. Hoxton's eyes meet mine, dark with desire and something . . . something deeper that I can't quite place. His gaze is intense and searching, as if he's trying to unravel the very essence of me.

Without a word, he leans in again, capturing my lips with his in a fervent kiss that steals the breath from my lungs.

Has kissing ever felt this good before?

I try to remember a time my body felt this alive, but I keep coming up blank.

Never, I decide. It's never felt this good.

I let out a soft, impatient moan as Hoxton pulls away from

my lips, but he doesn't go far. He peppers hot, frantic kisses along my neck, one hand coming up to gently curl through my braids and keep them out of the way.

His lips burn a fiery path down my neck, leaving behind a trail of goosebumps and heightened sensitivity. Every touch of his tongue, every brush of his lips sends shivers down my spine, and I can't help but arch my body into his, desperate for more.

If this ever ends, it'll be too soon.

His mouth reaches the hollow of my throat, and he gently sucks, pulling at the delicate skin there. The sound that comes out of my mouth is almost feral, coming from the deepest depths of my chest.

I feel him smirk against my skin and I tug at his hair a little tighter, my actions a silent demand.

Do that again.

Hoxton, I learn very quickly, doesn't need to be told twice.

I feel the hardness of his body against mine, and it only makes me want him more. My hands trace over the fabric of his sweatshirt, feeling the sweat that's forming there as we continue to kiss. He groans softly into my neck, and his hips start to grind gently against my own.

His lips move back to mine in a frenzied kiss, as if he's trying to consume me whole.

I'd gladly let him.

I drop my hands from his hair and fist the collar of his sweatshirt, pulling him in as close as he's going to get. His hands come down to cup my ass and I don't hesitate hooking a leg over his waist and grinding into him, matching the pace he set earlier.

A groan rumbles from his throat and I feel it vibrate through him and right into me.

'*Alex.*' His name falls from my lips like a desperate hiss. 'God, *Alex*—'

Hoxton pulls away abruptly, leaving me gasping for air and panting heavily. Our eyes lock, each other's breath swirling in the hazy air between us. I'm not sure if it's shock or something else that's caused the abrupt halt, but my heart races and my mind scrambles to catch up to this new sensory onslaught.

He stares at me, eyes wide, lips swollen and red.

He shakes his head, visibly trying to gather his thoughts. 'Noelle,' he says finally, his voice a mix of urgency and vulnerability.

My heart stutters in my chest.

'We shouldn't . . . I mean, *I* shouldn't . . .'

I stand frozen, the taste of strawberry cream still lingering on my lips, which just seconds ago were happily pressed against *his* and it felt like every Christmas light in the universe had suddenly sparked to life inside me.

Hoxton takes a step back, a crease of regret – or is it panic? – etching his brow.

'I'm sorry,' he mutters, a deep flush spreading under the tanned skin of his cheeks.

'It's fine,' I manage to stutter out, my heart rate slowing down just a bit. 'You didn't . . . I mean, I wanted to, so . . .'

But he's already retreating, all wide-eyed and ready to bolt. A small part of me finds it a little endearing – the whole deer-in-headlights look he's got going on right now, but then he twists away from me and starts making frantic strides towards the door. A wave of hurt slams into me but I push through it and fix what I *hope* is a nonchalant expression onto my face.

'Hold up,' I call out, snatching a wooden spoon from the countertop with more flair than necessary. Hoxton ignores me, one hand on the door. Hurt makes way for a flash of panic and I raise my voice ever so slightly, praying that he mistakes the crack in my tone for something else entirely. 'You think you can just waltz in here, turn my kitchen upside down, kiss me senseless, and then what?' I force a dry laugh, like I'm not actively fighting the feeling of rejection that's currently seeping into my very bones right now. 'Sprint to safety and leave me to clean everything up? Not on my watch.'

He stops, hesitating in the doorway. He turns to face me, a kaleidoscope of emotions flashing over his face. 'I don't want to make—'

'Make things awkward?' I finish for him, a brow raised,

hands on my hips. The picture of indifference. 'Too late for that.'

He winces, but I ignore it and turn away so he can't see the hurt that must surely be written across my face.

'Fine,' he relents. 'But only because I'm partly responsible for . . . this.'

I'm not entirely sure if he means the flour-dusted counters, the splatters of icing here and there, or the crackling tension between us. Whatever the answer is, he's not wrong.

My heart is still racing. I can still feel the heat of Hoxton's body lingering on mine. Can still remember exactly how he tasted as his tongue slid against mine.

I take a deep breath, trying to steady my nerves and focus on the task at hand. We can't *both* have mini panic attacks now, can we? One of us has to keep their head and it seems like Hoxton's unilaterally handed that role over to me.

Rude.

His movements are deliberate, almost robotic, as he wipes down the counters and sweeps up the mess of flour that spilled everywhere. He keeps a deliberate distance between us, never getting close enough for our fingers to accidentally brush as we work. It's hard to believe that just five minutes ago we were wrapped in an embrace so tight, we could put a pretzel to shame.

As we work, I steal glances at Hoxton out of the corner

of my eye. His face is flushed, practically the same colour as the strawberries we'd been working with earlier. His eyes are downcast, focused on his task, but I can see the tension in his jaw and the way his hands grip the dishrag tightly as he methodically runs it along the counter.

I can't decide how I'm feeling right now. Relief that our brief moment of intimacy has passed.

Longing for it to return.

Frustration at the interruption.

Annoyed that Hoxton has decided to retreat into himself instead of using his words like a grown man.

And curious, so damn curious, about what might have happened if he hadn't pulled away.

★ ★ ★

Eve answers on the first ring. It's my first nugget of human contact in hours bar Hoxton and just the sight of her grinning face makes some of the tension I'm feeling evaporate.

The man in question has been dodging me since our baking session-turned-clash-of-lips earlier, and I can't pretend like it's not getting to me. It's ridiculous how one kiss – or rather, the abrupt end to one – can make this huge house feel so empty. The lack of human contact, or any noise aside from the violent *whooshing* of the wind outside, has been gnawing at me for hours. Even if Hoxton wasn't stubbornly freezing himself to death just to avoid me, I'm not sure he'd cut it in the human contact department right now anyway.

I need to talk to someone who doesn't short circuit at the first sign of anything vaguely emotional.

Luckily, I have a twin.

Eve answers the call wearing a Santa hat and I'm pretty sure that's gold tinsel wrapped around her neck in lieu of a scarf. I can hear the sound of raucous laughter in the background and Christmas tunes playing softly in a nearby room.

A pang of longing hits me. I should be there – with my sister, with my family, enjoying Christmas the only way the Joneses know how. Not cooped up in a glorified cell with only the company of a man whose two emotional extremes seem to jump from passionate kissing to passionate ignoring.

'*Noelle!*' Eve coos, and the slight slur to her voice is unmistakable. I'd bet any money that someone – probably Uncle Lloyd – has broken out the Christmas rum, and Eve has definitely had her fair share.

Urgh. I'm so jealous.

'Looks like you're having fun,' I laugh, trying and failing to keep the bitterness out of my tone, as Eve uses her free hand to take another swig from something in a mug. Definitely the Christmas rum, then.

'Ain't that the truth,' a voice says from off-screen. Eve scowls and then flips her camera over, putting me face to face with her fiancé, Nathan. He's also wearing a Santa hat and there's a tipsy glint in his eye.

'Hey, Noelle. How's it going?'

I give my future brother-in-law a wave. 'I've been better.'

He winces and I realise I'm probably not doing a great job at masking my bitterness. 'Yeah. Eve filled me in on everything. How's SC?'

'Don't you start calling him that too.'

Nathan shrugs, his lips curling at the corners. 'Eve still hasn't told me his name.'

'It's Alex,' I mutter, because having my brother-in-law refer to Hoxton as *Sexy Client* might just be what finally does me in. 'Alexander, actually. And yeah, things aren't going great.'

The camera blurs suddenly as Eve flips it back towards her without warning. When her face comes into view again, she's staring at me with a strange intensity. 'What did you just say?'

Except she's slurring a little and it sounds more like 'whayoudjussay?' It's a testament to our twin telepathy that I even understand her at all.

'Things aren't going great,' I repeat, my shoulders sagging a little. 'He's been avoiding me for—'

'Not *that*,' Eve says, rolling her eyes like I'm purposely misunderstanding her. 'Before that. You told Nathan what SC's name is.'

I frown at my sister. Maybe she's drunker than I thought. 'Yeah. Alex.'

Her eyes light up and she pulls the camera a little closer to her face. '*Alex*. Not *Hoxton*.'

My frown deepens. 'Not sure what you're getting at. That is literally his name.'

'Not once,' Eve declares, her voice rising with each syllable, 'not once over the last two years have you ever called that man Alex. It's always "Hoxton this" or "Hoxton that" or "Hoxton's a miserable prick".' She tilts the camera down a little so it's hitting her face at an awkward angle. '*Never* Alex.' She takes another swig of her drink, a wicked glint in her eye. 'But now you're dropping his name like it's all natural, like you guys are on a first-name basis or something. Like you're *friends*.' She gives me a self-satisfied smirk. 'What gives? What's changed?'

We are, I realise with a jolt, technically on a first-name basis now. Hoxton's been calling me Noelle for the last forty-eight hours and, apparently, I'm happy to call him by his first name too.

When did *that* happen?

My mind floods with the memory of Hoxton deftly squeezing my ass, my fingers fisting against the fabric of his sweatshirt. The sound of his deep groans mixing with my moans and the word 'Alex' falling from my lips just before he pulled away.

Ah. So that was it.

'You guys fucked, didn't you?' Eve says suddenly, still looking irritatingly smug. Outside of the camera frame I hear Nathan groan and chide her gently, 'Babe, the kids are still running around' and Eve shoots him an apologetic grin.

'Sorry,' she says in a dramatic stage whisper, the best her drunken self can do with dropping her voice. 'But you did.' She turns her attention back to me. 'Didn't you?'

'No!'

Eve purses her lips, clearly unconvinced.

'We didn't,' I insist, my face warming with each passing second. 'We just ... well. We did kiss. A little bit.'

A whole lot.

Eve squeals. 'I knew it! I *knew* it.'

'Technically, you didn't,' I point out at the exact same time Nathan does.

Eve scowls at the two of us in turn. 'I knew *something* happened. I could tell.'

'How?' Nathan and I ask, again at the same time.

'Twin telepathy,' Eve says sagely. 'I felt it. A disturbance in the air.' She raises a brow, clearly impressed with her own drunken explanation.

I can't help but laugh. 'That's insane. *You're* insane.'

'And drunk,' Nathan chimes in cheerfully.

'And drunk,' I agree.

Eve isn't bothered by my dismissal. 'Either way, you guys kissed and now you're calling him Alex.'

She's got a point there.

'And now you say he's avoiding you?'

My thoughts circle back to Hoxton. The memory of his lips on my mine, his hands leaving a scorching trail over every inch of skin he touched, makes my stomach twist in the most delicious kind of way.

How the hell has one kiss managed to turn my entire world upside down like this?

'Right,' I confirm for Eve before she gets irritated. 'We kissed—'

'Was it good?'

I don't want to answer – I want to keep something for myself – but I suppose the look on my face gives me away because Eve cheers loudly.

I roll my eyes and continue, explaining, as briefly as I can, the odd situation I've found myself in. Hoxton is avoiding me, and I don't know if it's because he's afraid of the repercussions that might come with us leaning into this sudden attraction we've found ourselves in, or if he's dealing with his own world of chaos that he keeps hidden from me.

Maybe it's a bit of both.

When I finish speaking, I let out a deep breath, feeling drained from spilling all the details to Eve – and Nathan,

I suppose. She tightens her lips and swallows hard before taking another big gulp from her drink.

'Okay,' she starts slowly, sieving through her thoughts to gather the right words. 'First things first, what do *you* want from this?'

I don't even have to think about my answer. 'I don't want things to be awkward between us. We're stuck together in this house for God knows how much longer, so it'd be nice if I didn't feel like I was alone.'

Eve looks disappointed. 'That's it?'

I snort and roll my eyes because I know exactly what she's getting at, but I'm under no delusion here. 'There's nothing between me and Ale— Hoxton,' I correct myself quickly. 'Nothing but a little bit of cabin fever.'

And I'll keep telling myself that. Never mind that I can still feel Hoxton's touch ghosting over me like a persistent shadow, or the fact that I've committed the taste of him to memory – one that I'll no doubt replay on lonely nights if I ever get out of here.

Cabin fever. That's all it is.

Eve purses her lips, looking like she wants to say something, but something seems to catch her eye outside of my line of vision. I watch, slightly amused, as Eve and Nathan engage in a silent conversation consisting of raised eyebrows and the puckering of lips.

'*Fine*,' Eve huffs after several seconds of wiggling her

brows at her fiancé. I have no idea what silent conclusion they've come to, but when Eve looks at me again, I'm sure I see a hint of something mischievous dancing in her eyes. 'Let's say it *is* cabin fever.'

'Which it is.'

'You're right. You two shouldn't be avoiding each other. The longer this storm goes on, the less likely it is you'll make it here for Christmas and I will *not* have my sister spending Christmas alone.'

That pang of longing from earlier hits me again, as Eve reminds me of everything I'm about to miss this year.

'So you guys need to get it together,' Eve continues. 'I'm going back to my first suggestion.'

I frown, trying to wrack my brain and remember what Eve's first suggestion even was.

'Like I said yesterday, maybe you're here so you can let some of your Christmas spirit rub off on him.'

That is definitely *not* the answer I was expecting, and I can't help but scoff. 'Haven't we been through this? Ale— Hoxton is a Grinch through and through. There's a better chance of this storm breaking in the next ten seconds, than Alexander Hoxton getting in the Christmas spirit.'

CHAPTER THIRTEEN

Alex

I'm pretty sure I lost all feeling in my toes about two hours ago.

I've pulled on another sweatshirt and I've tripled up on socks, but the chill in my office is biting, seeping into my very bones with each passing second. I rub my hands together for warmth, trying to stave off the numbness that threatens to take hold.

My mind keeps wandering back to that kiss, that stolen moment of heat and passion that seemed to ignite a fire inside me. Noelle's lips on mine, her touch so tantalisingly soft yet electrifying at the same time. I can still feel the ghost of her fingers tracing along my jawline, sending shivers down my spine. Every time I close my eyes, the memory dances behind my eyelids, her scent – warm and cosy – lingering in the air around me.

But now, as I sit here in this freezing office, the memory of our kiss only serves to frustrate me further. I can't focus on anything else, can't shake the longing that has settled deep inside me, working its way into the deepest caverns of my chest. The cold only seems to heighten my awareness of every sensation, every desire towards Noelle that burns inside me.

I try to distract myself by focusing on my budget spreadsheets but it's useless. My thoughts keep wandering back to Noelle. To the way her body fit against mine so perfectly. To the sound of her quiet moans. The way her skin felt like fire beneath my lips. The way my name – *Alex* – spilled from her kiss-bruised lips and sounded like warm honey as it reached my ears.

How did she manage to invade every fibre of my being with just one kiss?

How can I get her to do it again?

Would she even want to?

Do *I* even want to?

I shake my head and return to my spreadsheet, desperate to push her out of my mind. At least, I try to. But the numbers and equations in front of me all morph into an unreadable blur and it's clear that I'm not getting anywhere with this anytime soon.

Another distraction then.

I pull up my internet browser, intent on flicking through

today's headlines but my fingers move of their own accord and, before I know it, I'm typing '**homemade Christmas decorations**' into the search bar.

Dear God, what have I become?

Images of intricate paper snowflakes, foil Christmas tree toppers, and handmade wreaths flood my screen, and each one leaves me feeling completely uninspired and more than a little bit irritated.

I scoff at a photo of a meticulously hand-painted ornament, its colours vibrant and flawless. It's too much. Too pristine. Too cookie-cutter perfect. The delicate snowflakes look like a hassle to create, the tree toppers too gaudy for my taste, and the wreaths seem like a pointless endeavour. Too much work for twenty-four hours sitting centre stage – and that's even if anyone notices it amongst the deluge of all the other Christmas crap that'll undoubtedly surround it.

With each click of the mouse, I delve deeper into the world of DIY Christmas decorations. Glitter-covered baubles, intricate garlands made of dried oranges and cinnamon sticks, and even a tutorial on how to create your own doll-sized gingerbread house. I can't help but roll my eyes at the absurdity of it all.

Who has time for this?

Who needs their home transformed into a winter wonderland just to celebrate a single day?

Why am I *still* scrolling through them all?

But then it dawns on me, as I scroll through countless DIY Christmas decoration ideas, I'm only doing this because I know it'll make Noelle smile.

As the realisation hits me, a wave of frustration washes over me. Why am I bending over backwards, searching for things that don't even interest me, just to please her? Why should I have to change who I am just because, like everyone else in the world, she has an insane need to celebrate Christmas?

I know the answer, even as I voice the question to myself.

The truth is, I think I would do pretty much anything to see that smile light up Noelle's face. The thought of her turning that smile on me fills me with an inexplicable warmth, the kind that spreads from my chest to the tips of my fingers. It's a feeling I can't quite comprehend, one I don't think I've ever felt before, but I know that I crave it more than anything else right now.

I shake my head and close out the five – *five* – tabs I currently have open dedicated to DIY Christmas decorations.

This is just because the kiss is still fresh in my mind. Nothing more. Nothing less.

★ ★ ★

Noelle doesn't knock on my office door as the evening creeps up on me, but the mouth-watering scent of something simmering in the kitchen wafts up towards me.

Curiosity – and the fact that I'm certain my toes are seconds away from falling off – gets the better of me, and before I can second-guess myself, I find my feet carrying me downstairs.

As soon as I step into the warm glow of the kitchen, I'm met with a familiar sight. Noelle is sat at my kitchen table, tension carving deep lines on her forehead as she stabs a bowl of what looks like spaghetti. She looks up as I enter, her eyes immediately going wide.

I give her a small smile in response to her surprised expression and she clears her throat, fidgeting with the fork in her hand.

'I wasn't sure if you wanted to come down and eat, so . . .' She trails off and shoots me an apologetic wince. 'But there's plenty in the pot. I'm nearly done, so I can get out of your way if you give me a couple of minutes.'

Guilt shoots through me like an electrical current at her obvious uncertainty.

'You don't need to rush,' I say as I make my way to the stove and help myself to a generous portion of spaghetti. She looks unconvinced, so I take a seat next to her at the table, much to her obvious surprise. The silence between us is palpable as I start eating and the clinking of cutlery against our plates is the only sound in the room.

I steal glances at Noelle as we eat. Her eyes are downcast, focused on her food, and there's a tension in her posture that definitely wasn't there before.

My fault, I think with a pang of a regret. *This is my fault.*

After a few moments of uneasy silence, I clear my throat to speak up, but she gets there before me.

She puts her fork down with a heavy *clang*, tilts her head, and looks at me, her gaze piercing. 'What is your *deal*?'

Of all the things I was expecting her to come out with, '*What is your deal?*' definitely wasn't at the top of my list.

'My deal?'

She nods, a frown twisting her lips. 'I don't get you.'

'Believe it or not,' I say, trying to inject a bit of lightness into the strange turn this conversation has taken. 'That's not the first time I've heard that.'

Noelle's expression doesn't shift. 'It's like, one minute you can't stand me—'

'One minute I can't *what*?'

'And the next, you're all over me,' she continues, like there's been no interruption. 'Roland told me that the holidays aren't a great time for you.'

I make a mental note for me and Roland to have a nice, long chat in the new year about what is and what isn't acceptable to tell people.

'And is this just the result of that?' she asks, gesturing between us as if she can see the wall of tension that's currently dividing us. 'Because if it is, then I've got the same question: what is your deal with Christmas?'

I stab at my spaghetti and avoid all eye contact. 'It's

nothing but an overhyped, overcommercialised excuse for excessive spending and false cheer.' The words tumble out of me with dismissive ease – it's the same argument I've rehearsed every year when December rolls around.

Noelle raises an eyebrow, her full lips finally curving in a sardonic smile. It's clear that she's not buying it, and why should she? It's an obvious cop-out.

'There's got to be more to it than that.'

'There isn't,' I lie.

She exhales deeply and we fall into another silence. For a moment, I think I've got out easy. That she's going to accept my lie and let us ride out the storm without any further interrogations.

'You can do Christmas your own way, you know,' she says suddenly, her voice breaking through the silence. 'If you don't like the commercial side of it – which, neither do I, by the way – you don't have to lean into it. Christmas is more than tinsel and sales.'

I glance up. There's no judgment in her eyes. 'Like what?'

'It's about family. For me, anyway,' Noelle says, her hands gesturing wildly as if she's trying to paint a picture for me to see. 'My parents, my sister, cousins, aunts, uncles, family friends who aren't technically related but might as well be? They're scattered all over the country. And you know what life is like. Everyone's busy. Everyone's got their own shit to deal with on a daily basis. But Christmas?' She grins, bright and wide. 'That's our magnet. Do a documentary about the Jones family and have David Attenborough narrate it, and he'd probably describe it as some kind of homing instinct, the way we all descend on my grandmother's home in the run-up to Christmas.'

She leans forward and drops her chin into the palm of her hand, a wistful expression taking over her face. A soft smile plays at her lips. 'It's the one time we can count on being together, sharing stories, eating good food, catching up on lost time.'

'Sounds . . .' I click my tongue, searching around for the right word to use here. Something that won't offend her and send her hackles right up. 'Cosy?'

'Cosy doesn't even begin to cover it,' she laughs, shaking her head. 'It's loud, messy, and there's guaranteed to be at *least* three fights – and my mother will be involved in at least two. But it's ours, you know?'

'That's the problem,' I say. 'I *don't* know.'

My Christmases have never been like that. They're not about family spending time together and catching up. Sharing laughter and jokes and joy.

'But you said your mother is hosting Christmas this year?' Noelle says, frowning. 'So, your family *do* get together, right?'

I think back to the last Christmas I spent with my family. I was . . . twenty-two maybe? Twenty-three? It was a façade of togetherness, a performance for the sake of performance.

The air was thick with tension, our forced smiles barely hiding the fractures beneath the surface.

'It's not like that for me,' I say finally, the words heavy on my tongue.

'Then what is it like?' Noelle sighs in obvious exasperation. 'Paint me a picture.'

I've never been one to shy away from confrontation. I've built a career off being able to dive headfirst into uncomfortable or difficult situations without fear or nerves holding me back. So why the hell am I hesitating now?

It's not like Noelle's the first person to ever ask – and I doubt she'll be the last – but she's the first to ever ask like *this*. Like she's genuinely interested in the answer and isn't just waiting for a lull in the conversation so she can start listing all the things she loves about Christmas and how I'm inherently wrong for not agreeing.

Noelle waits patiently for my answer, even as the silence between us stretches into something uncomfortably awkward.

'It's . . . complicated,' I manage to get out, struggling to find the right words to describe the tangled mess of emotions that Christmas stirs up for me.

Noelle's expression softens. 'Complicated, how?'

I'm fighting the urge to run my hand down my face and groan. 'Do you bother all your clients like this?' I snap, my words coming out harsher than I'd like.

Noelle visibly stiffens. Her jaw sets and the soft expression in her eyes hardens into something I'm more than familiar with. Whatever goodwill I've managed to amass with my personal chef over the last two days is long gone. I'm not sure whether to feel relieved or disappointed that we're back on familiar territory once again.

'Sorry for being such a *bother*,' Noelle sniffs. 'But it's obvious you're going through something.'

I bark out a dry laugh as I push myself up from my seat. 'It's obvious, is it?'

Noelle's eyes narrow into thin, irritated slits. 'And I thought you could use a friend.'

That familiar feeling of guilt hits me again, so hard I'm almost drowning in it. The smart, rational part of me knows that Noelle doesn't deserve my Christmas ire, but what else am I supposed to say?

'Christmas doesn't have to be complicated,' Noelle calls after me as I stride towards the door. 'I don't know what kind of Christmases you've had before, but it doesn't have to be that way. You know that, right?'

I swallow hard, her words stirring something inside me that I didn't know was there. An emotion I thought I'd suffocated, from disuse, years and years ago.

'You can do your own thing,' Noelle continues.

I grab the door handle and wrench it open, cold air slapping me in the face as I step out into the hall. I don't turn around, but I hear Noelle slump against the table before she mutters, 'You can still make it whatever *you* want it to be.'

The problem is, I haven't made it anything in so long, I'm not sure I'd even know how to.

CHAPTER FOURTEEN

Alex

This is ridiculous. Utterly and entirely ridiculous. And yet . . .

My lips dip into a scowl as I cut my finger against yet another piece of foil as I try to mould it into this damn shape. Try and fail.

I glance up at the YouTube video currently playing across my screen. EASY ALUMINIUM FOIL CHRISTMAS STARS . . . And yet there is nothing easy about this. I let out an exasperated sigh and flick the offending scrap of foil off my finger, watching it skitter across my desk like a tiny, shiny, mocking entity. The video on my screen shows someone's hands moving deftly, folding and twisting the foil into a neat, perfect star. There's even festive music playing in the background, but the only thing ringing in my ears right now is the sound of my own frustration.

'Okay,' I mutter under my breath, taking a deep breath. 'Focus, Alex. Focus.'

I grab another square of foil, careful this time to keep my hands steady, my grip light. But it's like the foil has a mind of its own. It's irritatingly slippery and crinkles and folds in all the wrong places. Why does it look so easy in the video? The person on screen isn't bleeding from most of their fingertips.

I try again, folding the corners just like they showed. First one side, then the other. I can feel the tension building in my shoulders, but I refuse to give up. I'm not about to let this piece of flimsy metal foil beat me.

After what feels like hours but is probably only ten minutes, I hold up my creation. It's ... well, it's something. Not exactly a star. More of a wrinkled approximation of one. A deformed blob of shiny metal with vaguely pointy edges.

I stare at it. It stares back. We both know it's a failure.

I toss my latest attempt into my pile of increasingly worse attempts and slump back into my chair with a groan.

How did I get here?

How did I, Alexander Hoxton, CEO and founder of the third-most successful tech company in the country get *here*? Freezing my toes off while I glare at the failed arts and crafts project in front of me.

If Luca could see me now, he'd be in hysterics. I can practically hear him, '*What's got into you, man?*'

At least I have an answer to that.

Noelle's frowning face fills my mind front and centre as I pick up another piece of foil and begin rolling and folding it into something vaguely star-shaped.

Christmas doesn't have to be complicated. You can make it whatever you want it to be.

I want Christmas to be nothing. For everyone to stop acting like the world stops spinning and nothing else matters for this one insignificant day of the year. But I'm clearly in the minority there. And I usually wouldn't care. But for Noelle.

Christmas means something to Noelle and I'm feeling increasingly guilty knowing her favourite day of the year is going to be spent here.

And so here I am, torturing myself with tiny pieces of foil, cardboard and some ridiculous tutorial I found online. I take a shaky breath and try to smooth the wrinkles out of the foil. My thumb presses into it too hard and tears right through. I hiss out another groan of frustration.

I glance back at the video again. The woman's hands are moving in fluid motions, as if she's been crafting foil stars since birth. Her smile is as fake as the twinkling lights in the background. It's not even like I want a star. Not really. What I want is . . . What I want is to see Noelle's smile again, that smile of hers that lights up the room. She'd probably laugh at my pathetic attempts with this foil, and maybe that's what I need. A little perspective. A little Noelle to remind me that it's not about getting everything perfect.

The thought of her smile, of how much I've missed it just over the last few hours, is enough to make my chest tighten. I lean forward, staring at the crumpled mess of foil in my hand. It's not a star. It's a wad of failure, a representation of how I've been trying – and failing – to make this whole holiday thing right.

I still don't get it. The frantic shopping, the forced cheer, the expectations. Noelle, though? She gets it. She feels it. And, damn it all, I want to help her feel it. Just a little bit.

The sound of footsteps shuffling down the hall jolts me out of my thoughts. I pause the video and listen out, half-heartedly hoping that she'll stop in front of my office door. She doesn't.

She passes by without breaking her stride and, from the sound of it, enters the guest room. I frown. Surely she's not thinking about sleeping in there, is she? Did I really make today *that* uncomfortable and awkward that freezing to death is a better alternative than rooming with me again?

Yes.

Yes, I most definitely did.

I groan again. I want to rewind time and bring us back to that delicious moment in the kitchen when I had Noelle in my arms and everything felt easy. Holding Noelle, feeling her, *kissing* her, it felt right. It felt easy.

But then she said my name – *moaned* my name – and the reality of the situation pulled me into the present like a bucket of icy water. Our relationship has been nothing but stony professionalism for the entire time we've known each other. Surely she couldn't want anything more than that.

Could she?

I shake my head and push away from my desk, slamming my laptop shut as I go. I'm a mess. I've *been* a mess for too long, focusing on work and control, shutting off everything that could possibly complicate my life and distract me from my goals. But Noelle? She complicates everything in the best way possible.

I yank open the bottom drawer of my desk, intending on shoving the failed foil stars in and forgetting about them forever, but something makes me pause.

The drawer is already half full of Post-it notes in various colours. I pluck one from the top of the pile and immediately smile.

Mr H
I have yet to meet another soul who doesn't LOVE my lasagne. Let me know what you think.
Noelle

I remember that lasagne. It was delicious. *Beyond* delicious. She made enough for me to eat leftovers for about a week afterwards, and I missed it as soon as it was finished. I don't think I ever told her that.

> Mr H
> It's getting cold out. This is a super moreish
> chicken pot pie – it's my go-to once winter
> gets into full swing, and I hope you like it!
> Noelle

Another flawless dish.

> Mr H
> Roland mentioned you're in back-to-back
> meetings most of this week. Hope they go
> well, and you enjoy this salmon and couscous
> as a quick lunch on your busiest days.
> Noelle

The meetings went spectacularly, and the salmon and couscous was phenomenal. I keep going through the drawer. There are two years' worth of Post-it notes in here, a paper trail of all the good Noelle has brought into my life since I first hired her.

How many thank yous has she received from me?

How many times have I vocalised how appreciative I am of her? How in awe I am of her skills?

A solid zero.

Urgh. It's no wonder she can barely stand me, though I don't suppose I've done myself any favours with my behaviour today. I've been the very definition of hot and cold, and even I'm getting tired of it. I wouldn't be surprised if, as soon as the storm breaks, she hands in her notice and I never see her again.

It's not even about the food at this point, though her dishes will be missed. It's about *her*. She's been within my reach for the last two years, but I haven't felt as close or connected to her as I have these last few days. The idea of going back to the cold, distant relationship we had before, or losing her entirely, is unpleasant.

Extremely so.

I sigh as I drop my failed foil stars into the drawer filled with Post-it notes and slam it shut.

I need to make things right.

CHAPTER FIFTEEN

Noelle

I don't think I've ever felt worse in my entire life.

I spit out the last dregs of mouthwash and grimace at my reflection in the bathroom mirror. My braids are getting fuzzy after three days of sleeping without a bonnet or head-scarf, my borrowed clothes from Hoxton dwarf me entirely, making me seem small and frail, there are circles forming under my eyes, and there's a deep furrow in my brow that I'm sure isn't normally there.

Guilt has a way of etching itself into your features, and I'm practically broadcasting my regret to the whole universe right now.

'Pushed too hard, Noelle. Pushed way too hard,' I mutter to myself, remembering the way Hoxton's dark eyes clouded over earlier when I prodded him about his aversion to Christmas. I take a deep breath and try to shake off the tension coiled in my chest.

It wasn't my place to pry; to attempt to unravel the threads of his pain without consent. And the way he flinched when I mentioned Christmas? The way his jaw tightened and his gaze turned distant? I've crossed an invisible boundary and I'm not sure if there's any coming back from this. It doesn't help that we were already on thin ice after our kiss earlier.

It only happened a few hours ago, but it feels like a lifetime has passed since we kissed. To me, anyway. I'm sure Hoxton's already forgotten about it. It's clear as day that he's already put me back in whatever box it was he'd categorised me in before this storm. Any chance of Hoxton and I having any kind of relationship – friendly, or otherwise – once this entire ordeal is over is non-existent.

As soon as the storm passes, I'm out of here. I've been keeping an eye on the Met Office website, desperately waiting for the alert system to downgrade to amber – no such luck just yet, but surely this can't continue for much longer. I give it another day. By tomorrow afternoon I'll be out of here and on my way to Gran's. Christmas will officially be on track again.

With a soft click, I switch off the light and make my way back towards the guest room, fully intent on camping out in there tonight. I'm not sure I can handle being bundled up beside Hoxton after everything that's gone on between us. But as I enter the room, an icy chill hits me like a wave and goosebumps spring to life all over my body almost instantaneously.

This heater situation is going to be the death of me, I swear it. At this point, I either freeze to death or die from a Hoxton-related aneurysm.

Both seem equally likely.

I wrap my arms around my body in a feeble attempt to warm up, but it feels like standing outside in the dead of winter.

With a resigned groan, I dive into the bed and crawl under the covers, tucking my knees close in an attempt to muster up some kind of warmth. But the cold seems to have made itself at home under my skin and nothing works. I glance longingly at the door that leads out into the hall and towards Hoxton's room.

It's just heat, I think to myself. *A basic human need.* Surely he wouldn't begrudge me that?

I dismiss the idea as soon as it pops into my mind. After everything that's happened today, seeking refuge there of all places feels like tiptoeing through a minefield.

But, after ten minutes of teeth-chattering contemplation, I finally cave. I've joked about it several times over the last three days, but I genuinely think if I spent the night in this room I *will* freeze to death. I push off the covers, stand up and make the possibly regretful decision to brave the potential awkwardness between me and Hoxton all for the sake of some warmth.

And, you know, not dying.

I slip out of the guest room and pause in the doorway. The hallway is shrouded in darkness, and the only pinprick of light is coming from the crack beneath Hoxton's door. I heave a quiet sigh of relief. At least he's not sleeping yet.

I knock lightly and wait. I can hear the sound of bedsheets ruffling and then—

'Come in,' he murmurs, and he doesn't sound at all surprised that I'm here at his door.

I take a deep breath and then tiptoe into the room. 'Sorry,' I say brusquely. 'I really didn't want to bother you again, but . . .'

I cut myself off, mouth agape. Hoxton is lying in bed, still as a statue, his duvet pulled up to his chin, and beside him—

'What the hell is that?' Any hope of not starting another argument with Hoxton and just hunkering down to get some sleep evaporates in an instance. I point an accusing finger at what I can only describe as 'The Great Wall of Pillow' set up down the centre of the bed. Hoxton has used his surprising collection of decorative pillows to create a neat line going down the middle of the bed, effectively dividing the king-sized mattress into two.

It's absurdly meticulous, and each pillow is fluffed and positioned with the precision of someone who spends all day dealing in algorithms and code.

I stifle a laugh because *really*? This is the kind of ri-
diculousness that could only make sense to someone like
Alexander Hoxton.

He cracks open an eye. 'I wasn't sure if you were coming
in and I thought if you did, this set-up would be preferable.
Given . . .' He trails off and I arch a brow.

'Given the fact that we're currently stepping on eggshells
around each other?'

Hoxton's jaw tightens and he gives me a stiff little nod. 'I
wouldn't put it that way.'

'How would you put it?' I ask as I shuffle across the room
and settle down on *my* side of the bed. Hoxton doesn't
respond. When I glance over at him, both eyes are closed
again.

I sigh.

I guess this is all the conversation I'm going to get out
of him.

I slip under the covers on my designated side of the bed,
careful not to disturb the pillow wall. Despite the ridiculous
makeshift border, the bed is a vast improvement over the
arctic zone of the guest room. The warmth envelops me like
a cocoon, and I let out a contented sigh, feeling the tension
in my shoulders slowly unwind.

Even Hoxton's presence beside me is oddly reassuring
in the quiet darkness of the room. I steal another glance
at him over the pillows. His side profile is sharp against

the dim light of his bedside lamp, his jawline chiselled and defined.

That tight feeling in the pit of my stomach is back. I remember just how good the stubble on his jawline felt scraping against my skin as he pressed me up against the countertop and devoured my mouth like a man starved.

God, what I wouldn't give to feel like that again.

Every single inch of me that his hands touched felt as if they'd been touched by a loose wire buzzing with electricity. It was like the world outside had gone completely silent, like the storm didn't exist, and there was nothing left but the hum of our connection.

On second thoughts, given the events of today, maybe sharing a bed with Hoxton isn't the smartest idea I've ever had.

I shift on the bed until I'm facing the wall, trying to keep my distance both physically and emotionally. It's easier this way. The pillow wall is a ridiculous buffer, but it's enough to keep me from second-guessing everything. Because, honestly, if I let myself think too hard about what's been happening between us, about the way we've both been circling around each other, my brain will explode.

Time drags on, but sleep refuses to come. I can barely feel the cold that was gnawing at me in the guest room; instead the only thing I can focus on is the growing tension I can feel tightening in my chest. Hoxton's presence is like a quiet storm in the room, and I can feel the pull of it in the pit of my stomach, like I'm tethered to him in some way I can't untangle.

The silence is thick, and it's suffocating. Something needs to give.

Finally, I can't take it anymore.

I push myself up onto my elbows and peer over the make-shift wall.

'Thanks, again,' I whisper tentatively, testing the waters. He doesn't respond, but I don't miss the way he tenses ever so slightly. I don't know whether to feel encouraged by this small reaction or worried, but I press on. 'For letting me crash in here again tonight. And I'm sorry if I overstepped earlier. I didn't mean to pry or make you uncomfortable. I promise I'll be out of your hair as soon as I can. Hopefully tomorrow.'

There's a pause before he finally speaks, his voice low and rough. 'You didn't overstep, Noelle. You just . . . hit a nerve.' Another pause. 'And you don't have to thank me or rush to get away.' Another pause. 'Don't put yourself in danger just to get away from me.'

Is that what he thinks I'm doing?

'It's not you,' I start. I can't see him but I hear his disbelieving snort. 'It's not *just* you,' I amend before reaching out tentatively, my fingers hovering over the barrier of pillows between us. The urge to bridge the divide, to offer some semblance of comfort, is almost overwhelming. But I hesitate. I don't know if he'd welcome the touch or use it as another reason to push me further away.

Instead, I settle for a soft smile in the darkness, hoping he can sense it. 'Goodnight, Alex,' I murmur.

For a moment, there's nothing but silence – the kind that stretches taut between us. And then, just as I begin to think he won't respond, his voice cuts through the darkness like a beacon. 'Goodnight, Noelle.'

I close my eyes and try to find sleep, but it's like trying to catch a snowflake on your tongue – seemingly simple, yet impossibly elusive. My mind races non-stop with thoughts of today, of Christmas, of Hoxton's hidden wounds that I'd spent the evening unknowingly prodding at.

Hoxton, on the other side of his pillow barricade, seems perfectly at peace. Which is something, I guess. His breathing is even and deep, the rhythm of someone far away in dreamland. There's something so disarming about seeing him this way – guard down, defences up only in the form of pillows. A tiny snore escapes him, and I bite my lip to keep from laughing out loud.

Of *course* he's a snorer.

I can just about make out the steady rise and fall of his chest from over the pillow wall, and his breathing quickly becomes a lullaby that I'm all too willing to listen to. Maybe it's the proximity, or maybe it's the fact that, even divided by a cushioned partition, Hoxton's presence is oddly comforting.

Visions of our earlier kiss flood my mind again and heat crawls up my spine. *No. No, no, no,* I tell myself. *Stop it, Noelle.* I'm absolutely not going there. Not now. Not with Hoxton himself lying just a few inches away.

I'll save *that* for later, when I'm alone in my own bed and unbearably horny.

I turn onto my back and stare up at the ceiling shrouded in shadows. The minutes stretch on endlessly. Every fibre of my being is attuned to the presence of the man beside me, the rise and fall of his chest, the soft staccato of his breathing.

Sleep just won't come.

I roll onto my side again, tucking the blanket tighter around my shoulders. I curl into a ball, trying to trap any semblance of warmth beneath the covers. The mattress beside me dips slightly, and I freeze, listening. Hoxton's breathing remains steady, but I can't shake the feeling that he's not in quite as deep a sleep as he seems. He's not snoring anymore. Is he laying there, eyes open, staring at the ceiling just like me? Is he counting the cracks in the paint to pass the time, or has his brain managed to do what mine can't, and shut down for the night?

Minutes drag by, each one colder than the last, and I feel a begrudging gratitude for even the small heat source on the other side of the pillow wall. But it's getting ridiculous, really; this barrier between us is the kind of thing I would've put up when was a tween and forced to share a bed with Eve and my cousins every Christmas.

As if he's just read my mind, a heavy sigh breaks the silence, and suddenly, the pillow wall comes toppling down. Hoxton's arm emerges from the shadowy darkness, sweeping away the soft blockade. He doesn't say a word, doesn't look at me, but I smile anyway.

'Thanks,' I whisper, though I'm not sure if it's for the dismantled pillows or the unspoken truce hanging in the air. For a moment, I consider the possibility of conversation, of delving into whatever thoughts are currently keeping him awake. But now isn't the time. I've pushed enough for one day, and right now, the silent acknowledgment of our shared need for warmth is enough.

With the pillows gone, I allow myself to relax slightly and sink into the mattress. I'm sure that sleep is about to take hold of me any minute now.

But my limbs have a mind of their own. Despite the pep talk I give myself about personal space and boundaries and not pushing Hoxton any more than I have already today, my body ignores the memo. It's like every cell in my body is conspiring against me, inching closer to the source of heat beside me. Hoxton is magnetic, an undeniable force pulling me towards him with the promise of warmth in this icebox he calls a bedroom.

'Sorry,' I mumble as my arm accidentally brushes against his. But instead of retreating, his body shifts ever so slightly like he's welcoming the contact. The air between us is charged with something I can't quite name, and it's not just static from the duvet. There's an invisible thread pulling us together, and we're both fighting it and embracing it all at once.

'Stop apologising,' Hoxton's voice rumbles in the darkness, a hint of amusement lacing his tone. 'You're cold, aren't you?'

'How are you *not*?' I huff, wrapping my arms around myself – not that it does much to stop the shivers wracking through me. In a silent concession, I surrender to the cold, and to Hoxton. My body leans into his, and I feel the solid warmth of his chest against my back. His breath is steady, a calming rhythm in the otherwise quiet room. There's no denying the comfort his closeness brings. It's like snuggling up to a freshly baked loaf of bread – if that bread had biceps and was sporting day three of a five o'clock shadow.

'Better?' he asks, his voice barely above a whisper, as if speaking any louder might break the spell.

'So much better,' I admit, the last of my resistance melting away. I release a happy exhale, sinking into the hug. Our legs intertwine under the blankets, a playful game of knees and shins trying to get comfortable.

I shut my eyes, just enjoying the way his chest rises and

falls against mine, and how his arm is draped over me. I catch a whiff of that familiar vanilla scent again as Hoxton's body envelops me. It's like I can feel his heart thumping in rhythm with mine, even in the darkness.

I have one last coherent thought before sleep finally takes hold of me. *If I'm not careful, I could get used to this.*

CHAPTER SIXTEEN

Alex

December 24th

It's strange how quickly you can become accustomed to the warmth of another person pressed up beside you.

I've never been particularly obsessed with the idea of companionship. I've had partners of course, fleeting romances that have always ultimately fizzled out under some complaint or other about my working hours or, more than once, my personality. But I've never minded waking up alone. Never minded a quiet home with nothing but my own thoughts to keep me company.

In fact, that's what I've always strived for.

Being alone in my own space has always been the goal. I remember being seven years old, sharing a room with three of my brothers and dreaming of one day having a room all to myself, where I could read and play without interruption. Without having to share every single last thing with my brothers and sisters. I suppose I've taken that to the extreme now, but I can't say I don't like the life I've crafted for myself.

Or at least, if you'd asked me that question four days ago, I would've said that.

But now?

Now, as I lay here with Noelle curled up beside me, I think I never want to wake up alone again.

She fits so perfectly here, seamlessly slotting into the mundane parts of my life like this is where she was always meant to be. Just the sight of her right now, bundled up in *my* clothes, her legs draped between mine, the soft pinch to her brows as she murmurs in her sleep, and the rise and fall of her chest against mine, fills me with a sense of peace I didn't even know I was missing. It feels like she's always been here.

I glance over towards the window just as another gust of wind sends a flurry of snowflakes dancing across the glass. Yesterday the storm outside was powerful enough to make the walls creak, but it's more of a grumble than a roar today. Less intense.

I sigh, half out of relief that the weather seems to be finally turning, and half out of disappointment that that means *this* is ending soon.

How many more mornings like this do I have left to look forward to?

Noelle twitches in my arms and nuzzles closer to me. Something tight in my chest unfurls a little more. I've built walls so high and sturdy around myself that I'd almost forgotten what it was like to let someone in like this.

Her soft breath tickles my neck, sending a shiver down my spine. I close my eyes, trying to memorise this moment – the weight of her head on my chest, the way her heart pulses in sync with mine, the steady rhythm of her breathing.

I don't want to forget any of it. Once this storm is over, the memory of this will be all I have.

I could lie here forever, but reality has an irritating way of bringing you back down to earth when you least expect it.

Noelle's phone suddenly erupts with all the urgency of a fire alarm, shattering the silence. She stirs immediately, her entire body tensing as she rolls away from me and reaches for her phone, stuffed under the pillow she abandoned for my arm at some point during the night. Not that I'm complaining.

I'd take a thousand dead arms if it meant I got to wake up like this every morning.

'Sorry,' she mumbles, eyes barely open as she fumbles with her phone. 'One sec.' Her thumb swipes at the screen and she props herself up on one elbow as she holds the phone up to her face.

I roll onto my back, glaring at the ceiling and suddenly feeling like an intruder in my own bed. The warmth we shared is replaced by a cool draught as she moves away, back to her unofficial side.

'Hello?' Her voice is groggy but tinged with an underlying excitement I can't quite place.

There's another beat of silence and then, for the second time this morning, my bedroom erupts in noise. This time, it's not the high-pitched ringing of her phone or Noelle's own groggy greeting, but the sound of several people all excitedly talking at once.

'*There* she is!'

'Still in bed, huh? What time do you call this?'

'Is that her? Let me see! Let me *see*!'

'Merry Christmas Eve!'

And then, 'Oh my *God*, everyone back up.'

Noelle laughs and sits up in bed, leaning against the headboard. Her face lights up as she beams at the screen. Her smile right now could rival the morning sun, and there's a light in her eyes that wasn't there before. The sound of laughter, music and overlapping greetings grates on my ears but none of it seems to faze Noelle.

I glance over in her direction, not wanting to intrude, but my curiosity gets the better of me. There's a woman in the middle of the screen wearing a lopsided Santa hat and a wide grin. She looks just like Noelle, with wide brown eyes and skin the colour of warm caramel. The resemblance is uncanny, and I realise she must be Noelle's sister, the one I heard her talking to the other day.

Huddled around her sister are several people I can only assume are family. They've all got the same bright smiles, the same deeply expressive eyes, and I can practically feel the warmth and love radiating through the screen. Noelle's sister waves excitedly, her voice crackling through the phone speakers with a contagious energy.

'I *told* them it was too early to call,' she says with a playful roll of the eyes. 'But they insisted. Well, *she* insisted.'

'Because we're about to start cooking,' a voice cuts in. Noelle's sister tilts the camera a little until an older woman is in focus.

'Hi Gran,' Noelle says with a soft smile.

'Look at you, still in bed while we're all up and about ready to start the festivities!' Her grandmother tuts playfully, shaking her head in obvious mock disapproval. 'It's not the same without you, you know,' her grandmother continues, and Noelle practically deflates in front of me.

I know it's not my fault that she's still here, but a wave of guilt washes over me at how obvious it is that Noelle wants to be with her family. I've spent the last five minutes hoping to extend my time with her as much as I possibly can, and she's, rightfully, desperate to leave.

'I'll be there,' Noelle says, and it sounds like she's trying to convince herself just as much as she is them. 'As soon as the weather clears, I'll be on the road.'

'Don't do anything reckless now,' her grandmother says, a hint of motherly concern slipping into her words. 'We want you here in one piece, sweetheart.'

Noelle starts to blink rapidly. 'Right. Got it.'

'And wherever you are,' her grandmother continues, 'you'll be doing something to celebrate, won't you?'

I take that moment to look away as another wave of guilt hits me. She *could* be doing something, if I wasn't such a miserable prick. My thoughts drift towards my impromptu Google search yesterday for DIY Christmas decorations and my drawer filled with terrible foil stars. Maybe I *could* put them out for her? Or, I could go back to the YouTube drawing board and attempt some of the other tutorials I'd scrolled past. Surely it can't be too hard to pull together some garlands made from dried fruit and cinnamon sticks? Though I did say the same thing about the foil stars and look where that got me. I try not to think too hard about the fact that most of these projects are aimed at primary school children.

'Of course,' Noelle says dismissively, and I wonder if her family can tell that she's lying as easily as I can. 'You know I bring the Christmas spirit wherever I go.'

Her grandmother hums and then I hear her sister's voice crackling through the speakers again.

'And what about *Alex*?'

Noelle starts coughing loudly in an attempt to drown out her sister, but it's too late. I whip my head around again and raise a brow because, if I'm not mistaken, Noelle's sister just purred my name.

My *first* name.

Purred it.

My heart skips a beat as I catch Noelle's eyes darting towards me, a mix of panic and mischief dancing in them. She hastily sits up straighter, her cheeks flushing a deep crimson that spreads down beyond the neckline of my sweatshirt. I can just about make out the teasing glint in her sister's eyes on the screen, and suddenly the atmosphere in the room on the screen changes.

'Who's Alex?' another voice chimes in from the screen, and a ripple of laughter follows.

Noelle tries desperately to change the subject, steering the conversation back to their holiday plans and the food they're preparing, but no one is having it. If anything, Noelle's terrible attempts at trying to divert the conversation only seem to fuel their interest further.

'Is he your *boyfriend*?' a younger voice calls out, and Noelle's sister dips the camera a little to show a gap-toothed little girl peering up at the screen. 'Is he?'

Noelle looks like she's hoping the bed will miraculously open up and swallow her whole. 'No,' she says firmly, and I try not to take offence. 'He is *not* my boyfriend.'

'Then who is he?' someone asks.

The camera shifts again and suddenly Noelle's sister is centre stage once more. 'And *where* is he?'

I decide that I've heard too much. I don't think I've ever seen Noelle so red, and it's clear that this isn't a conversation she wants to be having – much less having in front of me. I move to swing my legs out of the bed and give her some much-needed privacy, but then she sighs and says—

'He's right here.'

And then Noelle does the unthinkable. She turns the camera in my direction.

CHAPTER SEVENTEEN

Noelle

If looks could kill, I'd be a dead woman right now.

Hoxton is frozen to the spot, eyes wide, a deer-in-headlights expression on his face. If I didn't feel so bad about throwing him into this madness without any warning, I might've laughed. I don't think I've ever seen Hoxton look so off guard. In fact, I don't think he's ever *been* so off guard either.

I shoot him an apologetic look and mouth '*I'm sorry*' as my family immediately start bombarding him with questions.

I can see panic blooming in his eyes as my grandmother's voice cuts through with a loud and questioning, 'I thought you said he wasn't your boyfriend.'

'He's not, Gran,' Eve says, and I don't even have to look at the screen to know that she's grinning deviously. '*Alex . . .*'

257

If she keeps saying his name like that – drowning in not-so-subtle implication – I'm going to scream.

'. . . is one of Noelle's clients.'

That triggers another round of loud, garbled questioning from my family gathered around the phone.

Hoxton looks very much like he's hoping aliens will descend upon Earth and beam him up. I can't say that I blame him. I'm currently hoping the aliens will take pity on me too.

On a good day, my family are a *lot*. There's a reason Eve waited two years before bringing Nathan to one of our annual Christmas reunions, and she always jokes that she had to secure the ring first so he couldn't change his mind. This is most definitely *not* the ideal scenario I would've had in mind for Hoxton meeting my family.

Not that I ever had any intention of him meeting them in the first place, but still.

Not ideal.

The man is practically vibrating with nerves. He keeps running a hand through his hair, like he's trying to smooth down his sleep-tousled curls but they're not cooperating. It's hard to believe that this is the same person who I watched scowl wordlessly at his Board of Directors from the head of the dinner table just a few days ago.

Where has that confidence, that bravado, that casual in-difference to everyone but himself gone?

'A *client*?' someone says; I think, from the sound of it, it's my cousin Jean. 'And that's where she is right now? In bed with him? That's a bit saucy, isn't it?'

Thank you, Jean.

They all start talking over each other like Hoxton and I aren't in the room. Which, I suppose we're not. But still.

'We can hear you; you know?' I say, raising my voice a little louder when someone – Eve, of course – starts running through Hoxton's credentials, telling everyone all about HoxTech. They don't acknowledge me because Eve's helpful bout of information-sharing has in turn elicited another round of *ooh*s and *ahh*s because HoxTech is a household name. One of my uncles starts gushing about a HoxTech vacuum he bought eight years ago that still works like it's brand new. A cousin asks if they can get a discount on the latest HoxTech laptop. Someone else mentions something about a phone.

I had no idea my family were such big fans.

The more they talk, the more it looks like Hoxton is about to bolt. He's sitting on the very edge of the bed, his body angled towards the door, and I know that the only thing stopping him from making a beeline for freedom is the fact that the camera is still on him.

I don't understand how my family can't feel his tension vibrating through the screen, but I know I need to intervene before that aneurysm Roland mentioned three days ago finally becomes a reality.

'I'm stuck here because of the storm,' I tell them, turning the camera back to me to give him a little bit of a reprieve. I half expect him to sprint out of the room the second the camera is off him, but I think he's still frozen in place because he doesn't move an inch.

'Hox— Alex was kind enough to let me use his spare room while we ride it out. That's all.'

'And you're *both* in the spare room, then?' Eve says and I swear to God, I'm going to throttle her as soon as I see her again. She knows exactly what she's doing.

I glare at the screen, but Eve's deceptively innocent smile doesn't waver.

'We had a heating issue,' I say through gritted teeth. 'Nothing scandalous, I promise.'

My family members exchange knowing glances, and it's clear that their curiosity hasn't been satisfied by my explanation.

'A shame,' Eve says with a dramatic sigh. 'You know how much we love a scandal.'

'Didn't you say you guys are about to start cooking?' I ask, still scowling at my twin. As usual, she isn't fazed.

'That's right,' Gran calls from somewhere in the background, her voice fading away in a way that tells me she's already wandering off towards the kitchen. 'Come on. Quick time now. If you don't help, you're not eating tomorrow.'

Everyone grumbles but, one by one, they all slowly disappear from the camera frame. Gran isn't playing when she says, '*If you don't help, you don't eat.*' It's another one of my favourite Jones family Christmas traditions. Christmas Eve spent in the kitchen – everyone pitching in however they can. Even the younger ones get given a job, mostly setting out the plates, cutlery and cups for the big day. It's hectic. It's fun. It's my family. And God, if I don't miss it.

Hoxton breathes a sigh of relief as the chaos dies down. I can practically see the tension draining from his shoulders, but the relief is short-lived because Eve is still grinning up from the screen.

'You're evil,' I mutter to Eve, shooting her a look that promises retribution later. She just laughs, delighting in the chaos she's caused. 'You know that, right?'

She shrugs and then makes a show of peering around, like she can somehow see through the confines of the camera. 'Is he still there, or did we scare him off?'

Against all odds, Hoxton *is* still here. He's still perched on the edge of the bed, looking borderline shellshocked. I don't think he's said a word since I answered the call.

He looks up suddenly, his eyes meeting mine. And then—
'He's still here,' he says, voice low and filled with something I don't think I've ever heard before. It's amusement tinged with something else, but I'm not sure what.

Eve squeals, obviously delighted, and claps her hands together. 'Put him on. Put him on!'

'Are you going to behave?' I ask, trying to inject as much sternness into my voice as possible. Though, given the way she quirks a brow at me, I'm not sure I've succeeded.

'Of course,' she says sweetly. And I've known my sister long enough to know that the tone of voice she's using right now promises nothing but chaos. But Hoxton's sitting next to me, listening to every word, and there's no point in delaying the inevitable.

I shoot him another apologetic grimace and then turn the camera in his direction.

Eve's smile widens. 'Alex, *darling.*'

Hoxton hesitates for a moment, glancing at me as if he's looking for permission, before he reluctantly scoots closer to the camera. The expression on his face is a mix of apprehension and curiosity. Eve has always had a way of luring people in with her charisma, a talent she flaunts shamelessly. I can almost see the invisible thread she weaves to draw Hoxton into her web, and part of me wants to warn him, but another part is curious to see how he'll fare against her.

'You must be Noelle's sister,' he says slowly, cautiously.

'Eve. I'm sure you've heard so much about me. All good things, I hope.'

Hoxton glances at me briefly, panic sparking in his eyes.

'She's messing with you,' I tell him, leaning forward so

I can get in frame and roll my eyes at her. The movement sends me brushing against his shoulder, but he doesn't pull back. 'Be nice,' I say, in warning.

'Right, right.' Eve waves a dismissive hand in front of her face. 'Aren't I always?' She pulls her camera a little closer to her face, like she's trying to inspect Hoxton. 'I just wanted to meet the guy who's keeping Noelle all to himself for Christmas.'

I expect Hoxton to blanch at that, but he only responds with a slight eyebrow raise. 'You mean the storm?'

Eve blinks silently for a few seconds and then bursts into laughter. In that moment, I know that Hoxton's got her. There's nothing Eve likes more than someone who can hold their own against her without getting flustered. It's about 90 per cent of the reason why she fell so hard for Nathan – he never lets her dramatics slide and can give back as good as he gets.

I feel myself start to relax; tension I didn't know I was holding onto falling from me in waves.

Eve's laughter fades into a smirk as she leans back, clearly impressed. 'That too. But ...' The smirk fades away into something serious. 'It *is* just going to be the two of you for Christmas, isn't it?'

I swallow. I've been desperately avoiding the reality of the situation but Eve has pulled it to the forefront and I have to finally accept that I won't make it home in time for Christmas. Even if the storm stopped right at this very moment, I wouldn't be able to leave. The roads would still be an icy death trap, so I'd have to crawl along at a snail's pace. If I'm lucky, I might get to Gran's by Boxing Day.

The soft snort of laughter I allow myself isn't enough to hide my dismay at the fact that this will be my first Christmas alone.

My heart pangs slightly.

'I don't know if you've realised, but Christmas is a big deal in our family,' Eve continues, that same serious expression on her face. 'Make sure Noelle gets to enjoy it, all right?'

I expect Hoxton to scoff, maybe roll his eyes and then launch into another mini tirade about how Christmas is nothing but a consumerist nightmare. But, to my surprise, Hoxton's face softens and he nods, his expression unexpectedly solemn.

'I'll do my best.'

I don't know what he sees on my face when he looks up to meet my eye, but whatever it is makes his lips curl upwards into a soft smile. Rare. One just for me. 'Noelle deserves a proper Christmas, even if it's not the one she's used to.'

Eve studies him for a moment, her eyes softening before she breaks into a smile. 'Good. Because if you don't, I know where to find you.'

Hoxton laughs – a real, genuine laugh that has the corners of his eyes creasing – and Eve smiles approvingly at him before turning her gaze back to me. 'And you. You better make the best of it too. Don't let the absence of our crazy family ruin *your* Christmas spirit.'

I nod, feeling a lump form in my throat. 'I promise I'll try.'

Eve gives me a satisfied nod. 'Good. Now I've got to go before Gran makes good on the whole 'no eating' thing tomorrow.' She beams at us one last time before hanging up.

The call ends and there's a moment of quiet between me and Hoxton. It's Christmas Day tomorrow and the reality of spending it away from my family settles in my chest like a lead weight. But I've promised Eve I'm going to at least try to make the best of it, so I shake my head, banishing any negative thoughts, and fix a smile onto my face.

'That was—' I begin.

'A lot,' Hoxton finishes for me. He gives me a sideways glance, his eyes searching mine for something I can't quite decipher. And then, as if deciding on something, he shifts closer to me on the bed. The distance between us closes until our knees are touching, sending a pulse of warmth through me.

I can feel his hooded gaze on me, intense and unwavering, like he's trying to read my thoughts. My heartbeat quickens in my chest as I meet his eyes, the air suddenly charged with an electric tension. For a moment, it feels as if the world has fallen away, leaving just the two of us in our own little bubble.

I clear my throat and the sound breaks the spell that's wrapped itself around us. Hoxton blinks, like he's just woken up from a trance, and I spy a faint, pink blush colouring his cheeks.

'Sorry for the madness that is my family,' I say softly. 'I didn't mean to put you on the spot like that.'

He shrugs like it's no big deal and he hasn't just spent the last ten minutes frozen in place while my family hurled question after question at him. 'It was . . .' He pauses for a moment, a frown furrowing his brows. 'It was nice seeing your family come together like that for you. You seem close. Especially with your sister.'

'We are. Like I said, Christmas is really the only time we can all get together like that, but that doesn't mean we don't keep in touch the rest of the time.' A wistful smile tugs at my lips. 'Everyone is always in everyone's business. That's just how we are.'

He lets out a quiet laugh. 'I can see that.'

'Sometimes I think I was destined to love Christmas,' I murmur, not really thinking about what I'm saying. 'I mean, you can't really name your kids *Noelle* and *Eve* and not expect them to be Christmas mad, can you?'

Hoxton laughs. 'They are very fitting names for the two of you.'

'You should meet my cousin Casper – guess what his favourite holiday is?'

Another laugh. I'm really starting to enjoy the sound.

Our conversation reaches a natural lull and, if this were anyone else, I'd take the opportunity to ask about his family. But I think I sense a tinge of bitterness in his words. Nothing overwhelming, but it's definitely there. The fallout from our conversation last night rears its ugly head in my memories and I quickly banish the idea of broaching it again with him.

Instead, I decide to switch topics and lighten the mood. I clap my hands together and push myself off the bed. 'So, what's the plan for today? More spreadsheets?'

Hoxton chuckles good-naturedly, and any sign of the bitterness from yesterday is gone. 'Not today. What do you want to do?'

The answer comes to me immediately. 'I want to cook.'

CHAPTER EIGHTEEN

Noelle

To his credit, Hoxton doesn't complain once when I insist he dons my Christmas apron for a second night in a row.

'Come on, it's Christmas,' I plead with faux wide eyes as I hand him in the apron.

'It's December 24th,' Hoxton deadpans even as he grabs the apron.

'Otherwise known as Christmas Eve,' I say brightly as he pulls the apron over his neck and smooths it out. 'And it's actually really starting to suit you,' I tease as he pulls the apron over his neck and smooths it out.

'Ha, ha,' Hoxton says with an overexaggerated eye-roll. 'Don't make me regret this.'

The threat falls flat though, because he's grinning as he ties the apron strings behind his back, the corners of his eyes crinkling in amusement. If you'd have told me three days ago that I'd be standing in Hoxton's kitchen watching him put on a garish Christmas-themed apron without even a hint of protest, I would've laughed in your face.

But here we are. I suppose stranger things have happened. Not that any come to mind right now. But still – they must have.

'Don't you mean "Don't make me regret this, *Chef*"?' I say, wagging a spatula in his face to emphasise the last word.

Hoxton rolls his eyes, but there's no irritation behind it. 'Yes, Chef.'

I beam up at him and then turn to the kitchen counter where I've pulled out everything I could possibly find from the depths of his cupboards, fridge and freezer that could make a traditional Christmas dinner.

I may not be able to spend Christmas with my family this year, but Eve is right. That doesn't mean I can't enjoy it how I want to. And I want to *eat*.

★ ★ ★

I found a small whole chicken at the back of Hoxton's freezer, so in lieu of a turkey, it's been slowly defrosting in the sink for the last few hours. It should be done soon, if the timer I've set on my phone is anything to go by. I vaguely remember ordering it a month or two ago, but never ended up using it.

Thanks to Hoxton's Christmas dinner with his Board, I've got plenty of leftover spices and seasonings, enough to make some delicious, homemade stuffing. We're going to have to veer off course from *traditional* a little bit when it comes to the sides, but I've found enough to make a creamy mac and cheese, along with a small portion of crispy roast potatoes.

It's not the Christmas meal I was expecting to be preparing today, but I can make it work.

I'm *going* to make it work.

I'm going to have *my* Christmas.

'Is there anything you want?' I ask, glancing over my shoulder. It's just hit me that I've been cobbling together this meal without any consideration towards Hoxton and what he might like. 'Remember, we're working with what we've got, but if it's in here, I can add it to the menu.'

I expect him to shrug off the question or throw out some non-committal response. Instead, he looks thoughtful, a small crease forming between those piercing dark eyes that I've caught myself getting lost in more times than I want to admit.

'You know what I'd really like?' he starts, his gaze fixed on mine. 'I'd like some mulled wine.'

I blink, caught off guard by his request. Mulled wine isn't something I had even considered making, but in my mind the idea of it fills the room with a warm, spicy scent.

'Mulled wine?' I repeat, unable to mask the curiosity in my tone. 'That's extremely ... *Christmassy* of you.'

Hoxton scowls. 'It tastes nice.'

'But you agree, it *is* a Christmas drink?'

'It's a *drink*,' Hoxton says flatly. 'I can't help it if the rest of the world only wants to have it once a year. A drink is a drink. I'd have a glass in the middle of the summer if I could find it anywhere.'

'Maybe that should be your next business venture,' I tease. 'A bar that only serves mulled wine 365 days a year.'

His lips twitch. 'Maybe. I'll be closed throughout December, of course.'

'Oh, of course,' I say. 'Can't have any Christmas joy seeping into things.'

The grin that takes over his face could light up a Christmas tree. 'Exactly. Glad to see we're on the same page again.'

'Thought of any names for the bar?' I ask.

'None. It'll be nameless. Only those in the know will be able to find it.'

'Ooh,' I laugh. 'How very exclusive of you. They'll love you on TikTok.'

'What about you?' he asks, tilting his head to the side.

'A name for your bar? I don't know, what about—'

'No. For your restaurant.'

I stare at him for a few seconds. 'I ... I don't have—'

'Noelle,' he says my name softly and bumps his arm gently

against mine. 'What's the name you've been *mulling* over in your mind for the last five years?'

The question, and the pun, catches me off guard, and for a moment, I feel my heart stutter in my chest. My fingers grip the spatula tighter, like it will keep me grounded in the here and now. *It's just Hoxton*, I remind myself. He's asking casually, like it's no big deal. But it feels like he's prying open a door I've kept firmly closed for a long time.

I try to brush it off with a nervous laugh, but the words slip out before I can stop them.

'Heart,' I say, quieter than I intended.

'Heart?' Hoxton repeats, sounding intrigued, but not mocking. His gaze doesn't leave me, and I suddenly feel very exposed, like he's waiting for more.

'Yeah,' I murmur, swallowing hard, shifting uncomfortably. I turn back to the counter and start shuffling around the ingredients laid out in front of me – anything to avoid eye contact. 'I've been thinking about it for years now. A restaurant called Heart.'

I don't say anything more, half hoping he won't press me further. But Hoxton doesn't let the silence hang for too long.

'That's an interesting name,' he says. 'What kind of restaurant is it?'

I hesitate. For some reason, this feels harder than it should. Maybe because it's something I've never really shared with anyone before. Not Eve. Not anyone. My real dream. Not the surface-level stuff about jobs or random ambitions, but the thing that's always been at the core of me.

'I don't know,' I admit, my voice soft. 'It's . . . it's about bringing people together. Food has this way of doing that, you know? The whole idea is to create a space where people can share a meal, but not just any meal. It has to be good food. Comforting food. The kind that makes you feel like you belong, like you're at home, even if you're far away from it. I want people to sit down, break bread together, and leave feeling full – not just of food, but of something more. Like . . . like they've rebuilt a connection.'

I can feel Hoxton's gaze on me, steady and intent. I try not to look at him, but it's hard. There's something in the way he's looking at me that makes my chest tighten, like he's truly listening. Really *hearing* me for the first time.

'Sounds like a good idea,' he says after a beat. 'What's the "Heart" part for?'

I pause for a moment, trying to put into words the feelings I've kept buried for so long. 'Just bear with me here, but food is the most important part of any relationship, don't you think? It's like the heart. People connect over meals. It's not just about the food on the plate – it's about what happens when you sit down together, the conversations, the shared experience. I've always believed that. And I want Heart to reflect that. A place where people can rediscover those connections, even when the world feels like it's pulling them apart.'

The words hang in the air, and for a moment, I wonder if I've said too much. The dream I've kept tucked away, afraid to chase, now feels real, like it's right in front of me, waiting for me to take it.

Hoxton is quiet for a moment, and then he asks, 'What would be on the menu at Heart?'

'I think I'd start with things like roast chicken, mac and cheese, roast potatoes. Comfort food, mostly. But with a little twist. Things you'd find at home, but with something special about them. Something to make you remember why food matters.' I gesture to the food we're preparing right now. 'Stuff like this.'

'Nice,' he says. 'I could get behind that.'

I smile, and I feel a real spark of excitement. It's been a while since I thought about this in any kind of real detail. 'I want it to feel like a family meal, you know? But even for people who don't have that anymore. Maybe they've lost it, or maybe they just never had it, I don't know. But food has a way of healing things. Of making people feel like they're part of something, even when they're at their loneliest.'

His smile falters slightly, and for a second, I wonder if I've said too much again, but then he looks at me with a look I don't think I've ever seen directed at me before. Respect, I think. 'That's what food does,' he agrees softly.

I feel a little breathless, like I've just shared a piece of my soul, and the air around us seems to settle a bit.

'You've put a lot of thought into this,' Hoxton says, and I feel a flicker of embarrassment in my stomach.

I shake my head. 'It's just a stupid pipe dream. I'd never be able to pull it off.'

He frowns. 'Why not?'

A dry laugh splutters out of me without my permission. 'Running a restaurant is hard.'

'And you're the best chef I've ever had the pleasure of meeting,' Hoxton says without missing a beat. 'And I've eaten at some pretty well-reviewed places. Nothing, and I mean *nothing*, Noelle, compares to the dishes you make me on a weekly basis.'

I swallow hard, and grip the spatula like it's the only thing holding me upright. 'You can't be serious,' I say, even though I know he is. My voice comes out rougher than I meant it to. 'I mean, yeah, I make decent food, but running a restaurant? It's a whole other thing.'

Hoxton takes a step closer, his gaze unwavering, and I'm struck by how easy it has become for him to disarm me. 'Noelle,' he says, voice low. 'I'm not saying it because I think it's just a nice thing to say. I'm saying it because it's true. From day one you've been amazing. You understood what I was asking for from the very beginning. I've never had to resend you my brief or rework any of your menus – you've always just got it down perfectly. You have something that the best chefs in the world don't have. You make food that isn't just about the ingredients, it's about the feeling. And that's what matters.'

I'm not sure how to respond to that.

'And that's just me talking about how good your food is,' Hoxton continues. 'I haven't even started talking about the admin of it all. How many other clients do you have? How many other briefs, menus, allergies, dietary requirements and more do you have to keep in your mind at any given point in time? You're *good*, Noelle. Brilliant, even. You can do it. You know you can.'

I look at him – *really* look at him – and there's something in his eyes that tells me he's not just trying to get me to blush or feel good for a moment. This isn't a game for him. He believes it. He really, truly believes what he's saying.

My heart thuds a little harder in my chest, and I feel heat rising in my cheeks. 'You really think that?' I ask, my voice barely above a whisper. I feel vulnerable and exposed, like I've let something important slip out of me and I'm not sure I'll ever get it back.

Hoxton nods, slow but steady. 'I do. Can I tell you something?'

I nod.

'I didn't even want to attend that meal at The Avalon a couple of years back.'

'What a surprise,' I snort. 'Alexander Hoxton didn't want to attend a Christmas meal.'

He glares at me half-heartedly before continuing. 'I only went out of obligation – I'd been invited by a potential new investor and I needed to do some schmoozing. The investment ultimately ended up falling through and I would've called the whole evening a colossal waste of time if it hadn't been for you.'

It feels like my heart stops and then restarts. 'Me?'

Hoxton nods and offers me a soft, warm smile. 'That was best meal I'd had in years. Going to that dinner was one of the best decisions I've ever made in my life because it led to you.'

A nervous laugh escapes me before I can stop it and I try my best to deflect. 'You're really laying it on thick now, aren't you?'

He shrugs, but his smile doesn't falter. 'Maybe, but I don't think you hear it enough. Definitely not enough from me, and you should. Because it's true. You're amazing at what you do, Noelle. *You* are amazing, Noelle.'

I shake my head. 'You don't even like me! I mean, well, you *didn't* like me until very recently.'

Hoxton looks vaguely amused. 'I've never not liked you, Noelle. I just . . . It's just easier to keep people at a distance. People can't disappoint you if you don't give them the chance to know you.'

'That's sad,' I mumble.

He shrugs. 'I've made my peace with it. And this isn't

about me. It's about *you*. And why you should follow the dream you've had for your entire life.'

There's a lump in my throat I can't swallow down, a strange mixture of gratitude and disbelief. I want to argue, to point out every reason why I couldn't do it, why I'll never be able to pull off something as big as a restaurant. But for some reason, it's harder to keep pushing that back. Something in me is starting to hope. To dare to think that maybe this dream I've had for so long isn't as impossible as it seems.

I shake my head, trying to regain some composure. 'I don't know what to say to that.'

'You don't have to say anything,' he replies easily, his gaze softening. 'But you should listen. You've got something good here, Noelle. Don't let it go.'

I feel something inside me stir, something that's been dormant for years – something that was so scared of failure, it built a fortress around itself. Hoxton's words are like a hammer to that wall, cracking through it, piece by piece.

For the first time in a long while, I let myself consider the possibility that I might actually have a chance. Maybe it's not such a stupid pipe dream after all.

I finally manage a small, shaky smile. 'Thanks, Hoxton. I ... I'll think about it.'

And when he smiles back at me, I realise just how much I needed to hear that.

I clear my throat. 'Back to you, though.'

He shoots me a quizzical look. 'Me?'

'If I'm going to open Heart, you need to think about your mulled wine bar. And I've got the perfect name.' I shoot him a devilish look. 'How about The Grinch's Lair?'

Hoxton's scowl returns, but there's no fire behind it this time. 'When are you going to drop this whole Grinch thing?'

I shrug. 'When you stop being one and drop your one-sided grudge against Christmas.'

He leans against the counter, arms crossed defensively over his chest. 'I don't have a "grudge". It's just another day.'

'And you spend it acting like you're auditioning for a role in *A Christmas Carol* – and *not* as Tiny Tim.'

'Tiny Tim?'

The look of confusion on his face is plain to see, and something dawns on me. 'You've never watched *A Christmas Carol*, have you?'

'Why would I?'

'Have you watched *any* Christmas film?'

'I vaguely remembering watching *The Nightmare Before Christmas* as a child.'

I let out a sigh of relief. 'Okay, good. Not a complete lost cause then.'

'But I stopped at around the halfway mark.'

I flick through the film in my mind, and then shoot

Hoxton a deadpan glare. 'Right as Jack decides to abandon Halloween and go all in on Christmas?'

Hoxton's grin is smug. 'Exactly. I thought he was a very reasonable character up until then.'

'Of course you did,' I mutter. I have to remember: this is the man who willingly sits and reads books entitled *The Return of Krampus* in his spare time. 'I'm just saying, letting some Christmas joy into your life isn't a bad thing.'

Hoxton heaves out a frustrated sigh. 'Yes, you keep saying.'

'Maybe you'll finally take it to heart,' I quip back, stubbornly.

'I'm not a bad person because I don't enjoy Christmas, Noelle.'

I pause. Is that what he thinks? That he's a bad person because Christmas isn't his favourite time of the year.

That *I* think he's a bad person because of it? I look up and meet his gaze. His jaw is set tightly but there's a hint of vulnerability in his eyes that I don't think I've seen before.

'I don't think you're a bad person, Alex,' I say softly. 'I just think—' I cut myself off. We're veering dangerously into the same territory as last night, and that didn't end well for anyone.

'What?' Hoxton pushes me. 'Go on, say it.'

'I just . . . I feel like you're the kind of person who makes himself intentionally miserable sometimes.'

Hoxton's eyes widen and he scoffs, but I keep on.

'It's like you don't believe you're allowed to enjoy yourself. Any spark of joy you get, you chase it away or lock it up as soon as it comes.' His gym. His bathtub. The bath bombs. How long is he going to make excuses for deferring enjoyment?

I remember our kiss and how quickly he pushed me away, even though it was obvious he was enjoying himself just as much as I was. And what he just revealed about purposely keeping people at a distance so they can't disappoint him? Despite all his riches, it's clear Alexander Hoxton has no idea how to enjoy life.

'And yes, that includes Christmas,' I continue. 'And other things too. The world doesn't have to revolve around work, Alex. You can find happiness outside of spreadsheets and making a million pounds every other minute.'

I mean the last part as joke, but Hoxton doesn't look particularly amused. He leans back against the counter, arms crossed over his chest. The sleeves of his sweatshirt are rolled up to his elbows, and the tense muscles of his arm peek out. For a moment, I wonder if I've struck a nerve too deep.

'That's quite an analysis, *Chef*,' he says, his voice dripping with sarcasm. 'But you're wrong. I'm perfectly capable of enjoying myself.'

'Prove it, then,' I counter. Those piercing dark eyes lock onto mine, but I don't look away. I hope he sees the challenge in my own gaze, daring him to step out of his carefully constructed comfort zone.

I take a step forward. And then another. And another. Then one last step until there's barely an inch of space between us. My heart is pounding but, with a rush of boldness, I close the gap between us and place a hand on his chest, feeling the solid, pounding rhythm of his heartbeat beneath my touch.

I wet my lips as I look up. A fire is smouldering in Hoxton's eyes, and I'm sure he must see the same when he looks into mine.

'How?' Hoxton asks, his voice rough and slow. Not much louder than a whisper.

I swallow, and then push myself up onto my tiptoes until my lips graze against his. 'Kiss me again.'

The words hang between us. For a second, it's like we both stop breathing, and the only sounds I can hear are gentle hum of the refrigerator and the soft rumble from the storm outside. And then I see it – the slightest twitch at the corner of his mouth.

'What was that?' Hoxton croaks out, even as he brings a hand to rest in the small of my back, pulling me flush against him.

'Kiss me,' I repeat.

'*Noelle*,' Hoxton groans, his grip on my lower back tightening. 'You can't just—'

'Kiss. Me.'

His eyes widen, searching mine for something. A hint of hesitation or fear or regret, maybe. But if he's looking for that, he's not going to find it.

Not now.

Not ever.

I snake a hand up the back of his neck and thread my fingers through his hair. 'Please don't make me ask again.'

'Okay,' he murmurs. 'I won't.'

CHAPTER NINETEEN

Alex

I feel like I'm on fire.

The world around us fades into nothingness as my lips crash against hers with an urgency that surprises even me.

Kiss me.

Kiss. Me.

The words echo in my mind like a mantra I'm going to have on repeat for the rest of my life.

How have two simple words unravelled me like this? And why don't I care?

All thoughts of the kitchen counter and the dinner preparations for tomorrow vanish from my mind as I focus solely on Noelle. She is all that matters in this moment – the way her body fits perfectly against mine, the taste of her kisses like the finest chocolate, rich and addicting. The thought of pulling away from her is unimaginable.

My hands slide up her back, feeling the soft fabric of her borrowed sweatshirt beneath my fingers. Noelle's hands tangle in my hair, pulling me impossibly closer as our kiss deepens. I part my lips, inviting her in, and she accepts the invitation eagerly, her tongue sliding against mine like she's done this a million times before. Like she knows my body intimately and knows just how to coax out each groan and spasm of pleasure that shoots down my spine.

Her free hand dips under the hem of my sweatshirt, her fingers tracing the contours of my back, leaving a trail of fire in their wake.

'*Alex.*'

She moans my name against my mouth like it's something to savour. Something to *revere*.

I want her to say it again. I want to commit the sight of her lips forming each syllable to memory.

I pull back slightly, gasping for air as our lips finally part. My eyes find hers, dark, desperate, and filled with heat. She looks as lost in this moment as I feel, her pupils dilated and her breath coming out in quick, sharp pants.

Her lips quirk into a half-smile, and I can't help but smile back, despite the overwhelming surge of desire that still ripples beneath my skin.

'Alex,' she says again, her voice barely above a whisper.

I don't even acknowledge my own name. I reach down and cup her face in my hands, bringing her lips back to mine.

Now I've had a taste, I don't know how she expects me to ever give this up.

Kissing her like this? It feels like my entire life depends on it. Like if we break away, everything is going to crumble to pieces around me. I can feel every contour of her face beneath my fingers, the warmth and passion in the way her lips part against mine.

Our first kiss was electric, but this feels cataclysmic in the best kind of way.

The kitchen is spinning around me and yet I don't think I've ever felt more grounded in my entire life.

My hands slide down her back and she lets out a pleased-sounding whimper as I slide further south and squeeze her ass experimentally. It's a very nice ass. Soft and pliable, even beneath the thick fabric of my sweatpants.

'Al-ex.'

I don't think I'm ever going to get tired of hearing her say my name like that.

I walk us backwards towards the table in the centre of the room without breaking the kiss. She lets out a tiny *ah* as her back brushes against the edge of the table but, before she can dwell on it, I'm lifting her up and her legs are wrapping around my waist as she goes. Her braids cascade over the edge of the table, a waterfall of brown silk I'm aching to drown in.

Noelle bites down on my lip and I let out a hiss of

pleasure. She chuckles against my lips, and then does it again. Bites and then runs her tongue along over the spot as if she's trying to soothe the prick of pain that appears.

Her lips trail along my jaw, her tongue leaving a trail of fire in its wake. She nips at the soft skin, sending shivers down my spine. Her thighs squeeze my waist and she bucks into me.

For the first time in three days, I'm hot.

Too hot.

Noelle seems to read my mind and she tugs at the hem of my sweatshirt. I don't need to be told twice, and lift it up over my head, taking the T-shirt I have on underneath with it too.

Noelle doesn't even hesitate. Her hands slide over my bare chest, her fingers running over my nipples in a way that sends shockwaves shooting through me.

While she explores my chest, I grab her hips, lifting her higher, nearly right up off the table. She lets out a soft moan, her eyes fluttering shut.

I press my lips to her neck, trailing my tongue along the delicate curves of her throat. She lets out a soft gasp, her body arching up into mine. My hands explore her body, running up and down her spine, tracing every curve and dip, and she melts into my touch.

'Put me down,' Noelle moans. 'Put me down and—'

Within seconds of dropping her gently back down onto the table, my hands are tugging at the hem of her sweatshirt.

She lets me pull it up over her head and I toss it mindlessly into a nearby corner, too entranced by the sight of her heaving breasts spilling out of a black lacy bra to care where it lands. She gives me precisely three seconds to admire her body before she's pulling me back into a searing kiss while I fumble with the clasp of her bra.

My heart stops for a brief moment the second the fabric falls away. The curve of her hips, the fullness of her breasts, the way they sway slightly as she breathes.

Beautiful is an understatement when it comes to Noelle Jones.

I'm in a daze as I lower my head and take one of her nipples into my mouth, rolling it between my lips. I flick the tip with my tongue, savouring every inch of her. I cup her other breast with my hand, massaging it gently while my thumb brushes over her erect nipple.

Noelle lets out little moans and sighs with each touch, her breathing quickening, and I know we're both about to reach a breaking point. Her hands are back to running through my hair, pulling me closer, as if she can't get enough.

I know the feeling.

I don't want this moment to end, and a thought suddenly strikes me. *I could do this forever.* Stay in this kitchen, kissing and touching Noelle until the stars burn out.

And so, of course, the timer on her phone chooses that moment to go off.

The alarm is piercing, cutting through the heavy, heated sounds of our deep breathing. Noelle jolts backwards in my arms with a shriek of surprise.

'Shit!' she murmurs, pressing a hand to her chest as she struggles to catch her breath. She tries to lean away from me to reach for her phone and switch off the alarm, but I pull her back towards me until she's flush against my chest. Her nipples, hard little peaks, brush against me and that sends another wave of arousal shooting straight through me.

'I should—' she begins, but I cut her off by capturing her lips in one last searing kiss. She's stiff in my arms for all of half a second, before she melts into my touch. Her hands come up to cup my face and we lose ourselves in each other again.

This time, when we pull away, I don't let her get too far. I press my forehead against her own and run my thumb along her jawline.

'What were you saying again?' I murmur.

Noelle blinks. 'I . . . What?'

'Something about me not enjoying life? You think I didn't enjoy that?'

She swallows and then laughs, pulling my chin down until I'm level with her lips again. 'Fine. You win.'

She pulls me in for another kiss. One I'm more than happy to give.

You win.

Except, it feels like we both have.

CHAPTER TWENTY

Noelle

'It's not like I'm asking you to put on a Santa suit and dance around singing carols all night,' I say, nudging Hoxton with my elbow as we stand in front of his giant TV screen that probably cost more than my rent for the year. *'Although . . .'*

Hoxton rolls those dark, brooding eyes – a look I've become well acquainted with in the short time I've been his temporary roommate – and folds his arms over his chest, which is admittedly a *very* nice chest. I'm allowed to say that, now that I've had first-hand experience of it.

'Don't get any ideas.' He shoots me a sideways glance before picking up the remote and switching the TV on.

I have to admit, when I first broached the idea of watching a Christmas film tonight, I was certain Hoxton would put up more of a fight. But he agreed without any hesitation at all. I'm not sure if that has something to do with the fact that he could probably still taste me on his lips *or* if it was because I was sitting on his lap, softly grinding against him as I murmured my request.

Either way, here we are.

Hoxton is dutifully scrolling through his various streaming services, looking for a Christmas film we can both agree on. I sneak a glance at him as he scrolls through the listings, the look on his face entirely too serious for what he's looking at right now.

Not once over the course of the last two years have I seen Hoxton looking anything other than meticulously groomed and poised. I've joked with Eve before that he's like a machine, appearance always perfect without a single strand of hair out of place.

But now . . .

His hair is still tousled, his sweatshirt hanging awkwardly from one shoulder from when he roughly pulled it back on minutes ago, and there's an unmistakable purple mark blooming at the base of his neck. I feel an unfamiliar sense of possessiveness as I take him in.

I did that.

He *wanted* me to do that.

Begged for it. Groaned into the crook of my neck as I alternated between biting and sucking along his jawline. If my alarm hadn't gone off, I have no doubt that his hands would've travelled below my breasts and dipped below the waistband of my sweats, finding me wet and waiting.

Just the thought of it makes me squirm in the best kind of way.

Suddenly, Hoxton stops on a title and raises an eyebrow in my direction. 'How about this one?'

The Grinch's crooked smile is slanted across the screen and I let out a snort of laughter. 'Seriously?'

He shrugs and then guides me towards the sofa, his arm coming up to rest casually around my shoulder like this is normal for us. Like touching me is second nature now. 'I feel like I should probably watch the film everyone keeps comparing me to.'

I grind to a halt, one knee on the sofa. 'Are you telling me you've never watched *How The Grinch Stole Christmas*? Not even as a kid?'

A look of amused disbelief flits across Hoxton's face. 'Why does that surprise you?'

He's got a point.

After everything I've learned about Hoxton over the last few days, it really shouldn't.

But still.

'It's The Grinch,' I insist as he pulls me down onto the sofa, tucking me into his side and holding me close like I'm something precious he never wants to let go of. 'You know the one with Jim Carrey? It's a classic.'

'Yes, I keep hearing,' Hoxton says dryly. 'Do you want to watch it or not? Because there are other things I'd like to be doing right now.' He leans back against the sofa, his eyes suddenly turning dark and hooded as his gaze drops and he stares pointedly at my lips. His tongue darts out to wet his own lips and I feel my pussy throb with anticipation.

I indulge him for just a second. I lean in and press my lips softly against his. One large hand immediately comes up to rest on my waist, eager to pull me onto his lap, but I pull away and bite my lip to silence the laugh that threatens to fall when Hoxton *pouts* at me.

Literally pouts.

That shouldn't be attractive. And yet, somehow, it is.

'Film first,' I say, settling back into the sofa.

Hoxton looks like he wants to argue, so I snatch the remote from him and hit *play* before he can say anything.

I half expect him to grumble and moan throughout the film, but he's surprisingly content. He sits upright, watching the whole thing with an air of seriousness that definitely doesn't compute with a children's film. If I didn't know any better, I'd say he's enjoying it.

'I like this Grinch guy,' Hoxton says with an appreciative nod as the Grinch loudly and dramatically declares that he hates Christmas and then promptly moves into a cave inside a mountain. 'Very relatable.'

I roll my eyes and reach for a cushion to swat him with.

'Are you implying that you want to hide from society and live in a cave alone?'

'At Christmas, sure,' Hoxton says with a shrug. Then he looks over at me, his eyes darkening ever so slightly. 'Maybe not alone, though.'

'See, there's your problem. I'm not living in a cave,' I say, leaning into him a little more. 'I've become accustomed to the finer things over the last few days.'

Hoxton scoffs. 'You mean a house without working heating?'

'There's been a few hiccups,' I concede. 'But, overall, not bad. I'd give you three out of five on Airbnb.'

And anyway, I barely feel the cold anymore. When we were back in the kitchen, I just put it down to the heat from the Aga mixing with the heat we generated from our kiss. But, now that I think about it, I don't think I've felt the cold all day today.

From when I woke up this morning till now, there's no sign of the biting cold that's been making itself at home in my bones for the last three days. The temperature actually feels quite normal. *Warm,* even. I allow myself the fleeting dream that the heater has heard my prayers and has kicked itself back into action but before I can voice my thoughts aloud, something catches my eye from the window.

For the first time in days, I don't see a snowy maelstrom in front of me. The snow is still falling, but the snowflakes are gently, slowly falling towards the ground. Not swirling around in a flurry of chaos.

The glass on the window is no longer completely blurred with icy frost and instead, I can just about make out the shapes of trees and bushes in the garden. I can even see the homes of Hoxton's neighbours again.

The storm is clearing.

The *storm* is clearing.

A sense of relief mixed with excitement suddenly washes over me. If I drove through the night, I might just be able to make it to Gran's house on time for Christmas. The pure joy of being able to go back home starts creeping into my mind, but then another, less pleasant thought pushes its way forward.

I'd be leaving Hoxton alone over Christmas.

I know he probably wouldn't care, but the notion feels wrong, almost unsettling. It's accompanied by a twinge of something I can't quite place. Guilt, maybe? Or something else entirely?

Hoxton laughs suddenly and I look up in time to catch the Grinch burning down the Whoville Christmas tree.

'You are absolutely not beating the Grinch allegations anytime soon,' I say, although I can't help but laugh too.

'He has his reasons for hating Christmas,' Hoxton says with a shrug. 'I respect that.'

I hum, thoughts of the storm and Christmas at Gran's

evaporating instantaneously as I realise we're teetering on historically rocky ground here. 'And you?' I ask quietly. 'Do you have your reasons?'

He stiffens a little beneath me and I immediately regret voicing the question. Hoxton's gaze flickers away, his jaw clenching as if he's debating whether to confide in me or shut me out. I can see the turmoil in his eyes, the memories stirring beneath the surface, and guilt threatens to drown me.

Why do I keep prying? There's obviously something deep-seated simmering beneath the surface. Something he's not ready to talk about. Maybe he will one day, but it's clear today is not that day.

'Actually, don't worry about it.' I wave an airy hand, trying to dispel the sudden tension that has settled between us. 'You don't have to tell me. I get it. You've been through some things.'

Things that have clearly scarred him deeply.

Hoxton exhales a deep breath and runs a hand down his face. 'It's not that.' He finally turns to look at me, something beyond pain flashing behind his eyes, and holds my gaze.

'Really,' I say, reaching between us to clasp his hand in my own. 'You don't have to say anything. Let's just enjoy the rest of the film.' I try to tug him back to settle into the sofa, but Hoxton just shakes his head.

'No,' he murmurs, tugging his hand gently out from my grip. 'It's time.'

Something unpleasant settles in the pit of my stomach as I take in the grim look on his face. 'Really, Alex, I mean it. You don't have to.'

He pushes himself up from the sofa and walks stiffly towards the window, his hands clasped tightly behind his back. My mind is racing with about a million scenarios at once – all darker and more depressing than the last.

What is he going to tell me? What could possibly have happened in his past to make Christmas such a dreaded day for him?

Worst-case scenarios flood my mind and I reflexively reach out to squeeze his hand in pre-emptive sympathy. I want him to know I'm here for him. That whatever he's about to reveal won't have me running for the hills. *I'm here.*

He's not facing me anymore, but I can see his reflection in the window. His lips are pressed into a thin line, and he's got a faraway look in his eyes. He might be here physically, but his thoughts are somewhere else.

'Christmas is …' Hoxton says slowly, still staring out of the window. He takes a deep, shaky breath and I brace myself for the worst. 'It's. Well. It's my birthday.'

I stare at him dumbfounded for a few seconds, certain I must have missed the part where he shared another reason for hating Christmas. 'Come again?'

Hoxton turns to face me, the look on his face no less

grim, like he's just given me earth-shatteringly awful news. 'It's my birthday.'

'It's . . . your . . . birthday?' I parrot weakly.

Hoxton nods. 'Tomorrow, I mean. Not today.'

Gears start to turn in my mind. 'Your birthday,' I say slowly. 'Is on Christmas *Day*? December 25th?'

'The one and only,' Hoxton says with another drawn-out sigh.

I try to keep a straight face.

I try *extremely* hard.

Because Hoxton looks so serious right now, his brows knit together in the middle, his jaw tight, and I can tell that this is something very important to him. Something that he's been holding onto for far too long, and I should feel grateful that he's willing to open up to me. I'm probably the first person he's told in years and I can't betray his confidence.

Must keep a straight face.

Must keep a straight—

I last probably less than five seconds before I burst into laughter.

'Oh my *God*,' I cackle, my sides literally aching because I'm laughing so hard. 'You're not serious. *Please* tell me you're not serious.'

He doesn't say anything, just narrows his eyes. He still hasn't moved from the window.

'Okay, okay,' I say, trying to get a hold of the situation

before he pulls all the way back and we're back at square one. 'I'm not laughing at *you*.'

'You sure about that?'

'I'm laughing at the situation,' I say. 'Alex, come *on*. I thought someone had *died* or something equally devastating and that you were harbouring deep, deep traumatic memories related to Christmas because of that.'

'I never said anyone *died*,' Hoxton says, looking almost indignant that I would jump to that conclusion, despite it being a perfectly natural conclusion for literally anyone else on the planet to arrive at. He finally makes his way back to the sofa and drops down next to me. 'I can't be blamed for you having an overactive imagination.'

'But you're so dramatic about the whole hating Christmas thing,' I say, still laughing just a little. 'When you're that passionate about hating something, people are going to assume there's a serious, potentially traumatic, reason for it.'

'It *is* a serious reason,' Hoxton says, though I'm pretty sure I spy a rueful smile tugging at the corner of his lips, the absurdity of his words finally sinking in a little. 'For me anyway. Imagine being seven years old and watching all six of your siblings have their birthday celebrated properly all throughout the year. Seeing them get cakes and parties and gifts, and having a whole day dedicated to them. And then when your turn comes around, you know that you'll be lucky to even get a card.' He wrinkles his nose and shakes his head. 'And when you *do* get one, nine times out of ten, it'll be Christmas-themed and addressed to everyone else in your family anyway. *Dear The Hoxtons, Merry Christmas and Happy New Year! Oh, and happy birthday to little Alex too.*' His lips curl in disgust. 'I'm an afterthought every December 25th.'

I try to put myself in his shoes. As a twin, I've had my own fair share of birthday disappointments over the years. I remember when Eve and I turned twelve and we couldn't agree on what cake we wanted. Eve's choice, a disgusting mint chocolate chip abomination, won out over my tried-and-tested vanilla raspberry and I remember refusing to blow out the candles or even have a slice. Partly because I can't stand the taste of mint chocolate, but mostly out of principle. It was *my* special day too, and I was suddenly an oversight. Expected to happily play second fiddle to some-one else and go along with whatever they wanted to do.

I remember exactly how angry and upset I felt. How bitter. How I wanted nothing more than to toss Eve's cake – because I absolutely refused to claim it as mine – out the nearest window and make us both suffer. And that was just *one* birthday. The thought of having to deal with that every year would turn even the most reasonable person into ... Well. Would turn them into Hoxton.

'As a kid,' Hoxton says, watching my expression carefully, as if waiting for my judgment on his childhood revelation. 'You expect to feel special on your day, right? But for me, it was just another excuse for my parents to throw a bigger party. Not for me, but for *Christmas*. Everyone all together, celebrating and swapping gifts and eating food. But nobody ever celebrated me.'

My mind conjures up images of a child Hoxton, seven years old and excited for a day of birthday surprises and special treatment that never came.

Four days ago, I would've gladly let this man walk into traffic without batting any eyelash. But now? My heart breaks for him.

'I get it,' he continues, that sad smile lifting his lips again. 'I know it sounds childish and ridiculous but, after years and years of the same thing, I've just become numb to Christmas. It's a symbol of everything I never got as a child.' He lifts his shoulders in a self-deprecating shrug. I can see real pain in his eyes, the lingering disappointment from years of neglected birthdays and I suddenly feel awful for laughing.

'Alex, that's . . .' I reach for his hand again and give him a little squeeze. 'I mean, that's actually kind of heartbreaking.'

'Tell me about it,' he says, forcing a chuckle that doesn't quite reach his eyes. 'I guess I am a modern-day Grinch. Every single birthday I've ever had has been lost in the Christmas frenzy – it all just blends into one big, forgettable event where I'm an afterthought.'

'I'm sorry,' I say softly. And I mean it too. 'No child, no

person, full stop, should feel overlooked on their birthday, especially not year after year. Christmas or not.'

He gives me another small shrug. 'It is what it is. I've made my peace with it.'

'But it still hurts,' I insist. I can tell from the look in his eyes how vehemently he's kept up this anti-Christmas personality for decades. 'Every Christmas, you still feel the same pain.' I give his hand another light squeeze. 'Let's make a pact. Next year, December 25th is going to be an Alex-only event. Christmas can wait another 365 days. Next year is only going to be about you.'

I realise, belatedly, that what I'm offering implies that *I'm* going to be around next year too. That this, whatever it is, has the legs to make it another year at least.

Hoxton swallows, and I know he's currently thinking the same thing. 'That would be . . . *nice.*'

CHAPTER TWENTY-ONE

Alex

If next year is going to be all about me, this year needs to be all about Noelle.

Somehow.

I'm still working on that, hoping that an idea to bring Christmas to life for the beautiful woman lying across my lap will spring to mind in the next— I glance at my watch. In the next hour and a half. Definitely cutting it fine.

Noelle stretches as the credits start to roll, a content smile on her face. 'Thoughts on your first official Christmas film?'

'It was decent,' I concede, though I'm pretty sure the grin on my face betrays me.

Noelle hums, seemingly satisfied and sits upright. I feel the absence of her body against mine as soon as it's gone, and the urge to pull her back down and press her flush against me again is overwhelming.

'I think I'll shower and get ready for bed,' she says, springing to her feet with more energy than I currently possess. She hovers on the spot for a second or two, looking strangely hesitant, and then says, 'I'll . . . I'll meet you in your room?'

I nod, not entirely sure why she feels she even has to ask. We've spent the last two nights pressed up against each other and, with everything that's happened between us today, she can't really believe there's any reality where I don't fall asleep with her by my side. Can she?

She gives me a relieved grin and then disappears down the hall, her braids swaying behind her with each step she takes. She's humming something under her breath as she goes, and I'm pretty sure it's a song from *How The Grinch Stole Christmas*.

The fact that it doesn't irritate me – the sound of Christmas music echoing in my home – is a testament to how far I've come over the last three days.

I rise from the sofa, suddenly feeling restless. I meant what I said earlier – if Noelle is determined to celebrate *me* next year, the least I can do is make sure she has a Christmas to remember this year.

She deserves that much and so much more. But how?

How do I go about making this Christmas something truly special with only – I glance at my watch again – an hour before midnight strikes? My thoughts drift, once again, to my foil stars hiding away in my office.

Surely I can do better than that. Can't I?

I'm lost in my thoughts as I absentmindedly walk over to the window. The sight of the snow outside beginning to melt snaps my attention away from my mental dilemma and I press my face against the glass, peering into the darkness outside. Moonlight casts silver outlines on the melting snow and I can see the roof of Noelle's car. Three days ago it was buried in a sea of white, but now the thaw has begun and I feel a twinge in my chest.

A slight pang of regret mixed with something else.

She's going to want to leave, isn't she?

And I wouldn't blame her. Wouldn't stop her either. As soon as she realises that the storm is over and the roads are safe, she'll be out of here in a flash. Part of me is happy for her – I know how much she wants to be with her family, her loved ones, for Christmas. But another part of me, the inherently selfish part, desperately wants her to stay.

But Noelle deserves more than my own selfishness right now.

I shake my head and turn off the TV before I clamber upstairs. I hear the sound of the shower running as I walk past the guest bedroom. I hesitate outside for a moment, half-heartedly wondering if I should knock and let her know about the storm, but I guess I'm a coward because

I keep on walking. I want to savour this for just a little while longer.

I reach my room and take a deep breath. Guilt gnaws at me as I step into the shower and underneath the cascade of blissfully warm water.

I should tell her.

She *deserves* to know.

And besides, she'll realise sooner or later anyway. I'm surprised her phone hasn't been blowing up with calls and texts from Eve, telling her to hurry up and get on her way.

I step out of the shower, steam billowing around me, and wrap myself in a towel. The air is cool against my damp skin as I make my way back to my bedroom, intent on pulling on some clothes. As soon as I open the adjoining door, I freeze.

Noelle is lying across my bed like some sort of Christmas gift waiting to be unwrapped. My fingers twitch by my side as I take her in. She's wearing an oversized sweatshirt of mine, the green fabric hanging off her shoulder, revealing just enough skin to set my heart racing.

And that's it.

Nothing else.

Her long, bare legs stretch out across my white sheets, her skin glowing under the soft lamplight in a way that makes her look almost ethereal.

My heartbeat pulses at the sight of her, and I can feel desire coiling in the pit of my stomach.

Without a word, I cross the room and stand in front of her, reaching out a hand to caress her cheek. Her skin is soft beneath my touch, warm and inviting. She leans into my hand, her eyes fluttering closed for a moment before she meets my gaze again, a silent question lingering between us.

I lean down, capturing her lips in a searing kiss that sends a jolt of electricity coursing through both of us. Noelle responds eagerly, her arms winding around my neck as she pulls me closer, deepening the kiss.

I don't think I'll ever get tired of kissing her.

It feels brand new every single time. I could drown in the sensation, in the way she moulds herself against me, like she can't get close enough.

I'm still slightly damp from the shower, but Noelle doesn't seem to mind. She drags a hand down the length of my chest, stopping where I've got the towel wrapped around my waist. Her long fingers dip under the fabric, and I feel her smirk against my lips as she pulls me backwards and onto the bed with her.

I topple over her, our bodies fitting together perfectly, and her laughter bubbles up between our kisses.

I could very easily lose myself in Noelle. In the softness of her skin. In her panted moans. In the way she arches against me with a quiet desperation that mirrors my own.

But then that guilt rears its ugly head again and I pull back.

Noelle blinks up at me blearily, frowning. 'Is everything all right?'

I glance at the window, where moonlight now seeps through the gap in the curtain. I turn back to Noelle and pull away just enough to meet her questioning gaze, hating myself for halting the moment. 'I think the storm is over.'

Her brow furrows in confusion, and I imagine she's trying to process why I'd bring up weather when there are clearly more pressing issues at hand.

My dick, for example, which is currently straining against the loosely wrapped towel around my waist.

I sit upright on the bed, trying to subtly adjust myself. 'I noticed about an hour ago. If you left now, I think you could make it to your grandmother's house before sunrise. I can call a car for you if you're worried about your one making it the whole way.'

Noelle makes a sound that's a mix between a scoff of disbelief and a dry laugh. She sits up too and fixes me in place with a sharp stare. 'Are you asking me to leave?'

'No,' I say quickly. 'That's the last thing I want.'

'Then why are you saying anything?'

'Because it'll be Christmas in about five minutes,' I say with a wry grin. 'And I know how important it was for you to spend it with your family. So . . .' I shrug. 'Now you have your chance.'

Noelle considers me for a few long moments. 'And if I said I wanted to stay?' She lifts herself up onto her knees and then straddles me, draping her arms loosely around my neck.

'If I said that it's your birthday in about four minutes, and I wanted to stay and celebrate with you?'

My hands immediately go to her thighs and I have to bite back a groan as my fingers dig into soft, supple skin.

She smirks and grinds into me, sliding over my already painfully hard dick. 'Answer the question, Alex. If I told you that I wanted to stay? Then what?'

'If you really wanted to—'

She leans in and nips at my neck. 'I do.'

I swallow. 'Then—'

'Then what?'

I'm tired of playing games. I pull her flush against me, my towel falling by the wayside so my dick can run along the fabric of her panties. 'Then there's nothing else to discuss,' I growl against her lips.

Noelle lets out a happy sigh. '*Finally.* We're on the same page.'

Her lips meet mine in a frenzy and we tumble back onto the bed, our bodies writhing together in a desperate need for each other. I slip a hand between us and she practically purrs in approval as my fingers run along the thin, damp strip of fabric that's keeping her pussy from me.

'Are you just going to tease me all night?' she murmurs against my lips as I press my thumb over her clothed clit and watch as she hisses and arches further into me.

'Seriously considering it.'

She pulls back slightly and rolls her eyes. 'Hilari—'

'Take them off,' I say, my voice rough with desire.

Her eyes widen a fraction, but she doesn't ask for any clarification. Just drops a hand and tugs her panties down her leg before tossing them into a dark corner of the room.

Noelle crawls back up my body, and I can now feel the damp heat of her core against me, begging to be touched. And I desperately want to touch her. But not like this.

I slide down on the bed until I'm lying flat against the sheets. 'Here.' I point to my face and enjoy the way Noelle flushes immediately. I can actually feel the warmth spreading through her where my hands meet her skin.

'You want me to—'

'*Sit.*'

Her tongue darts out to wet her lip before she gives me a tiny nod, and crawls up my body until her thighs are bracketing my head. I give them both a squeeze, signalling for her to sit down fully, but she hesitates.

I look up, watching as she curls her fingers around the edge of the headboard. I can feel her entire body tingling.

I wait a beat, but she doesn't move. I raise a brow and give her thighs an encouraging squeeze. 'Weren't you the one who said that you wanted to ... What was it? Ah, yes. "*Wipe that smirk right off my face*"?'

Noelle freezes, her legs still hovering over me. 'So, you just eavesdrop on all my conversations now?'

'Pretty sure it was the same conversation.' I feel my lips curve upwards into a familiar smirk. 'Anyway. Now you have your chance.'

She yips as my fingers sink a little deeper into her thighs so I can firmly, but not painfully, bring her down over me. Once she's down, I give her half a second to get her bearings before my tongue slides along her slick entrance and her back is arching.

I can't see her now, my vision blocked by the sight of her riding my face, but I can *hear* her. Can hear each delicious moan that slips from between her parted lips. Every gasp, every whimper, every breathy utterance of my name heads straight to my dick.

I don't think I've ever been so hard.

I reach up and place my hands on her ass, pulling her closer to me, and causing her to increase her pace. She whimpers softly, my name falling from her lips like she's begging me for something.

Faster.

Slower.

More.

Her words blur together into a nonsensical moan.

I let my fingers slide between her cheeks, just barely touching her entrance with each swipe. She mewls loudly, and I can feel her pussy quivering.

'Alex, I'm ... *Fuck,* I'm ...'

I hear the creaking of wood as she grips the headboard tighter and I imagine her knuckles turning pale as her orgasm builds.

I don't stop running my tongue along her entrance. Our rhythm has synced up perfectly. Each buck of her hips in perfect time with my long, languid strokes.

I want to shower her in praise – tell her she's doing so well; tell her she's beautiful, ethereal, deserving of every good thing in this world – but I don't want to stop. Not when she's so close.

'*Al-ex.*' She chokes my name out, breaking it down into two long drawn-out syllables before she lets out a long moan and her orgasm washes over her.

She goes limp above me, legs trembling as she slumps against the headboard. But I'm not done yet. I let her catch her breath for a moment, my tongue still inside, teasing her, sending little aftershocks through her body. Then, I sit up quickly and pull her into my arms so she's straddling me again. My dick runs along her slick entrance and she shudders against me.

'I'm gonna need a minute or two,' she laughs, eyes fluttering shut as she rests her head against my chest.

'Does it look like I'm in a rush?'

I let my hands roam over her body while she catches her breath, tracing the curves and valleys of her skin. Her scent, a mix of sex and vanilla, fills my nostrils, and I inhale deeply.

My dicks aches against her thigh, demanding release.

She giggles as it twitches against her. 'I didn't realise you were the impatient type.'

She smiles, a playful half-smile that turns every bone in my body into melted butter. Without another word, she reaches down and takes hold of my dick, stroking it experimentally. My eyes never leave hers as her hand moves up and down, creating a delicious friction.

My breath hitches and she leans in and kisses me softly, her lips warm and wet. My mind is a blur right now, but my hands somehow find their way to her hips, urging her to straddle my waist again. She obliges, her eyes never leaving mine as she lowers herself onto me, inch by achingly slow inch.

I groan as she finally envelops me, her tight heat engulfing my entire length.

She feels amazing.

Beyond amazing.

Out of this world.

'*Fuck*,' I groan, my head falling forwards to rest against her shoulder. 'You feel so good.' With slow, deliberate strokes, I thrust into her.

Noelle moans, her fingers digging into my shoulders. She starts to match my rhythm, her hips moving in sync with mine. The room is filled with the sound of our skin slapping together, our ragged breaths, and our cries of pleasure.

'Alex, I—' A loud moan courses through her and she throws her head back to let out a needy half-scream. 'I want more. I *need* more.'

She arches her back, her chest pressing against mine as her nipples harden with every thrust.

'I want you to come for me again,' I tell her in between strokes. 'I need to see you like that.'

I grab her hips, urging her to move faster against me. She moans softly, her breaths turning ragged as her climax approaches.

'Faster,' I murmur, one hand gliding up her spine to tangle in her swaying braids.

Noelle whimpers, her hips bucking wildly against me. I catch her eyes again, watching as they glaze over with desire. I groan, my hips bucking as I thrust harder, deeper into her. I can feel myself reaching the tipping point.

I can't hold on any longer. My thrusts become more frantic, each stroke more desperate for release. Noelle lets out a strangled cry, her body shaking as she climaxes once again. I pump my hips, groaning loud and low, my own release coursing through me as I empty myself into her.

I collapse back against the pillow, spent and breathless, my heart pounding in my chest. Noelle collapses on top of me, her weight pressing me into the mattress as she pants, her face buried in my neck.

'Holy fuck,' she whispers, her voice still shaking with the

aftershocks of her orgasm. 'That was . . .' She shakes her head and slumps against me, her breathing slowly evening back out.

I laugh. 'Yeah.'

She shifts slightly in my arms, raising her head to peer at something I can't quite make out. When she resettles again, she's got a wide grin on her face.

'What is it?' I ask.

'It's gone midnight.'

'Oh.' I blink at her. 'I guess, Merry Ch—'

'Happy Birthday, Alex,' she murmurs before leaning in to press a soft, sweet kiss against my lips. She shifts her weight, repositioning herself so that she's lying next to me, her head on my chest. I wrap an arm around her, pulling her close as a soft smile takes over my face.

It's only just getting started, but this is already the best birthday I've had in a long while.

★ ★ ★

Noelle's steady breathing fills the air. She's tucked in beside me and I've spent the last hour or so just watching the steady rise and fall of her chest as she sleeps. I trace the curve of her hip with my finger, relishing the warmth and softness of her skin, even as guilt continues to gnaw at me.

Yes, Noelle chose to stay.

She could've easily left hours ago and been on her way to her grandmother's house.

The fact that she's still here, softly snoring beside me, is because *she* made the decision to do so.

I should respect that.

I should feel grateful that she's willing to give up Christmas with her family in order to spend the day with me.

And I am, don't get me wrong. Just the thought of it fills me with the kind of happiness I haven't felt in years. But I still feel like I owe her something. She deserves more than a lacklustre Christmas and that's all I can give her at this stage.

My resolve hardens and I slide out of bed, careful not to wake her. She stirs slightly but doesn't wake as I pull on some clothes and pad out of the room, taking care to close the door softly behind me.

When I reach my office, I power up my laptop and search for a file I haven't so much as glanced at once in the last two years. Noelle's employee form fills my screen and I scroll through it quickly, getting to the section that has the information I need:

EMERGENCY CONTACT
Eve Jones

I grin as I dial Eve's number.

Noelle is going to get the Christmas she deserves. I'm going to make sure of it.

CHAPTER TWENTY-TWO

Noelle

December 25th

I think I'm hardwired to wake up early on Christmas morning.

It's been like this since I was a young girl. Eve and I would try to stay up all night on Christmas Eve in an attempt to catch Father Christmas in the act, only to inevitably fall asleep before midnight and miss all the action. But we'd always wake up at the crack of dawn on Christmas Day, and that habit has apparently followed me into adulthood.

It's why I'm up before the sun right now without setting an alarm. I stretch out in the bed, forgetting for a minute where I am. For a moment, I wonder why it's so quiet.

Why I don't hear the sound of my little cousins shrieking and playing as they tear open the handful of gifts they're allowed to open before breakfast. But then Alex stirs beside me, curling his body into the space I've just made by sitting upright and everything floods back to me.

I watch him for a little while. His features are softened in sleep, the frown lines that often crease his forehead are smoothed away. He looks more peaceful and content than I've ever seen him before.

I slide out of bed carefully, not wanting to disturb him, and pad softly across the room. I open the curtains just enough for me to confirm that it's no longer snowing at all. The sky is a pinkish-blue, and the snow that covers the world outside is melting rapidly enough for me to spy patches of green and brown in the fields in the distance.

Not quite a white Christmas but, given what we've endured over the last four days, I'll take it.

A jolt of excitement shoots through me suddenly as I remember that it is, in fact, Christmas Day. I try to imagine what my family are up to right now. I have no doubt in my mind that Eve is up just as early as I am. I can picture her and Nathan cuddled up in bed together, swapping their gifts before they head downstairs into the chaos that is the Jones family's Christmas morning.

I bet my younger cousins are already running wild around the Christmas tree, sorting their piles and piles of presents into neat stacks ready for when the adults come down and give them the go-ahead to tear into them.

A handful of people will be in the kitchen getting breakfast ready, the smell of frying bacon and sausages and egg quickly filling Gran's house.

I'm actually surprised Eve hasn't messaged or called yet. I half expected to wake up with a flurry of notifications of missed calls and increasingly agitated texts, but my phone remains silent. I fire off a quick:

Noelle

MERRY CHRISTMAS!!!!!!
CALL ME WHEN YOU'RE UP

and expect my phone to vibrate in response almost immediately after, but nothing comes.

Weird.

But I don't have time to dwell it on right now. I've got a plan and the success of it depends largely on how much I can get done before Alex wakes up. Luckily, it seems like he's dead to the world. He clearly hasn't been hard-wired to wake up at the crack of dawn on Christmas Day.

I pull on some clothes and tiptoe out of the room and downstairs into the kitchen as quickly as I can. I pull out the food Alex and I prepared last night and stick the chicken in the oven to roast for later.

Once that's cooking on low, I turn my attention to the whole reason I'm down here in the first place.

Today isn't just Christmas, it's Alex's birthday and I'm determined to make it special. For once. I throw open the cupboards and pull out the ingredients I need for a simple cake. I'd love to go all out, especially now I know Hoxton's history with Christmas, but we're running low on the core ingredients. There's just enough flour, butter and eggs to make a small, but tasty, cake. The decadent, three-tiered genoise sponge I have in mind will have to wait until next year. This year it's all about just letting him know that he hasn't been forgotten. That the years of birthdays spent playing second fiddle to Christmas are over now.

I gather all the ingredients I need and start mixing the batter, the rhythmic sound of the wooden spoon against the metal bowl a comforting background noise in the silence of the kitchen. It helps to ground me and keep my thoughts from drifting back towards my family.

Why haven't they called or messaged yet?

It's not like Eve to be silent on Christmas morning – or, ever actually. A small seed of worry starts to bloom in my chest, but I try to push it aside. Maybe they're just caught up in their own festivities, caught up in the chaos of Christmas.

The worry morphs into bitterness because, if that's the case, it means they've forgotten me.

Out of sight, out of mind.

I could, in theory, just call Eve myself, but something makes me hesitate. I feel like an outsider in my own family and that I'd be intruding if I called now.

The cake serves as a timely distraction from the increasingly depressive train of thought I'm heading towards. I take my time tidying up after myself and getting some of the dishes Hoxton and I will be having for our small, cobbled-together Christmas dinner. By the time I'm sliding the cake out of the oven and setting it to cool, I haven't thought about Eve and the rest of family for about an hour.

Unfortunately, leaving it to cool before I ice it leaves plenty of time for my thoughts to wander. I pull out my phone again and grimace at the lack of notifications flashing across my screen.

I hit 'call' on Eve's contact card, but she doesn't answer. Same goes for my mother, my cousin Jean, Gran, and even Nathan. Every single call goes straight to answerphone.

For my sanity, I set my phone aside and focus on finishing Alex's birthday cake. The sweet vanilla scent fills the kitchen as I spread a smooth layer of icing over the top and a sense of warmth and happiness washes over me.

This was definitely not the Christmas I had in mind for this year, but I don't hate it.

Just as I'm put the finishing touches on the cake, I hear footsteps approaching from behind. I whirl around to see Alex standing in the doorway, a look of pure relief flooding his features.

'I thought you'd left,' he says, shuffling into the kitchen with a yawn. His gaze lands on the cake and his eyes widen in silent question.

I laugh as he comes to a halt in front of me, and reach up to pull him down for a quick kiss. It's funny how natural it feels to reach for him like this now. 'I never would've left without saying goodbye.'

'But you wanted to leave?' Alex asks quietly.

'No,' I say, without even having to think. The response clearly surprises Alex, and it surprises me too. 'I thought I would want to. That I'd want to get out of here and get over to Gran's as soon as I could, but I meant what I said last night.' I reach out for another kiss and he happily obliges. 'I told you I wanted to be here, and I meant it.'

He hums against my lips, his hands snaking down towards the small of my back to pull me in close. 'I wouldn't have minded—'

'Yes, you would,' I say. 'You wouldn't admit it to yourself or to anyone else, but you would have. And I would have just joined the long line of people who prioritised Christmas over you.'

His eyes crinkle slightly in the corners. 'Noelle—'

'And I'm not going to be that person.' I pull apart from him, eliciting a tiny whimper, and gesture to the small cake on the counter. 'Happy Birthday!'

He grins, his eyes sparkling with genuine surprise and delight. 'You made this for me?' he asks.

I nod, watching as his gaze flits from the cake to me and back again. His smile grows wider before he leans in to press another quick kiss to my lips. 'Thank you, Noelle. You really didn't have to do this.'

I shrug nonchalantly. 'This is just the warm-up. Next year, now I've got a bit more notice, I'm going all out.'

'Next year . . .' Alex says quietly. He pulls me in closer again, holding me tight like he doesn't ever want to let go. He opens his mouth to say something else, but the gates to his drive suddenly swing open and we both watch as a mini-parade of sleek black cars park up just outside. 'Oh. They're early.'

'What's happening?' I ask, breaking free of Alex's grip to peer out of the window. There are six identical cars in the drive, and I can spy several more parking up on the street outside Alex's house. 'Are you getting raided by MI5 or something? Is this where I find out that you've been evading taxes for the last decade and the government have finally had enough?'

Alex laughs and comes to stand behind me, his arms bracketing me in as we watch the scene outside unfold.

'That,' he points to the fleet of cars outside, 'would be your Christmas gift.'

My heart stops, starts, and then stops again as one of the car doors opens up and I watch as my sister tumbles out of it, followed by my parents. From another car, Gran steps out, helped by Uncle Morris, and from the rest I watch as various aunts, uncles, and cousins all spill out.

A million questions are rushing through my mind: How is this possible? Did they drive through the night? Where the hell have all these cars come from? And ... *God*, do we have enough food for everyone?

I swivel around in Hoxton's arms, my heart in my throat, my eyes bleary with the sudden onslaught of tears. 'What—' is all I manage to croak out before he interrupts.

'I'm glad you didn't leave earlier. For multiple reasons, but primarily because you would've ruined your surprise.' Then, he lifts my chin with a finger and presses a soft kiss against my lips and says three words I never thought I'd hear coming out of Alexander Hoxton's mouth. 'Merry Christmas, Noelle.'

CHAPTER TWENTY-THREE

Alex

I don't think there have ever been this many people in my house. Up until three days ago, the record had been taken by my Board and I hadn't been anticipating breaking it anytime soon.

And yet . . .

Everywhere I turn there's another unfamiliar face and someone rushing to introduce themselves to me. In the span of about five minutes, I meet and shake the hands of just about every single member of Noelle's family – extended too. I meet aunts, uncles, cousins, cousins twice removed, grand uncles, and at least two family friends who aren't sure when they became pretty much family, but have been rolling with it for years.

Someone has managed to get into my sound system and

Christmas carols blast from the speakers throughout the house. Another someone – I have no idea who, or how they've managed it – has set up a small Christmas tree in the middle of my living room. The fact that they *had* a mini Christmas tree to bring with them from Noelle's grandmother's house to here is insane, but nobody seems to question it. The fact that a three-foot tree, complete with colourful decorations, has suddenly appeared in my living room is apparently the most normal thing in the world to the Joneses.

Some of them have brought plates of Christmas cookies and cakes, their sweet fragrances wafting through the air, mingling with the fresh pine scent of the Christmas tree.

Laughter, chatter and music fills every room as everyone mills around excitedly. There are even little children running around, their giggles and shouts echoing off the walls.

It's loud and busy and hectic and just so Christmassy.

Surprisingly, I don't hate it.

I remember how I felt having the Board in my home. How uncomfortable it had been to have these people – effectively strangers – wandering through my home, my safe space. I don't feel any of that right now.

I think I quite like it actually.

I watch as Noelle floats around the room, her smile radiant as she chats with each member of her family, pulling them into tight hugs and making sure that everyone feels welcome.

'What're your intentions with my sister, *Alex*?'

Eve sidles up next to me and wiggles her brows. I've known Eve for a grand total of fifteen minutes, but I get the distinct impression that she's the kind of person who says whatever's on her mind.

If I'm being honest, I respect it.

'I'll take whatever she's willing to give me,' I say, in the spirit of honesty. I'm well aware that whatever it is Noelle and I have developed these last four days, we need to sit in it some more. Figure out exactly what it is we want from each other and how we'll fit into each other's lives. But it doesn't feel like a hopeless task; I feel like we could build something good – something *great* even.

I catch Noelle's eye from across the room and she grins over at me, before her gaze slides over to her sister and she narrows her eyes.

Eve blows her a kiss and then turns her attention back to me. She surveys me for a few seconds before giving me a satisfactory nod. 'All right. I approve. The whole *hiring cars to bring us all up here* thing definitely chucked a few bonus points your way.'

I laugh, and I'm surprised at how easy it comes to me. I don't think I've felt this light, this free, in a very long time. 'Thanks?'

'You're welcome,' Eve says absentmindedly, her dark brown eyes scanning the room for someone else. She settles on a tall man laughing in a corner with a group of people and her expression turns soft. 'I just want Noelle to be happy.'

'Me too.' I don't even have to think about it. I know, like the way you know deep, core truths about yourself, that Noelle's happiness has quickly climbed the list of my priorities and claimed the number one spot.

Eve smiles and gives my arm a gentle squeeze before she floats across the room to drape herself over man she was looking out for.

I take a moment to observe the scene playing out in front of me, the warmth and laughter of Noelle's family enveloping me in a way I never knew I craved. For so long, I've been content with my solitary existence, but I'd be lying if I didn't admit that maybe I'm starting to want more.

A little bit of this every now and then wouldn't be so bad, would it?

Noelle catches my eye from across the room, mutters something to the group she's currently talking to, and then breaks free from their circle to come and stand directly in front of me.

I don't get the chance to say a word before she's wrapping her arms tightly around me, pulling me into a deep hug. I freeze for a moment – PDA is still a slightly foreign concept to me – but my arms start to move of their own accord, and I'm hugging her too.

I'm dimly aware that her family are watching – I'm pretty

sure Eve has pulled out her phone and is recording – but I can't bring myself to focus on that right now.

The only thing that matters is the woman in my arms.

She leans back, just enough so she can see me fully, and smiles. 'Thank you for all of this,' she murmurs, her voice filled with genuine gratitude. 'I know it's probably – *definitely* – way out of your comfort zone, but it means the world to me.'

It means the world to me.

Maybe I am the modern-day Grinch, because I swear my heart grows about five sizes when she says that.

She stands up on her tiptoes and I pull her in close. I tilt my head down, meeting her halfway for a kiss that's soft and sweet and makes my heart race like it never has before.

Noelle melts into it, her hands coming up to frame my face gently, and I have to resist the urge to pull her even closer.

When we finally break apart, she rests her forehead against mine, our breaths mingling in the small space between us.

'Can I give you one last gift?' I murmur against her lips.

Noelle pulls back slightly and laughs. 'You don't owe me *anything*, Alex.'

'Just humour me.'

She nods and lets me guide her upstairs. Someone – Eve, I'm sure – hoots loudly as we disappear up the staircase.

'I'm going to kill her,' Noelle murmurs as we disappear

the sound of music, laughter and general merriment fades slightly. 'Sorry, by the way. I must've absorbed all the filter between us in the womb and now she has none.'

'It's fine,' I say. And I mean it too. 'It's . . . it's nice seeing your relationship with her.' I think about my own relationship with my siblings. We've never had anything even remotely close to the camaraderie I see between Eve and Noelle, and maybe that's more my fault than I've been willing to admit.

Though, not one of them has messaged to say 'Happy Birthday' yet, so maybe I'm giving them too much credit.

I shake my head and push out the thought of my family and focus on the beautiful woman beside me. This is about her and making Christmas something special.

'Here.' I open my office door and usher her inside. Noelle watches me with vague, curious amusement as I walk over to my desk and pull open the bottom drawer. My foil stars look even worse in the harsh light of day but I pull out a few and sheepishly hand them over to her.

'What, um . . . What are these?' she asks, barely concealing a smile.

'They're supposed to be decorations. You know, like stars for a tree.' I rub the back of my neck, feeling the heat that's already crawled up there. 'I wanted to try and bring some of the Christmas magic to you, but arts and crafts isn't my forte unfortunately.'

Noelle presses a hand against her mouth to smother her laugh. 'No. No. This is ... um ... This is really, really, sweet. And so thoughtful and ... um ...'

'That's not the gift,' I say abruptly. 'And you can laugh, it's okay.' I reach back into the drawer and pull out the stack of Post-it notes. 'I wanted to show you this.'

I hand her the pile and her eyes widen.

'Alex ... Are these ...?'

I nod. 'These are all the notes you've left with the dishes you've made me over the last two years.'

'You've *kept* these?' she asks, voice crackling slightly. She flips through the pile and shakes her head in disbelief. 'I didn't even think you *read* them; I've kind of just been leaving them on autopilot recently. But you ...' She looks up at me, eyes shining. 'You've kept them all?'

I take a step closer to her, gently pluck the pile from her hands, and place it on the table. Then I wrap my arms around her waist and pull her in close. 'I've kept every last one. I meant what I said, Noelle. Your cooking? It's something special. And I want you to know that I mean that from the bottom of my heart.' I lean in and press my lips against hers, enjoying the way she immediately melts into my touch and reciprocates. When we finally break apart, I rest my head against hers and murmur, 'Merry Christmas, Noelle.'

She grins and I swear, I'm never going to get tired of seeing the way it lights up her face. 'Merry Christmas, Alex.'

EPILOGUE

Noelle

One Year Later

'But it's Christmas!' Eve whines.

'It's Alex's *birthday*,' I remind her.

I get an overwhelming sense of déjà vu as I watch my twin sister pout at me through the screen. 'Can't you do both?' she asks.

'Not this year,' I say. 'Maybe next year, we'll see.'

Eve's pout intensifies, not that it does any good. 'But Gran is asking—'

'Gran already knows I'm not coming,' I cut Eve off halfway through her ridiculous attempt at guilt-tripping me. 'She's fine with it.'

'Urgh.' Eve scoffs and rolls her eyes. 'It's like I'm the only person who cares about tradition these days.'

'You just don't want to deal with Mum and Aunt Valerie alone for the second year in a row.' Though, *technically*, she only had to deal with them for a few days last year.

'That too.'

I laugh and toss my phone onto my bed so my hands are free to finish rifling through my suitcase. I've packed and unpacked at least ten times over the last few days, and I *think* I've got everything I need. 'Red set or black set?' I ask, holding up the two lacy pieces of lingerie sets for Eve to see.

She wiggles her brows. 'How long are you guys going for?'

'Five days.'

'Another wiggle of the brows. 'Both, then. You'll need them.'

I roll my eyes, but can't help but agree. I restuff both sets into my suitcase. I'm heading off to a secluded, luxury cabin in the Scottish Highlands with Alex for the next five days. I had a whole year to plan the perfect birthday getaway for a man who hates Christmas, and I think I've done pretty well.

No carollers. No decorations. No Christmas songs. No Christmas *anything*. Just us, nature, copious amounts of mulled wine, and the chance to really relax and enjoy each other's company. If we're lucky, we won't see a single person for the entire five days we're there.

I don't mean to toot my own horn, but this may just be

the best birthday Alex has ever had. Not that there's a lot of competition in that regard, but still.

'And you're not going to miss us at all?' Eve's voice sounds slightly distant from my bed, but I hear the slight pang of pain it in either way.

'Of course I am,' I call, as I double-check I've safely packed away another gift for Alex — a basket of luxury bath bombs I'm determined to make good use of on this trip. 'But it's just *one* Christmas. I'll survive and so will you.'

Eve makes a displeased sounding noise. 'And he's worth it, is he?'

I roll my eyes even though she can't see the gesture. 'You adore Alex.'

'Not when he's stealing you away at Christmas I don't,' she says, but there's no bite in her voice. In fact, I'm pretty sure I can hear her smile. 'He really makes you happy, doesn't he?'

'We make each other happy,' I say, and it's the truth.

After our snowy adventure last year, I wasn't entirely sure what a future with Alexander Hoxton might look like. We both agreed that there was something there, something worth exploring, but I had no idea what that would look like in practice. A small part of me wondered if it wouldn't take long for me to be relegated to the very end of Alex's priorities list, especially knowing just how busy he is running his company, and whether the *something* we'd sparked while snowed-in together would ultimately fizzle out into nothing.

I've never been so happy in my life to be proven wrong.

I jolt backwards suddenly as the doorbell rings. 'Shit. I'm running late.'

'Tell Loverboy I said hi,' Eve says as I fumble for my phone. 'And if you can spare a moment in between bouts of intense *alone time* over the next few days to check in on us at Gran's, that would be nice.'

'We're not—' I stop myself. What's the point in lying to my twin? 'I'll do my best,' I say with a wide, Cheshire cat-type grin. 'But no promises.' With one last wink at the camera, I cut the call and then hurry down the hall to buzz Alex up.

It takes him a minute or two to navigate the labyrinth that is my particular apartment block, and then he's knocking at my door and I'm throwing it open and jumping into his arms.

He catches me with well-practised ease and walks us both back into my flat, kicking the door shut behind him as he goes. I barely have the chance to let out a breathy 'hi' before he's got me propped up against my shoe cabinet, and my legs are instinctively wrapping themselves around his waist to pull him in deeper.

He murmurs something that sounds vaguely like a gruff 'missed you' before his lips are on mine and I'm losing myself in him again.

Every kiss is like this.

Every kiss feels like the first time.

I keep waiting for things to dull a little, for it to start feeling mundane, but it never does. I feel my toes start to curl as one of Alex's hands wanders down my back and dips under the hem of my T-shirt.

'We don't have time for this,' I mutter against his lips.

'We have all the time in the world.'

Technically, true. But . . .

'I wanted to be on the road by now,' I say, and reluctantly pull away.

Alex full-on *pouts* at me. Eve would be proud.

'Come on,' I say. 'Help me bring my suitcase down and then we can hit the road.'

Alex mutters something vaguely mutinous-sounding under his breath, but otherwise follows me into my bedroom.

'And you're *sure* this is okay?' he asks as I zip my suitcase shut and heft it upright. 'Missing Christmas and your family?'

'If one more person asks me that, I'm going to have an aneurysm.'

Alex laughs. 'I'm just making sure. I don't want you to do anything you're going to regret.'

I stand up straight and prod him sharply in the chest 'Let me make something very clear, Hoxton.'

He quirks a brow. 'Hoxton?'

I can't help but smirk. 'Mhm. I'm perfectly capable of making my own choices and right now, I'm choosing *you*. I want to celebrate *you*. What's so hard to understand about that?'

'Celebrating me doesn't mean we have to pretend like Christmas doesn't exist,' he points out.

'Oh, how the tables have turned,' I laugh. 'A year ago, that sentence never would've come out of your mouth.'

Alex gives me a wry grin and shrugs. 'Am I wrong, though?'

No, I think.

'Yes,' I say. 'Just this once, you're wrong. We'll figure out Christmas and your birthday next year. But this year? This year it's all about you.'

I expect him to argue with me a little more, just like he's been doing ever since I told him what my plans for his birthday were this year, but he just gives me a resigned little shrug.

'Fine.'

'Fine?' I echo, eyeing him suspiciously. That was easy. Too easy.

'Fine,' he says again. 'This year it's all about me. And next year it's all about you. We'll trade off. That'll be our Christmas tradition.'

Something warm settles inside me when he says the word 'our'. It sounds so permanent. I'd very much like it to be.

'Christmas slash *birthday* tradition,' I correct him.

'That works too,' he says. 'But before we get to the next five days being all about me, can I give you something?'

I glare at him. 'Giving me a Christmas present kind of defeats the whole *all about you* thing, doesn't it?'

'Then it's not a Christmas present,' he says. 'It's an *I love you* present. Can I give you one of those?'

A warmth spreads through my body and I feel like I could melt on the spot. It's not the first time he's said those three little words – and I've said them back to him as well – but it gets the same reaction out of me every time.

I swallow and force myself to nod. 'I guess that would be fine.'

'Excellent.' His grin widens as he pulls out his phone, taps something into it, and then turns the screen to face me. 'This is the one you were looking at, right? Your top choice?'

Pretty sure my heart stops for a second.

Up on Alex's screen is the listing for the commercial property I've had my eye on recently. I've finally saved enough that it's looking like Heart could become a reality in the next year or so, and I've been indulging myself in a few late night Rightmove searches.

This one in particular is perfect. The location is wonderful. It's not *too* expensive. And, best of all, I can see myself inside it.

Alex must have noticed me pulling up the listing over and over again, and staring at it with wistful, longing eyes.

'Er, yes?' I say. 'I was just looking. I'm not ready to buy just yet and—'

'Great,' Alex says. He turns his phone back to him and quickly taps something in.

'What're you doing?' I ask, suddenly frantic.

'Having Roland book in a viewing for the new year,' he says, like it's the most normal thing in the world. 'And when you step through those doors, and you know officially that it's The One, I'm also buying it for you as well.'

If I wasn't sure before, I am this time. My heart *does* stop.

'Alex . . .' I croak out. 'You don't have to . . . I mean, this is too much for a Christmas present. You can't—'

'It's not a Christmas present,' he says, looking ridiculously smug. 'It's an *I love you* present and *I believe in you and want to help you chase your dreams* present.'

'You just made that up.'

'Maybe. It's still true, though.' He reaches forward and swipes his thumb against my cheek. 'Don't cry, Noelle.'

I blink. *I'm crying? Shit, I am crying.*

'I promise, these are happy tears,' I sniffle. 'I just . . .' I feel like there's so much more I need to say, but I don't even know where to begin. I settle for leaning into his touch, wrapping my arms around his neck, and pulling him in close. 'Thank you.'

His arms settle on my waist as he pulls me flush against him. 'Thank *you*, Noelle.'

We stand there holding each other for a little longer before I pull away. I'm sure my eyes are bloodshot and my cheeks are tear-stained, but Alex looks at me like I've just hung the moon.

'I love you,' I say.

His smile stretches from cheek to cheek. Just for me. Only ever for me. 'I love you too.'

Acknowledgements

I still can't quite believe that I get to write the stories that rattle around in my head 24/7 *and* that people enjoy them. I might be the one putting pen to paper, but none of this would be possible without some pretty amazing people:

Thank you to my husband for his eternal support, my best friends M&M who provide me with countless hours of laughter and encouragement, my editor, Molly, who seems to understand me and my writing on a level I did not think possible, the wonderful Misha who has kept me on track throughout this whole process, Clare who, like Molly, just seems to *get* me, and my agent, Emma, who is one of the most patient and dedicated people I have had the pleasure of knowing, and this book simply would not exist without her support.

And, as always, the biggest thank you goes to my readers. Thank you all so much for your continued support, words of encouragement, and just general love you send my way. It is very much felt and I hope you know how much I appreciate you all.

Until the next one . . . xoxo

Do you want to find out more?

Scan the QR code to get an extra spicy bonus chapter by signing up to Anise's newsletter.

DISCOVER MORE FROM
ANISE STARRE

AVAILABLE NOW

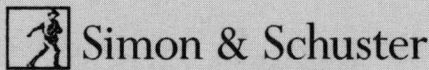